The Wailing
A Thriller Novel
By James Dobie
Published 10/31/2022

The Wailing

Wallowa Lake Series, Volume 1

James Dobie

Published by James Dobie, 2024.

THE WAILING

First edition. October 31, 2024.

ISBN: 979-8987133842

Written by James Dobie.

This novel is dedicated to my loving parents, Ruth and Nevill Dobie—may they rest in peace—who instilled in me at an early age a burning curiosity and a voracious desire to read and explore exciting new worlds.

Last, but certainly not least, my dear sister and Editor-in-Chief, Dianne Dobie. Without her infinite patience and constant encouragement, none of my novels would have ever seen the light of day.

JAMES DOBIE, 10/31/2022

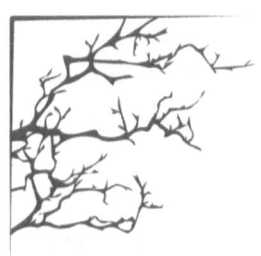

Chapter One

2:00 a.m., Sunday, October 28th, Wallowa Mountains, Oregon

Jake Anderson was running for his life. The horrible creature chasing him was quickly closing the gap between them. He didn't dare look back to see how close—if he tripped and fell, it would be on him in a heartbeat. He dodged trees in slow motion, every bush extended spiny tendrils to impede and hinder his flight from the monstrosity stalking him. Liquid fear flooded his mouth, turned his blood to ice water, with every beat of his heart. Adrenaline flooded his brain, urging him to run faster or die. He couldn't move fast enough, it gained on him every second. The terrible growling grew closer, closer—he could feel and smell it's hot, fetid breath on the back of his neck as the wickedly sharp teeth sank deep into the back of his neck and ...

JAKE JERKED AWAKE IN his bed, cold sweat soaking the bed sheets. *Holy shit!* His heart was racing hard from the nightmare. An unfamiliar sound had ripped him out of the horrid dream—thank God. He listened intently as his heartbeat slowly returned to normal. At first, he thought he'd imagined it, until another high-pitched, mysterious wail pierced the early morning silence of the forest surrounding his house. *There it was again!*

What the hell? he thought, the hair on his nape rising. It was 2:00 a.m., he should have been fast asleep after working late on his novel.

His jet-black hair was tousled, dampened with sweat. He rubbed the sleep out of steel blue eyes and hauled his sturdy six-foot-two frame out of bed with a groan. Jake Anderson had grown up here in the State Wallowa Forest outside the city of Joseph, but he'd never heard anything out there that sounded quite like the strange sound that had woken him.

A cold autumn chill pervaded the old house as he dressed warmly and trudged into his kitchen. Opening the back door, he stepped out onto the covered porch that ran the length of his house. The north wind sent icy bumps down the back of his neck, caressing it with its wintery fingers. The temperature had plummeted with the passage of a strong front.

Jake plopped down in a decrepit looking rocking chair, its wooden staves bent, and warped with age. He felt unusually anxious as he stared out into the forest's impenetrable dark, beyond the feeble reach of his old seventy-five-watt security light. He supposed it was the result of his nightmare and the strange sound that had interrupted it. He was usually comfortable, at one, with his isolated environment.

His thoughts were suddenly disrupted by the eerie noise again, echoing off the tall poplar pines that encompassed most of the 50 acres he called home.

"Probably just a damn coyote or panther," he observed aloud, trying to convince himself.

Abruptly, the undulating wail stopped as if a switch had been thrown. Chirping crickets and the occasional *who-who* of an owl were now all that he heard. He reached over, opened his ancient refrigerator, popped open a cold can of diet cola. He took a couple of quick gulps, grimacing as he wiped his mouth. Breakfast ... yum.

Shivering, he stood up, walked back inside the relative warmth of the house. The cast iron pot-bellied stove inside barely put forth any heat, as his old man had never installed a proper heater. Jake had forgotten to stoke the fire before going outside. He'd have to chop more wood to keep any warmth in the drafty two-bedroom house. No time like the present.

He grabbed his blue-jean jacket off the coat rack by the back door, his LED flashlight from the kitchen drawer and stepped back out onto the porch. Pulling the jacket on, he walked out to where the light ended abruptly and darkness took over. An ax-scarred chopping stump sat about twenty feet from the porch. He switched on the beam of light, splaying it out and around the woodpile, spotting the ax. Setting the flashlight on the log pile for light, he yanked the ax out of a large chunk of wood, raising it to split some logs.

He'd only chopped a few pieces of wood when something large dashed in front of him just beyond the stump. Out in the darkness, the crickets halted their chirping. A tingle of alarm ran up his spine as he dropped the ax to grab the light, shining it in a wide arc out into the forest and shrubs that bordered the fifty-foot clearing around the cabin. The flashlight's beam had reached the porch when a creature with razor sharp claws leaped onto his right thigh, digging in. With a startled shout, he stumbled back into the woodpile, then fell on his ass, nearly losing his grip on the light.

Stunned, he stared down at his leg as feral, yellow eyes gleamed back at him from a face surrounded by fur.

"Damn it, Jinx, get the hell off me, I nearly crapped myself, you furry fuck!"

He was addressing a twenty-five-pound bobcat that was domesticated only in the broadest sense. The big cat came and went as he pleased, disappearing for days before showing up, usually hungry.

He'd occasionally allow Jake to pet him once or twice after he'd gulped down his cat chow. More often, he gave him wary looks while he ate, disappearing again—until a day or two later, when Jake least expected it.

Three years ago, Jake had found the cat abandoned by its mother out in the forest when it was about two months old. He'd brought the kitten home to raise as a pet, but there would be no taming him. Which suited Jake *and* Jinx fine.

Jinx retracted his claws giving Jake his smug, *I got you, sucker!* cat stare. Leaping off, he ran up onto the porch, promptly disappearing into the shadows. It was a game the cat never tired of, though the sneak attacks were frequently unpleasant for Jake. He had scars all over his legs as souvenirs, despite his thick jeans. Now, the bobcat had vanished again, so Jake put bowls of food and water on the porch for him.

Jake smiled, shaking his head, and was once more reaching for the ax when the plaintive shriek rose again.

"What the hell is that?" Jake muttered aloud. His inquisitive nature was captivated by this enigma. He felt compelled to pursue the sound right then—come hell or high water.

Not a wolf, he thought, starting in the general direction of the sound. He paused, reconsidered, turned and strode briskly back into the house. Grabbing his nine mm pistol off the nightstand, he made sure a round was chambered, holstering it. He threaded it onto the right side his belt, snagged the flashlight from the kitchen and headed back out.

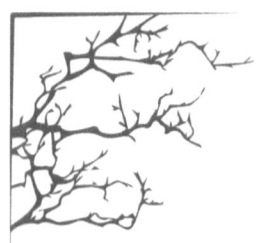

Chapter Two

The north wind had strengthened, dropping the temperature to around forty-five degrees, making it hard to determine the direction of the eerie sound. Jake's property abutted Wallowa Lake on the south end. The lake itself was relatively large, surrounded on three sides by lofty 9,000-foot mountains—a beautiful area of Oregon.

The lake was about eight miles long, with the town of Joseph at its north end. The water's edge was roughly a quarter mile north of his house, and that seemed to be the direction from which the keening wail was originating.

With his light leading the way, he began walking, weaving his way through the forest until he found a game trail about 100 yards in, leading in the general direction of the undulating sound. The path thickened with pine needles, softening his footsteps along the way. Moths fluttered in the beam of his flashlight.

A couple mosquitoes buzzed around his face, looking for an early breakfast as he made his way through shrubs and thick stands of trees. Jake estimated he was about 100 yards from the cliff overhanging the lake, when he stopped to catch his breath. He stood still, listening intently.

Suddenly, a low growling startled him. He swung the beam around in a circle, trees and shrubs throwing shadows everywhere, but nothing moved. He shrugged, turned back toward the lake, took three steps—and was knocked savagely to his knees from behind.

Jake yelled, "Damn it, Jinx, not *again*!"

Kneeling, he reached behind him to pull the bobcat off. But it wasn't Jinx. Something much heavier and vicious with needle-sharp teeth that bored into the flesh and bones of his right hand, ripping, pulling at the tendons in a spray of blood. He screamed and rolled, trying to dislodge the fierce creature's grip to end the ghastly agony shooting up his arm like a lightning bolt. Jake still held the flashlight in his left hand. Using it as a club, he managed a glancing blow to its body, which only made it angrier. It growled, shaking its head, pulling back ferociously on his hand. Terror fueled the adrenaline flowing like the blood from his shredded hand as he frantically beat at the beast.

The gun. He'd forgotten about the gun—but unfortunately, it was on the right side of his hip. He'd have to drop the flashlight to draw, then shoot blindly at the animal chewing its way through his appendage.

Jamming the flashlight awkwardly between his legs, he finally caught a good look at the creature attempting to separate his hand from his body. A Wolverine. A fucking wolverine the size of a medium-sized dog. He reached over, desperately trying to get a grip on the gun's blood-slicked handle. Jerking it out, he dropped it, continuing to kick at the frenzied animal as it snarled, teeth buried to the hilt, its muzzle covered with his blood.

He was gasping for breath when he finally retrieved the gun, got a firm grip, aimed between the creature's eyes and rapidly pulled the trigger twice, bullets exiting the animal's skull in a crimson mist of blood, bone and brains.

The shots were deafening. Jake wearily dropped the gun. Even in death, the wolverine refused to relinquish its hold on his hand. Holding the flashlight between his knees, he dug his folding knife from his pocket with a shaking left hand, took the folded blade between his teeth. Clamping down, Jake opened the blade and used it to pry its bloody jaws open, removing his hand. In the light, the flesh around his palm looked like hamburger, the back of the hand was torn and abraded, white metacarpal bone showing through the torn tissue. Kicking the dead animal away from him, he groaned in agony.

Pulling his flannel shirt tail out of his pants with his good hand, he took the bottom in his teeth, ripped a long, ragged strip off, wrapping it tightly around the severely damaged hand. Wincing with pain, he took one end of the flannel in his left hand and the other between his teeth and pulled the knot tight. Then he collapsed onto his back, sweating, sucking air.

Oh shit! I've got to get out of here! he thought, trying not to panic as he saw blood rapidly soaking through his flimsy, make-shift bandage.

Slowly, unsteadily, Jake got to his feet, swaying, he reached down to pick up the blood-smeared pistol, managing to holster it. He grabbed the flashlight and shined it on the bloody corpse.

Damn, that's a big bastard. Just hope it's not ... the word *"Rabid"* came to mind, then quickly dismissed it.

"Can't worry about that right now, gotta get help," he muttered, through clenched teeth. Cold sweat poured down his face. He'd never been afraid of the dark or of any animal out here in the mountains. A healthy respect, yes. It was very isolated out here, you had to be careful. He'd never experienced an attack like this in his life.

The nearest doctor was in Joseph, nearly ten miles to the north end of the lake, the nearest neighbor he knew, miles away. He was aware that wolverines were an endangered species, but at the moment, he could care less. Shock was setting in as he surveyed his surroundings, hoping he'd be able to find his way back to the game trail.

He stumbled forward, shivering as the temperature continued to drop. He walked on at an unsteady pace past trees and bushes that rustled and swayed with every step he took—hoping it was only the wind. The game trail had disappeared; he was thoroughly disoriented.

"Getting weak, gotta find the trail," he mumbled, stumbling over a tree root, twisting his ankle and going down hard, face first.

He tried to break his fall with his left arm, but in doing so, dropped the flashlight. It hit a rock, the beam flickered and died.

"Motherfuckeerr!" he screamed, in distress and frustration. His mangled right hand was trapped between his body and the forest floor.

Darkness was a living thing surrounding him. Panic spread, starting in the center of his rapidly heaving chest, eating its way outward until he felt it start to consume his reasoning and sanity. Jake spit dirt and pine needles out of his mouth.

"I'm *really* having a bad fucking day!" he shouted, groaning as he pushed himself to a sitting position, freeing his damaged hand. Then he stood, testing his left ankle, already swollen and throbbing like a bad tooth. He tried to put his weight on it and collapsed on his ass.

What the hell do I do now? he thought miserably. He groped around on the ground in front of him until he felt the familiar shape of the flashlight. He clicked the button a couple of times while shaking it. No good.

He didn't like his options—none were good. First, he could stay put and wait for sunup to determine at least his general location and possibly die of hypothermia and shock. Second, he could hobble blindly through the trees and bushes, hoping he didn't meet any more creatures with sharp teeth and claws or fall into the lake and still die from exposure and shock.

If he didn't decide on a course of action soon it wouldn't matter, he *would* die. Jake decided to keep moving. He stuck the useless flashlight into the back of his jeans and started shuffling carefully forward, his left hand sweeping the air in front of him back and forth, until his right foot caught another unseen obstacle, almost throwing him face-down again.

"This isn't gonna work, I need a damn cane, a stick or something to keep my balance," Jake moaned, feeling around in the dark for something, anything, to use as a crutch.

He could find nothing. He was about to give up when his hand brushed against a low branch. The limb was about an inch in diameter and maybe five feet long. Unfortunately, it was still attached to the tree. *Shit!* With his good hand, he dug out his Woodsman knife and repeated his earlier maneuver to open the four-inch blade, still covered in blood.

Luckily, the top of the blade had a serrated edge for sawing things. He'd never used that, but he had to try it now. He wedged the branch under his right armpit and started sawing the limb where it met the tree. He had to pause every couple of minutes to catch his breath as a wave of dizziness and nausea rolled over him. His left hand was getting blisters as he put his full weight on the knife sawing the branch.

Finally, with a loud *cr-ack* the branch came free, and Jake stumbled forward. Then, bracing himself against the tree, he refolded the knife and shoved it in his pocket. Gripping the branch in his left hand, he tested his weight on it. It bowed a little but seemed to hold up.

If only I had a little light to see where I'm going, Jake thought despairingly, alternately using the branch as a cane and a probe, slowly moving forward a couple of feet at a time. The night sky was as dark as the inside of a cave, overcast with clouds, no starlight.

He thought he had maybe moved thirty or so paces in perhaps the past ten to fifteen minutes, but he had no way of knowing how much time had passed. Jake didn't have a watch. Nobody seemed to wear them anymore with the advent of cell phones. He'd left his cell charging on the table by his bed. The phone wouldn't have done him much good, as he couldn't get a dependable signal out here at the best of times.

"I should have brought the damn thing with me. Could have used the flashlight on it. Yeah, hindsight's not worth shit," Jake muttered, as he stubbed his left boot against a hidden rock, sending waves of agony shooting through his swollen left ankle.

Suddenly there seemed to be no more trees. He could see a ghostly glow ahead in the distant dark that seemed to be moving slowly ... but, up and down?

"What the hell?"

The light was dim, but it was certainly a lantern or flashlight of some kind. He couldn't tell how far away it was, his depth perception impaired by pain and the dark.

He yelled out, "Help Me. Anyonne out there? Please," trying to move toward the brightness. No answer.

Jake took three more steps and as he leaned on the branch cane for support, it seemed to suddenly give way under him. He fell forward, bracing himself to hit the ground again, but instead found himself plunging weightlessly through air. He'd gone the wrong direction and reached the edge of the cliffs surrounding Lake Wallowa. They weren't all that high off the water, but that didn't matter—he knew the water temperature would be in the sixties this time of year and that would be enough to finish him!

Terror flooded him as he fell about ten feet before hitting the icy water. He felt like a bug squashed on a windshield, the air forced from his lungs as if someone had punched him in the stomach. Panic seized him as he desperately struggled to rise to the surface, his boots and jacket weighing him down, along with the heavy, damaged flashlight stuck in his jeans. He managed to dislodge the light and frantically kicked to the surface, gulping a breath before sinking again.

The shock of the frigid water had overridden the pain in his right hand, he managed to get his jacket over it, pulled it off and let it sink, but he needed air. Exhaustion was a lover, pulling him into its deadly embrace. Jake broke the surface of the Lake for a split second, sucking in another lungful of water. Gasping for a breath, he briefly thought he saw the glow of a light moving toward him.

He croaked out a feeble, "Hel..." before the icy water again sucked him down. As he began to sink, he saw a brilliant light shine above, blinding him.

I'm dying, he thought, expelling his last bubble of air as something tangled in his hair—yanking his head back to the surface and holding it above water. Jake coughed up water and banged his head hard against something solid. He looked up and saw brightness only a few feet away, partially illuminating a face that leaned down toward him.

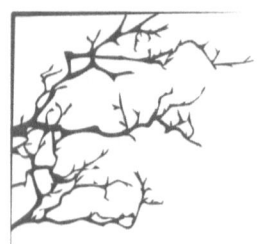

Chapter Three

"You're damn lucky I decided to fish this side of the Lake, friend," gasped a husky female voice, as she grunted with the effort to keep his head above water.

Jake coughed up more lake, reached out with his left hand and grabbed the side of a fourteen-foot V-hull Jon boat. The pressure on his scalp relaxed as the woman reached down, grabbed him under his left arm and pulled him halfway into the boat, tipping it dangerously close to the water.

"Mister, you're gonna have to help me—otherwise we're both goin' into the drink," she said in a tight voice, struggling to keep a grip on his left arm. "Throw your left leg over and pull your ass in," she commanded, leaning back to the opposite side to counterbalance the boat.

Jake swung his left leg over and into the boat, knocking the lantern off the seat and onto the floor of the rocking craft. Thankfully, the light didn't shatter and go dark. He rolled the rest of the way in and lay panting on the bottom between the metal seats, fishing tackle and poles.

"Th...th...thank y...you," he managed through chattering teeth, shivering uncontrollably.

The woman just stared at him, then shook her head, studying him in the glow of the lantern. Whitecaps began appearing on the Lake's surface.

"Mister, you oughta be at the bottom of the Lake, between that anchor you're wearing on your hip and those gunboat boots you've got on."

Jake stared down uncomprehendingly at the gun still on his hip.

"If I hadn't heard those two shots earlier, I wouldn't even be here. Fish 'not bitin' tonight, maybe the new moon, hell if I know, probably just the front moving through. I was gettin' ready to pack it in when I heard the splash you made when you decided to go swimming in sixty-degree water—it's damn near freezing out here."

She picked up the lantern and looked him over. Seeing the make-shift bandage on his swollen hand, she shook her head again, mumbling something that sounded suspiciously like "stupid damned men," as she dug around in the bottom of the boat, came up with a rain slicker and handed it to him.

"Here, I'll trade you—give me the gun, you won't need it. Then put this on, it's insulated and warmer than that wet flannel thing you're wearing."

Jake gratefully took the slicker and slowly inserted his right arm into the sleeve, moaning once when his hand caught on the inside lining.

"Thanks, m-miss, for saving my sorry ass. I owe you big time," Jake grunted, as he got the slicker wrapped around him, handing her the pistol.

She nodded, "You're welcome. Ya' know, you almost got it right, the name's Melissa, but I go by Missy to most folks."

Shaking with cold and fatigue, Jake eased himself up and leaned against the seat facing her. He tried to see her features, but her face was hidden in the shadows and covered by the hood of the heavy jacket she wore.

She added, "We'd better get you somewhere warm, but quick."

She turned in her seat, tossed the gun into an open tackle box, then cranked the twenty-five hp outboard motor. It started on her second pull of the cord, chugging out blue smoke that the north wind quickly snatched away. Jake laid down in the boat as the bow began to plane when she throttled to its top speed of about seventeen knots, the bottom bouncing and skipping over the smaller whitecaps as she made for the unseen shoreline.

Missy's boat had a fish/depth finder and GPS. She punched in the return coordinates to her small dock on the back-lit LCD display and turned on the powerful 1200-lumen spotlight mounted on the bow of the hull. It lit up the whitecaps of the Lake for fifty yards in front of the boat as she concentrated on watching the depth finder and closing the distance to her dock.

The Lake was only about three-quarters of a mile across from side to side at its widest point. She had plucked Jake out at about the half-way point, so the ride was only a few minutes. To Jake, it felt like forever. His shivering increased dramatically as the boat slowed, the bow rising then settling as Missy cut back on the throttle. She spotted her solar-powered dock light, adroitly guiding the boat parallel to it and cut both engine and light. The boat bumped into the old tire that served as a boat fender, and she secured the craft to the dock with a rope looped around a cleat.

She climbed out and onto the dock and glanced back at Jake. "You're gonna have to help me get your butt up here. Think you can stand without falling?"

She reached down for Jake's left hand. Grunting, he stood slowly, swaying as the boat shifted, with his weight mainly on his right leg. He grabbed onto her hand as she pulled with both of hers and he managed to get onto the dock before his left leg gave out and he collapsed to his knees.

"You're gonna have to do better than that. We got a-ways to go yet to get to my 'mansion,'" Missy said, pulling him to his feet and draping his arm over her shoulders.

"Y-you... y-you g-got a m-m-mansion?" Jake asked dubiously through chattering teeth, as she helped him limp down the dock and onto the shoreline.

She turned, cocked her head and looked at him, "Sure, doesn't everyone?"

She pulled a small flashlight from her coat pocket and turned it on, illuminating a stairway that inclined at a thirty-degree angle with about fifteen stairs. To Jake, it looked like fifty.

"Think you can make it up, Mister?" she goaded him.

"Th-th-the name's J-J-Jake. I'll r-r-race y-you t-to the t-t-top," he replied sarcastically, groaning with each step as, with her assistance, he slowly wobbled his way to the top of the steps where a walkway was connected. Jake stopped and stood there, staring.

Missy announced, "Well, there it is—home sweet home," as she shined the flashlight down the walk and onto her "mansion," illuminating the structure. It was a log cabin that might have been all of twenty square feet.

"Let's get you inside, quick," she undid the lock and shoved the door open, helping Jake to limp inside.

With the aid of the flashlight's beam, she steered him to a battered old recliner. With a sigh, Jake slowly eased into the chair that was more comfortable than it looked.

She said, "I'll be right back, don't run off," as she turned and went back outside, plunging Jake into inky darkness.

He suddenly felt uneasy and claustrophobic, cold sweat dripping from his face as his breath quickened, heart galloping in his chest.

He shouted, "M-Missy, y-y-you out t-t-there?"

Then he heard a motor fire up, sounding like a lawn mower or tractor. Almost immediately two bare light bulbs came to life in the cabin.

A generator, thank God! he thought, as Missy returned and slammed the door, bolting it with a two-by-four-inch board set into steel brackets on either side of the frame.

His heart rate slowed, the mounting panic subsided, and Jake got his first good look at Missy since he'd been pulled from the water, as she pulled her hood back. She looked to be in her late twenties, was about five foot six, with curly, brunette hair that she'd tied back in a ponytail. Her tanned face was angular, eyes a dark emerald green, and she had a cute, button nose—much more attractive than her rather gruff voice had led him to believe. Beyond that, he could tell nothing of her, as she still wore the bulky coat.

"That, Jake, brings us back from stone age. Now I'll get you as warm as possible, make some tea and have a look at that hand."

She moved to an antique style iron-framed bed in the corner of the cabin, picked up a thick blanket patterned with what looked like Native American symbols and brought it to him.

"Let's get the raincoat off, this'll warm you faster," she said, as she helped Jake stand and pulled the raincoat carefully off his arms, dropping it on the floor.

"The shirt's next, Bud. I'd take your pants, too, but I have nothing that could replace them."

She helped him unbutton the ripped flannel shirt. He grimaced when she pulled it off, wadded it up and tossed it on the floor with the raincoat. Throwing a small towel from her tiny bathroom to him, she made hair-drying motions, then wrapped the blanket around his shivering body and eased him back into the chair.

Turning, she walked to a sink with a small wooden counter on each side. Lighting a small propane stove which sat on the right side, she put a pan of water on to heat. Jake watched as she opened a canister and took out two tea bags, dropping them in a Mason jar, then turned, pulled up a wooden chair and plopped down in front of him. Now that his hair was halfway dry and pulled away from it, she saw a craggy, halfway handsome face framed by black, slightly wavy hair and a rough beard to match and light blue eyes framed by black lashes and brows.

"You wanna' tell me why the hell you decided to take a swim on a cold-ass night, in a cold-ass lake, fully dressed at... what, nearly 4:00 a.m., Jake?" she queried huskily.

The heavy blanket was beginning to thaw his upper body out, but not his lower extremities, as his pants were still soaking wet.

"Hold on a minute, let's get some tea in you first, then I need to check out your hand."

She turned off the burner on the little stove, poured the hot water over the bags, dumped in about a tablespoon of sugar, and brought it to him in the Mason jar, stirring as she came.

"Sorry I don't have anything fancier—function over form. I don't get many guests here," she added, handing him the canning jar.

Jake took it carefully in his left hand, holding it by the top rim of the jar to keep from scalding his palm, and slowly sipped, letting the hot liquid slide down his throat.

He made a face, "Too sweet, tastes funny."

Missy smiled, "It's chamomile, and you need the sugar to give ya' some energy. You burned a lot of calories out there, trying your best to drown. Now let me take a closer look at that hand."

Carefully, she untied the make-shift bandage on his ravaged hand, pulled the blood-and-water-soaked material off, then gasped. It looked like something that had been caught in a tree-shredder. The hand was swollen to twice its normal size, blood now oozing from the bitten appendage again.

"My God, what the hell did this? You need a doctor, and more stitches than Frankenstein's face ASAP," Missy exclaimed, frowning with alarm at the extent of damage.

Jake looked at her, "Wolverine—a damn big one."

The tea was doing its job warming him from the inside out, but the pain in his hand also said "howdy," inviting itself back with a vengeance. The cold air, water and adrenaline had numbed it considerably, but waves of agony now came flying back at him like a boomerang.

Still in her heavy jacket, Missy quickly got up and went to the small bathroom, rummaging through a cabinet until she found peroxide, triple antibiotic cream, a pillowcase and some scissors.

"This is gonna sting like hell, so hang on to your hat," she warned, as she poured peroxide over the bloody mess, making the blood foam up and causing Jake to jerk with an electric shock of pain.

"*Shiitt* ... that fucking *hurts*!" he snarled, as she blotted the torn flesh with part of the pillowcase.

Missy gave him a tight grimace, "I'll bet it do'. Now for the fun part."

She cut a long strip off the pillowcase and coated it with antibiotic cream, then carefully blotted the foamed blood and peroxide off his hand, with Jake gasping each time she touched it. Covering the bandage material with antibiotic cream, , she gently wrapped the it around the savaged hand, starting at the tip of his fingers and working up to his wrist.

"Shit ... hang on, I need something to hold it in place."

She got up, muttering to herself, and dug around again in the cabinet drawer, finally locating what she required.

"Here we go, this'll have to do for now," she said, as she came back with a roll of silver duct-tape, tore off a piece and secured the end of the bandage to his swollen wrist.

Then she moved to the nightstand by her bed and pulled out an orange bottle, shook out a couple pills and brought them to him.

"Here, take these—it's the only thing I have for pain."

Jake looked suspiciously at the pills but only hesitated a couple seconds before downing them with the remains of the tea.

"What did you just give me?" he asked, after he'd choked them down.

"Oh, just some left-over acid from a party last week," she deadpanned.

Jake's eyes got wider. "You're shittin' me—right?" he sputtered.

She waited a beat and smiled, "Yeah, I am. It's just a couple of Perc's I had left over from having a root-canal. Believe me, you'll thank me in about thirty minutes, Bud. You know the nearest hospital is in Joseph, so we better haul ass before the Percocet kicks in or it'll take a fork-lift to get you into my Cadillac."

She helped him to his feet, then took a sweater off a clothes tree near the front door.

"I'll never fit into that," Jake said, nodding toward the sweater.

"It's not for you, Aqua-man," and Missy pulled off the over-sized coat she'd been wearing, revealing a well-toned figure, and handed her coat to him.

She helped ease Jake into the coat, which barely fit. Then she slipped the sweater on, after which he threw his left arm over her shoulders as she led them through the front door.

"Hold on, I'll be back," Missy said, leaning Jake against the door jamb. She went back inside, got her purse and returned. "Almost forgot my keys."

She closed and locked the door behind them, switched on her flashlight and grabbed Jake left arm again. As she led him slowly across a graveled driveway, the beam of light reflected off the side of what appeared to be an old model Volkswagen micro-bus.

"THIS IS YOUR 'CADILLAC'?" he asked, as she opened the passenger-side door and helped ease him onto the ragged, worn-out seat.

He was feeling a little nauseated, from either pain or the pills.

Missy climbed into the car, proudly stating, "Hey, it's a classic '67, and it cost more than a damned Escalade. Don't look a gift horse in the mouth, Bud, I'm your only ride."

She cranked the engine over and pushed up the rpms to try to get the engine warm enough to run the heater. Jake felt chastised and a bit ashamed—after all she had just saved his life.

"I'm sorry, I didn't intend to insult your car. I appreciate everything you've done for me... I, uh, guess my sense of humor is crap right now, along with my hand." He groaned as he accidentally bumped it against the door's armrest.

She smiled tightly at him and reversed the bus, throwing up a cloud of dust as she drove up a narrow one-car lane, avoiding potholes that looked like they could eat a tire whole and ask for more.

"So, what's the story? How did all this happen?" she questioned, concentrating on the road.

"Well, earlier, an hour or two back, I heard a weird wailing sound coming from the forested area in back of my house, about a mile from here, I guess," Jake said, holding his left hand in front of the air vents as he would near a fireplace to warm it. Heat had slowly begun to blow from the orifice.

"'Wasn't familiar at all. Didn't sound like a coyote or panther, I know it wasn't a wolf. Almost like a shriek and a howl combined. So, I was awake... and I decided to have a look. Before I could get going, my damn bobcat, well... he's not really my cat, you can't own a cat, especially a bobcat. Anyway, Jinx attacked me from behind. He's always doing that—scared the shit out of me this time, though. I was already a little spooked by that strange wail."

Missy glanced at him and smirked, "Is that why you were packing heat? Not because of the bobcat but because of this mysterious sound you heard?"

Speaking of cats, Jake suddenly felt like a "pussy." The way she phrased that made it sound like he was chicken-shit, scared of the night sounds of the forest. Well, maybe he was, a little.

"Well, I wasn't gonna' go out there in the forest without any protection. As it turned out, it's a damn good thing I brought the gun," he said defensively.

Missy countered, "You know wolverines are endangered and a protected species, right?"

Jake stared at her, angrily rising to the bait, "Yeah... ya' know, at the time, I was feeling pretty endangered, so I did what I had to do to protect my ass from getting eaten alive."

Missy turned her head briefly and smiled at him, "Well, for your sake, I hope that wolverine wasn't rabid. 'Course, you're gonna need to get the shots, Jake, you know, just in case."

She came to the end of her graveled road and turned onto Wallowa Lake Highway 351, heading north toward the town of Joseph.

Jake shuddered as she echoed the same thought he'd had shortly after being attacked. *He imagined the virus circulating in his blood stream, slowly working its way up to his cerebral cortex, where it would begin to incubate, then start replicating like crazy until*—he shook his head and felt a shiver that had nothing to do with the cold whip through him. *Shut the hell up!* he told himself. *You'll just have to get the shots, that'll take care of it!*

They drove along in silence for a couple miles, until Missy hollered, "Shit," swerving to narrowly avoid a rabbit that darted out in front of her and disappeared across the road.

"Jake, that wailing sound you heard—did it go up and down in pitch, or did it stay the same?" she asked, glancing over at him.

Jake tried to concentrate. "Uh, I'm pretty sure... it went up and then down some before it stopped." He frowned, attempting to stay focused on her question.

She nodded slowly but said nothing else.

He turned his head and looked at her expectantly, "You've also heard it, then?" his speech slightly slurred.

Missy looked lost in thought as she concentrated on the road. They passed the city limit sign that read, "This little town is Heaven to us, don't drive like Hell thru it." She hit the brakes as she passed it, slowing the bus to just slightly over the speed limit as she turned onto Main Street, then on to Wallowa Mountain Medical. She screeched to a halt in front of the Emergency entrance—almost throwing Jake out of his seat. She got out, rushing toward the entrance.

The hospital's double doors slid apart, swallowing her like a hungry mouth. Jake stared groggily out the windshield, trying to recall what he'd just asked Missy, as the doors to the ER slid open again and a male nurse came out, pushing a wheelchair up to the passenger side door.

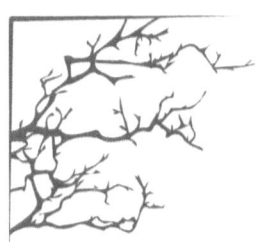

Chapter Four

The nurse opened the door and smiled, "Hello there, I'm Larry, your ride from here on, let's get you out and comfortably situated."

He took Jake's right arm and gently eased him out and into the chair.

Jake just grinned up at him, "So-kay by me, but my han' ain' dooin' too good, Doc."

"Well, I'm not a doctor, sir, I just play one on TV," the nurse joked with a grin, wheeling Jake through the doors and into the waiting room of the ER.

Missy was talking to the registration nurse through a little window.

She turned and told Jake, "They need your last name, I never got that far, too busy trying to patch your ass up. Also, do you have any insurance?"

Jake frowned and said, "Nope, no insurance, *lass* name *ish* Annerson... A-n-d-e-r-s-o-n," he spelled out, his tongue thick and dry from the Percocet.

The registration nurse wrote down the information. "We'll get the rest of the forms filled out later. Larry, take him to triage STAT."

Larry wheeled Jake back to a little curtained-off room with a bed and medical equipment, eased him up and into the bed, and proceeded to put an IV in his left arm and hang a bag of plasma, then inserted a drip line.

"Something really did a number on this hand," Larry exclaimed, excising the bandage from Jake's shredded appendage and carefully examining it, as an aide covered Jake with a warm blanket. Then he injected some pain medicine into the PICC-line in Jake's arm.

Missy came in, saying, "I gave him a couple of Percocet about thirty minutes ago—the only thing I had, he's in a lotta pain."

Larry gave her a look. "*Now* you tell me, I just gave him another twenty milligrams. *Oy vey*! It wasn't in the chart."

Missy shrugged guiltily, "My bad ... I forgot to tell the lady at the desk."

Jake gave her a goofy, opioid-induced grin as a tall, red-headed female doctor approached the end of the bed with chart in hand.

She looked up from the chart, "I'm Dr. Lowery. This says patient's hand was bitten by a wolverine. He's suffered blood loss, hypothermia and a twisted ankle?"

She looked at Jake, then Missy, and asserted, "Let's take a look at that hand first."

She turned on a little head lamp with a magnifying loop on it while Larry carefully removed Jake's left boot from his swollen foot and ankle. Under the bright light, the damage to the hand was more clearly visible. Missy grimaced and looked away, as the doctor irrigated it with a large syringe of saline solution. The doctor muttered to herself as, with a pair of hemostats, she picked something small, white and shiny from the back of Jake's hand.

The object appeared to be a tooth. She dropped it into a vial, capped it and handed it to Larry.

She spoke to Jake, "We've got to get you into surgery, STAT! Larry, give him a tetanus shot. Your hand has sustained a great deal of damage, Mr. Anderson. Normally, I'd call in an orthopedic surgeon to do the work, but there isn't time. The closest one would have to be flown in from Portland, and that's too long to wait.

"I am a general surgeon and that will have to suffice. Larry will get you prepped; I'll need to operate as soon as possible!"

She turned to Missy, "Are you his wife?"

Missy replied, "No, I just fished him out of the lake after he fell in ... um, I guess we're kinda neighbors. He said his place is about a mile away from my cabin, in the National Forest."

"Well, I'd love to hear the specifics of how he managed to survive all this, but I've got to prep for the surgery. You'll have to sign some papers, as I'm guessing he has no one else to serve as power of attorney.

"When I finish up, I'll come and discuss his prognosis. The waiting room's out front," Dr. Lowery finished, shaking Missy's hand, then she turned and hurried off.

Missy stood close to Jake's bed. "Well, Bud, good luck. I'll see ya' when the dope wears off," she patted his shoulder reassuringly.

Jake was in "la-la land," but managed a smile and slurred, "Than'ss for youu hep, Missshy." Then he fell promptly fell asleep.

Missy grabbed her purse, walked down the hall to the waiting room, found an uncomfortable looking chair and plopped down in it. She filled out some of the paperwork and took it to the registration desk, then asked the lady behind the glass where the kitchen area was.

The woman pointed to a sign on the wall, then pointed down a hallway to the right, "It's too early for breakfast, but there's coffee and tea."

Missy thanked her and made her way to the dining room, filled a Styrofoam cup with black sludge that passed for coffee and found a vending machine. She got herself a bag of cheese puffs, then returned to her seat to wait. She fell asleep almost immediately after eating the cheese puffs, leaving orange grunge on her fingers that clutched the empty coffee cup.

Sometime later, Missy felt someone shake her gently by the shoulder. She blinked awake—Dr. Lowery was sitting beside her.

"Sorry to wake you, but just wanted to give you an update."

Missy yawned, "What time is it? How long have I been asleep? Doesn't matter, how is Jake?"

The doctor said, "Well, there was extensive damage to his tendons and the ulnar nerve was damaged, which could lead to clawing of the small and ring fingers and cause weakness of most of the hand muscles.

"Several metacarpal bones were fractured and there is a real possibility of his needing skin grafts to complete the healing. I've done the best I could under the circumstances. It will be a long recovery, but with time, along with some physical therapy, he should recover the use of most of his hand."

Dr. Lowery smiled, "He seems pretty tough, and with some encouragement, should be able to regain some strength within a month or so. He will have to undergo a series of rabies prevention treatments which we've already started. He'll have to get four more over the course of the next fourteen days."

She continued, "He also could need some plastic surgery if the wounds don't heal properly. I've started him on some Amoxicillin that should head off any infection. His left ankle is just a light sprain, keep it elevated and iced. We'll keep him a couple of hours for observation, but he can probably go home this afternoon."

Missy thanked her, and the doctor turned and added, "Call me if you need anything else, goodbye."

Well, Missy thought, *better find out where he is.* She asked the receptionist, who said, "That would be room 315." Missy walked to the elevator and pushed the "up" button which flickered twice, then stayed lit until the elevator car arrived with a ding.

The doors opened, and she stepped inside quickly. She had phobias about elevator doors, picturing her hand or foot getting caught between the doors and being scissored off as the car passed between floors. She imagined the doors snapping shut on the unlucky appendage like a ravenous beast with steel teeth.

But her *biggest* secret phobia was it getting stuck; sandwiched in like a sardine amongst a bunch of total strangers terrified her. She shivered at the thought, as the elevator stopped with a sharp jerk on the third floor.

"Thank God," she thought with relief as the doors slid open. Stepping out quickly, Missy passed the nurse's station and found Jake's room at the end of the hallway.

She knocked twice and said quietly, "Hello? It's Missy, are you awake?" as she pushed the door inward and stepped into the room.

Jake lay in the dark room, covered with a blanket.

"Can I turn on the light? Or will it bother you?" she asked him.

He made kind of a grunt, then said, "Hope you brought something to eat, I'm fucking starving."

She laughed, turning on the light. "Sorry, Bud, no room service, but I've got some slightly stale peanut butter crackers somewhere in the bottom of my purse, if that will suffice 'til lunch."

He sat up in bed and replied, "I could eat a porcupine, quills and all. But 'Nurse Wretched' says I gotta wait to have anything solid until the anesthesia totally wears off."

"Well, I think you can have ice chips and maybe a sip of water, if you're a good boy," she said, pulling up a chair.

She scooped some ice into a Styrofoam cup, poured a little water in it, then sat in the chair, and handed the cup to him. Jake took it in his left hand, jostling the IV in his arm, and sipped a little water, spilling some as he opened his parched lips and swallowed.

Then he asked a bit hoarsely, "Did the doctor divulge any details about my hand yet?"

She gave him a tight smile, "Well, you're not gonna lose it, but there's extensive damage, some broken bones and possible damage to the Ulnar nerve, whatever that is. Oh, and you might need skin grafts in the future. The left ankle is just sprained, you'll need to ice and elevate it. Think that about sums it all up. Oh yeah, the Doc started you on your first round of rabies vaccine. You'll need four more over the next two weeks."

Jake lifted his right arm, gazing at the hand covered in gauze and bandaged up like a mummy's. "How long do I have to stay?" he asked.

"Probably just a couple hours—you'll be free to go this afternoon at some point. Do you have anyone you can call to come pick you up?" she inquired, straight to the point.

Jake looked at her thoughtfully for a moment. "Well, not unless Jinx has learned to answer a cell phone and drive in the last couple hours. Maybe I'll call a cab?"

Missy pursed her lips, thinking. "I'm off duty for the next two days, I guess I could come back and give you a ride home. I take it you live alone?"

Jake gave her a tight smile, answering mischievously, "At the moment... except for an occasional nocturnal visit from Jinx. You know, the Chinese believe if you save someone, then you're responsible for him the rest of his life, or something like that."

She gave him a smirk, "Well, in case you hadn't noticed, Bud, I'm not exactly Chinese. I have more Nez Perce Indian blood than anything else, and they have a saying, 'He who wrestle wolverine and fall into cold lake have shitty luck.'"

She narrowed her eyes at him, "*Do* you have shitty luck, Jake?"

He smiled, "I guess not, seeing as you saved my stupid ass from drowning. I owe you my life. If there's any way I can pay you back...?" leaving the question open-ended.

She crossed her arms and laughed, "You can pay me back by getting well and taking care of that hand and ankle."

Jake looked at her, "You said you have the next two days off—what do you do for a living?"

She smiled, "I save big, strong men's asses for a living. All joking aside, I'm a Forest Ranger for the Wallowa-Whitman State Forest Service. But I haven't had to save anyone's ass since I started working here. You're my first—and hopefully my last."

Jake said, "Why is it I've never seen you around town? Of course, I don't go there much myself, except for groceries and supplies for work."

She answered, "I spend most of my off-time on the Lake, either taking water quality samples, sonar depth-mapping the lakebed or just some fishing when I feel like it."

She stretched and got up, looked at her watch, and stifled a yawn. "What do you do for a living, when you're not fighting off wolverines or trying to drown yourself?"

Jake smiled and shook his head as he contemplated his answer. "Well, I was a long-haul trucker years ago, but that didn't work out so well. So, I came back home. I was raised in the house that I'm in now. My old man left it to me before they made the land part of the state park. It was grandfathered in, but no money in the deal. I found I had a latent talent for writing fiction. I've got a potential best seller in the works and a bona fide one that's been on the best seller list for about six months."

Not a lot of money, Jake thought, *but better than the starving option!*

Missy squeezed her eyebrows together in concentration. "You're *that* Jake Anderson? I knew I'd seen or heard that name somewhere before."

Jake smiled modestly. "Yeah, well, the royalty checks keep me alive and happy. I don't go anywhere to spend much money, just enough for food, printer ink and paper—oh, and a lot of cat chow. Do you read a lot?"

She frowned, "Not as much as I'd like to, being a Ranger takes up most of my time—that, and fishing men out of the Lake. Joke. Maybe I'll find a copy of your book and give it a look-see, what's it called anyway?"

"It's called 'Finding Melissa," he deadpanned. She stared a hole in him until he grinned, "Just kidding. It's called 'Finding Atlantis,' but it has nothing to do with Atlantis. Just a metaphor for the times we live in, I guess."

"Sounds interesting. I'll have to try and find a copy to read when I get the chance," Missy said.

Jake replied, "I'll give you an autographed copy when I get out of here—least I can do."

She yawned again, looking at the clock. Just then Nurse "Wretched" walked into the room, reading a chart. glanced at Missy, then elbowed her way between her and Jake's bed.

"Time for your pain meds, Mr. Anderson," she said, producing a syringe with a needle the size of a pencil, or so it looked to Jake.

"Don't worry, not gonna stick you... yet!" she said with an evil grin.

Just do it and get it over with! thought Jake anxiously.

Nurse "Wretched," whose actual name was Beverly according to her ID badge, injected the contents of the syringe into the PICC line in his left arm, smiling down at him—a hint of evil surely lurked somewhere behind that smile.

"The doctor wrote you a couple of 'scripts for some antibiotics and Percocet for pain. They'll give them to you when you're discharged later."

She adjusted the drip-flow from the saline bag, then lifted his left leg up and placed an ice-cold gel pack on the red and swollen ankle. She took out a penlight and looked at both eyes, said "uh-hmm..." and wrote down the rest of his vitals on her chart.

"You missed breakfast. They'll bring you something to eat just as soon as I give the okay to the dietitian-aide. Can you eat with your left hand, Mr. Anderson?" she asked impishly, biting the inside of her cheek.

Jake looked at her, then at Missy, who'd been quietly observing the nurse's not-so-gentle ministrations. "Don't know, I've never had to try. Guess I'd better learn quick or I'll starve."

The nurse gave him an odd smile. "You'll learn quick enough—you'd be surprised what hunger can motivate you to do." She turned, taking her chart, and walked briskly out of the room.

Missy grinned at her back. "Well, I guess I'll go run some errands and wait for your call—oh, I better give you my number."

She found a piece of paper in her purse and wrote down her cell number, folded it and put it in the front left pocket of Jake's jeans that were hanging in a small closet.

She turned to go, and Jake asked, "Hey, what's your last name?"

Missy gave him tight smile, "Morning Star—told you I had Indian blood. My Mother is full-blooded Nez Perce, my Dad was French-Canadian. Gotta

go, Bud! Give me a call when you're ready to leave this 'pleasure palace'!"
Then she left without another word.

As she closed the door, Jake thought fuzzily, *despite her brusque attitude, she's nice, and she's damned attractive. If we'd met under normal circumstances, we could've been friends.* Then he dozed off again.

He jerked awake on the hospital bed, alarms going off on the machine next to the bed. He was soaked in sweat, breathing so hard he thought his heart would burst from his chest!

Nurse Beverly rushed into the room. She found Jake sitting up in the bed, then twisted a dial on the machine to turn off and reset it. The raucous noise ceased. The only sound was Jake's raspy breathing, finally beginning to slow.

She turned to him, "You gave us a start! Bad dream??"

Jake just nodded, "Yeah, pretty scary! Thank God it was only a dream!"

He fell back against the hospital pillow and released a long *woosh* of air.

Nurse Beverly the "Wretched" said calmingly, "Your food is on the way, oh, and as soon as you have a B/M, we'll get you discharged!"

Jake looked at her a little anxiously, "Thanks for the warning, what happens if I can't shit??"

She gave him a wicked grin, said in a bad German parody, "Ve hav vay's oov making you shite, ja??"

Jake didn't look comforted by her attempt at humor. Nurse "Wretched" laughed, then left the room closing the door behind her. An aide brought in a tray of something and set it on a rectangular table with wheels. She pushed it close to Jake and left.

Jake was ravenous—with his left hand, he lifted the domed lid that was meant to keep its contents warm. He placed it on the bed beside him. He looked at the plate—some "mystery meat" covered in green congealed gravy lay on a bed of overcooked noodles. Green beans so withered and dried-up that even the 'jolly green guy' himself would have said, "Ho-ho-ho, this shit's got to go," and banished them to vegetable hell. The mashed potatoes were cold and disgustingly tasteless.

Jake dug in awkwardly with his left hand and shoveled in a mouthful. *Tastes better than it looks!* he thought, masticating loudly, then dropped a forkful onto his hospital gown. *Shit, gotta get the hang of this, sooner than later!*

He managed to get most of it down, then tried valiantly and in vain, to open a small carton of chocolate milk. "These damn things are made the same as when I was a kid! Fucking impossible to open, even with *two* good hands!" He finally gave up, tossing the unopened carton in the trash can by his bed in frustration. He looked despairingly at his right hand, knowing his livelihood was in danger of being cut off for God knows how long, until the hand healed!

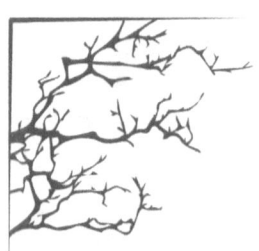

Chapter Five

After leaving the hospital, Missy drove around town a little aimlessly after running a few errands. She was thinking about the strange wailing sound that had brought Jake and her together on a collision course—ending with him in the hospital.

She *had* heard the wailing before. *It* had come *back*!! The thought ran shivers up and down her spine.

THE LAST TIME THE THING had appeared was in the summer of her youth. She was fourteen years old. Back then, *it* had come in the guise of a wolf—but it wasn't a wolf. She had been playing with her sister Elisa in a small field behind their house. It was just about sun-down, her sister had kicked a ball high and long into the forest surrounding their two-bedroom house.

"I'll get it!" Missy yelled, running after it.

She found the ball behind a small bush, just beyond the entrance to the forest proper. As she picked it up and was turning around, she heard the wailing for the first time. At first, it sounded like a woman in distress, then the tone would drop in pitch and start up again!

She turned and peered into the dark shadows of the forest, searching for the source. The wailing stopped abruptly! In its place, she heard a low growling, and nearly peed in terror as a large gray timber wolf stood facing her, about thirty feet into the darkening shadows of the forest! The low growling increased in pitch, the wolf's slit amber eyes locked on her, savage-looking canines exposed, dripping with saliva. She was frozen in place, the adrenaline pumping like mad through her body!

Elisa saw it at almost the same moment and screamed, "Missy!! Runnnnn!!"

As her sister turned and started running for the house, Missy threw the utility ball at the wolf with all her strength. It bounced off the wolf's snout, causing it to jerk back a few feet and hesitate. Missy didn't! She whirled and ran for her life toward the back door of the house. The wolf, sensing its prey was escaping, charged with a deep-throated growl. Her sister had just made it inside the back door. Missy ran with everything she had.

"I'm not gonna make it! I'm not gonna make it!" she cried as she raced. Then ten feet from the door, she tripped and fell face first into the grass.

The wolf was almost on her.

She started to get up, when Elisa screamed, "Stay down, Missy!!!"

She heard a loud *bang* and saw the wolf stopped abruptly about three feet away, knocked "ass over tea kettle," like a dog reaching the end of its leash. It gave a yelp of pain and anger, then rose on three legs and limped as fast as it could back into the shelter of the forest, looking back over its shoulder as it ran.

Missy jumped up and ran the rest of the way to the safety of her back door, seeing her sister holding her father's .30-.30 Winchester rifle pointed toward the forest and shaking like a leaf!

"Thank God—you remembered!!" she said, crying as she collapsed into Elisa's arms.

Her dad had always kept the Winchester handy by the back door.

"You never know when you might need it, better to have it close, 'just in *que-so*!'" he'd say with a smile and a wink. He had taught both girls gun safety and how to shoot at an early age.

The gun fell to the floor of the kitchen, as Missy embraced Elisa and said, "I don't know how you could have missed 'em from that range, but thank God you're okay!" Both girls sat down at the kitchen table, shaking with adrenaline.

"It would have been all over me in a heartbeat, if you hadn't shot when you did!" Missy said, gasping for breath. "You saw it limping off, right??"

Elisa just nodded, and Missy got up and hugged her again.

"You think it's dead?? Or maybe just wounded? I don't care... I'm just thankful to be in one piece!"

Elisa stared at her and spoke in a subdued voice, "We've never seen a wolf around here, have we??"

Missy shook her head. "No, but we know they're out there, we just happened to be in the wrong place at the wrong time, I guess!"

She got up from the table and walked over to the screen door, looking out to the inky darkness of the forest as the tall trees quickly eclipsed the sun.

"When did Mama say she'd be back?" Missy asked shakily.

"She said she had to stay late for the council meeting with the elders. Said not to stay up too late waiting for her, but she should be back around 10:00 p.m."

Just then, they heard the wailing again. It sounded far off in the distance, yet close enough that it sent icy shivers of fresh fear through them, the hair on the back of their necks stood up, goose-pimpled! Was it still alive? Or was it even the wolf making that awful sound? Missy wished with all her heart that her dad was still alive, so she could be comforted by his big arms wrapping around her tight, as he kissed her head and told her, "Everything's going to be okay, Sweetie"—but that was never going to happen again.

Her father had been a ranger for the Wallowa-Whitman National Forest Service for ten years before the 'incident.' He'd been on patrol late one night and had seen a car pulled over with its emergency flashers on. He stopped and walked over to the driver's side and, with his flashlight on, tapped the window. His body cam showed the big man inside grinning as he rolled his window halfway down—then shot the ranger twice in the head, killing him instantly. They'd caught the guy after he crashed his car into a tree five miles up the road. He'd come away with only a few cuts and bruises.

Turned out, the jerk was wanted in Utah for a double homicide. The murderer ended up on the receiving end of a bullet by firing squad. Ironic, perhaps poetic justice—but that was no conciliation to a wife and two young daughters now made fatherless. This had all happened two years before.

Their mother had taken it very hard. She had to provide for the girls, so she ended up working two jobs, but still made only half the income her husband had provided. She worked as a teller at a bank in Joseph during the day, then waited tables at night in a local cafe for low wages and tips.

Elisa was two years older than her sister, was taller and very reserved for sixteen-year old. Losing her dad had caused Elisa to shut down emotionally.

She didn't seem to have much empathy for anyone anymore but was always more sensible than Missy.

Now she said, "We can check and see if the wolf is dead or not tomorrow, there'll be a blood trail to follow—I know I hit the bastard! But for now, we need to eat something, do homework and get ready for bed, don't you think??"

Missy felt queasy at the thought of food! If her sister hadn't intervened as quickly as she did... She ate a bowl of canned soup, while Elisa had a frozen dinner.

They finished quickly, cleaned up the kitchen, then each finished her schoolwork. Afterwards, they brushed their teeth and got ready for bed. They shared a room, not much privacy for teenage girls, but tonight Missy was especially grateful to have Elisa's presence nearby. They had a night-light plugged in to read by, but she didn't feel much like reading tonight.

"Good night, Sweetie, I love you!" Missy said, yawning as she pulled the covers up to her chin.

"Good night!" Elisa murmured back.

Missy looked at the glow-in-the-dark clock by the bed, it was 9:45 p.m. She was just drifting off when she heard it—*Skritch... skritch... skritch*. The soft scraping sound seemed to be coming from behind her. Her bed rested against a window, with no headboard. Her eyes opened wide and her body went rigid as she listened intently! *Skritchhh... skritchhh... skritchhh...* the rasping noise was coming from her window and growing louder!!

"Elisa!! Do you hear that??" she asked in a fear-strained whisper. There was no response.

"Elisa!! Are you awake??" Missy implored, as she strained to see her sister in the dark.

Skritchhh ... skritchhh ... skritchhh—the sound of sharp fingernails on a chalkboard! Missy didn't notice the sudden warm wetness of her bladder releasing onto the bed as she slowly turned her head and looked out the window. A huge *monster* stood outside her window! All she could see was the blurry outline of something large, lurking a few feet away! Petrified with fear, she reached out a trembling hand, searching for the light switch on her bedside lamp, found it, turned the switch and light flooded the room.

The skeletal fingers scraping across the windowpane were—the untrimmed branches of the gnarled maple tree that stood six feet away, swaying in the wind with every little gust, scraping against the pane of glass.

Missy shuddered with a sigh of relief, angry at herself for letting her imagination run away with her so easily. She quickly changed into a fresh gown, stripped off the wet sheets, replaced them and crawled back into bed. She was reaching over to turn off the lamp when...

Tap ... tap ... tap. She turned, looked at the window again, and screamed in terror!! Plastered against the window—*a vision from hell*!! Staring back at her through the glass was the snarling face of a wolf-like creature leering in at her, except—the body was all wrong!! It stood upright on two legs, as a human would. But that couldn't be, could it??

Missy's scream woke Elisa, who turned toward the window and sang a duet of horror with her, seeing the monstrous thing capering at the window. Both girls jumped up and ran screaming into the kitchen.

Missy grabbed a butcher knife out of the knife block, while Elisa picked up the Winchester where it lay on the floor, working the lever-action to load a round. Missy threw the deadbolt on the back door, then without a word both girls backed into the corner of the kitchen. Suddenly there was a *scraping* noise that seemed to come from the living room door.

Missy frantically asked, "Did you remember to lock the front door before we went to bed??"

Elisa nodded yes, then shook her head, "I... I don't remember, for sure."

Missy grimaced, "Cover me, I gotta go check to make sure. Don't shoot unless you *have* to! And keep an eye on the back door, please!"

The front porch light was on. Missy crept into the darkened room, a little light shining through the curtains as she moved quietly to the door. She felt in the dark with a shaking hand for the deadbolt latch, found it and checked. It was locked! The door suddenly shook with a loud *thump!* Missy screamed and ran back to the kitchen! Someone or some*thing* was trying to get in!

She was hyperventilating as she told Elisa, "If *it* gets in, shoot the damn thing—and please don't miss this time!!"

Elisa gave her an annoyed look at the slight to her marksmanship but nodded. She drew a bead on the front door with the Winchester, using the back of a kitchen chair for a rest-aim. They heard the *snick* of the deadbolt turning out of its keeper in the door frame. Elisa's finger tightened on the trigger, starting a slow squeeze just as the door burst open, the porch light illuminating—their mother!! She was cursing the lock and struggling with a bag full of groceries.

"Don't shoot!! It's Mama!!" Missy cried out, shoving the barrel of the gun to the side just as her sister pulled the trigger with a deafening *boom*! Their mother shrieked, stumbled and fell onto the living room couch in a tangled heap.

Missy screamed, "Mommmm!" Elisa dropped the rifle to the floor, staring with horror at her fallen mother, as Missy went and quickly shut and bolted the door. She flipped on the inside light switch, then grabbed her mother's arm, pulling her up to a sitting position, and let out a huge sigh of relief, not seeing any blood or bullet wound.

Her mother looked from one sister to the other, wild-eyed and gasping to catch her breath. "What in the world is... going on here?? I saw something strange in the yard when I pulled up to park!"

Missy looked at her sister, who stood nearby. Elisa uttered stoically, "I almost shot you, Mama! I'm sorry—we thought it was the wolf-thing trying to get in!" She briefly hugged her mother, then quickly backed away as if embarrassed at the show of emotion.

Missy looked up at the door frame, shuddered as she saw the bullet hole there. The bullet had just missed her mother's head by maybe an inch!

Their mother looked at both girls and said anxiously, "*Wolf-thing*?? I saw what I thought was a man running from the porch in the headlights! Did he try to get in?? Did he try to hurt you??"

Missy sat down by her on the couch and recounted about the wailing they'd heard, right before the wolf's appearance, their mad dash to the house, and how her sister had saved her by shooting the wolf, or so they thought.

Her mother was staring at the bullet-hole in the door frame, muttering something that sounded like, "*You-know-Lucy*??"

"Lucy... who, Mama??"

Her mother was quiet for full minute, then said clearly and quietly, Yeenaldlooshi, a '*skin-walker*' or '*shapeshifter*,' it's an Indian word that roughly translates as '*He ,who goes on all fours*'!"

Their mother looked shaken as she told them of the old Native American legend. The girls listened intently as she related the story of an elder in the tribe who had sworn that he'd actually seen one. Dr. Mika Boucher, who was both a Doctor of Psychology and a shaman of the *Niimiipuu*, their people, claimed to have encountered a shaman who could transform into any animal at will. This power could only be accessed through killing a close relative or sibling. The *Yenaldooshi* presence was often heralded by eerie howling sounds. No one knew how or why they appeared, but it was never a good thing. They were supposed to be *evil* incarnate.

Missy was terrified, but Elisa sat quietly contemplating her mother's words.

Missy asked her mother, "But why did it come *here*?"

But it was Elisa who answered plainly and unemotionally, "Maybe it wants to *kill* us."

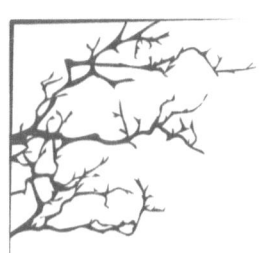

Chapter Six

A blaring car horn startled Missy, quickly bringing her back to the present. She found her van sitting half-way into an intersection, the traffic light was green. She frowned and shook her head, accelerating down the street toward the hospital.

Jake wasn't going to like—or even believe—her explanation of what she believed was behind the 'wailing' sound they had both heard, at different times in their lives. The wolverine attack was just too coincidental for comfort, at least to her. *Better not to bring it up at all, unless he asks again*, she thought, looking for a parking spot outside the hospital.

It was pushing 3:00 p.m. She was getting out of her 'bus, when her cell *rang* to the chorus of CCR's "Bad Moon Rising," a great old '70's rock song her mother had turned her onto. It brought back memories of an old werewolf flick she'd seen as a teenager. Now she wondered why she had chosen it as a ringtone in the first place!

She grimaced as she dug through her purse to find the damn phone, then reflected, *I'm gonna need to change that, and soon!*

She saw it was the hospital on the caller ID and answered, "Morning Star."

"Hi there, Missy, it's me, Jake. Uh ... the doctor said they were ready to kick me out. I kinda need you to sign some paperwork for me, being a 'southpaw' now really *sucks*! And it's definitely not going to improve my typing skills anytime soon."

Missy thought, *that's the least of his problems*, but said, "Sure, I just got back from running errands, are you downstairs yet?"

There was a pause. "Uh, Nurse 'Wretched' says I've got to take a crap first, so it may be awhile yet. Uh, oh boy, gotta go *now*, that orange stuff they gave me is working!" He ended the call abruptly.

Missy chuckled and made her way into the ER, got the paperwork from the clerk and sat down to fill it out. Then she realized she didn't know enough about Jake to complete it. Shit! She'd have to wait for them to release him or just fill in what she did know, which was next to nothing! She sighed and laid the clipboard with the forms on the chair beside her.

Twenty minutes later, the elevator opened, and an aide wheeled Jake over to where she was sitting. Jake gave her a weak smile.

"I was thinking maybe you might be having a little problem filling out those forms, you don't know 'jack' about me." He pushed the wheelchair up close to her seat.

She smiled. "I do know your curiosity just about got you killed last night, Bud! But you're right, I don't know 'jack' about you."

So, Jake dictated his information to her. As she filled out the forms, she learned he was divorced, no children, thirty-five years old, had a history with alcohol, didn't smoke, was allergic to penicillin, (like, who wasn't?) and—already apparent to her, had no common sense!

Typical man, she thought, as she finished up by signing his name on the forms and gave the clipboard back to the clerk and in return, got his 'scrips for antibiotics and pain.

"You ready to go? Or do you need to get anything before I take you home?" she inquired, as an aide wheeled Jake out into the overcast and chilly afternoon.

"I could use a six-pack of beer right about now," he replied, as he was helped carefully into the VW. Missy raised an eyebrow, looked at him, but said nothing.

He smiled, "Or maybe just a six-pack of soda, I'm still on the wagon." He named a few other items he thought he'd need.

She nodded and drove them to the drugstore, dropping off the prescriptions, then ran in and got the groceries he wanted. They sat in the car while they waited for the pharmacist to fill his order. Jake took a can out of the soda six-pack, then looked disgruntled, as he realized he couldn't easily open it with one hand.

"Could you pop my top, please?" he asked innocently, holding the can out to her.

Missy grinned. "You're trying my patience, Bud!" as she popped open the can with a snap.

Jake took a couple of gulps, belched, and looked for her reaction. Missy just rolled her eyes and shook her head.

He said, "Seriously, you know, it's gonna be pretty tough for me to do, like, the simplest tasks when I get back home, at least for a while. I was wondering if you might, uh, I mean, maybe you could ...?"

"No, Jake, I really can't. I'm sorry, but I have to work!" she responded, knowing what he was going to ask of her.

He sighed and just looked out the window at the gray clouded sky, wishing he'd kept his damn mouth shut. He felt ashamed for asking more of her than she had already done. She'd gone above and beyond the call of duty, saving his sorry ass from drowning and keeping him alive long enough to get him to the hospital. Plus, she had stayed and waited patiently to take him home. Hell, nobody else he knew would have been so generous. He couldn't ask any more from a total stranger.

"I'm sorry, Missy, I-I didn't mean to sound so selfish. I'm just tired and hurting, not looking forward to trying to 'type and wipe' with one hand, but I'll manage." Jake looked embarrassed at the pun, taking another sip from the can and thinking, *just shut your mouth and quit complaining to her!*

Missy pulled up to the drug window, got his prescriptions and paid for them, as he couldn't reach into his right back pocket to get his wallet.

She gave them to him saying, "You can owe me."

Jake muttered, "I already owe you my life, what's a few bucks more gonna matter? Listen, if I can ever do anything to repay your kindness, you just name it! If it's in my power to do, your wish is my command."

Now it was Missy who was flustered. "So now you're a writer-genie I've let out of the bottle?? Look Bud, you don't owe me anything! I did what any decent person would have done in my place, hell, saving your ass was just part of my job. I'm a Ranger, it's what I do for a living, for Christ's sake!

"I just wish I could've been there to save my father when he needed me, he was shot in the line of duty! But I was a kid. It will always haunt me. Maybe that's why I've tried to follow in his footsteps, to somehow make up for this helpless feeling of not being able to change what happened to him."

Jake looked at her solemnly for a minute, barely managed to open the pain med bottle with one hand, took two with a gulp of soda.

Then, changing the subject, he quietly said, "I'm sorry about your dad, I didn't know. Speaking of haunting, you said earlier you had heard that sound before. When... and where?"

Missy stared straight ahead, gripping the steering wheel hard, her knuckles white with tension as she thought about what to say to him. The road was beginning to curve back around to the south part of Lake Wallowa, toward the National Forest section where they both resided. She could smell the pines through the open window as they got closer. He gave her directions at the turn-off to the house.

"I was fourteen, my sister and I were playing out back of our house. My sis kicked the ball into the edge of the forest, I went to get it. As I picked it up, that sound—it was like a woman screaming, but *not*... I don't know, but anyway it abruptly stopped! Then I heard this *growling,* I looked around and saw this huge timber wolf about twenty or thirty feet away!" She told him the rest of it, about her sister shooting the wolf, then later the horror at the window, almost shooting their mother, and her mother telling them of an old Indian myth about *Shape Shifters* or *Skin-Walkers.*

"*Yeenaldlooshi,*" she called them. Supposedly, they were supernatural beings who could take the form of any animal they wished, but most often seemed to choose the form of a wolf. Usually, the medicine men of the tribe were attributed with these powers of transformation, but certain women of the tribe were also said to be able to transform at will on a full moon, all to inflict pain or suffering on others. The initiation was gruesome! To gain this immense power, they had to kill a close relative, cut out the heart and devour it while still beating! Yuck! And the transmutation elicited immense pain, often eliciting an unearthly wail as it transpired.

"These *Skin-Walkers* were said to be almost immortal, but they could be killed. Supposedly, anyone who tracked a *skin-walker* and learned their identity could in theory call them by their full given name under a full moon. Then the evil one would die for all the pain and cruelty they had caused. Or fire could kill them if all else failed.

"Anyway, my sis and I went out the next day, hoping to track the wolf to where it had died. Nothing! We couldn't find a single spot of blood on the ground—we know he was hit, because he was limping on three legs into the forest. But there were no tracks either. No spoor, nothing! It was like a bad nightmare, like it never happened at all. We never saw it again after that night, thank God! My sister thought it was there to kill us. I'll never forget that awful night."

Missy finished her explanation, pulling into Jake's driveway, and coming to a halt in front of his house. She turned and looked at Jake. He was pale and a thin sheen of sweat ran off his face, even though the temperature outside was in the forties.

"Are you okay?? You look like you swallowed something nasty!" she asked.

Jake answered a little queasily, "Yeah, I think it's called bullshit! I'm sorry, but I'm having a hard time believing the 'wolf-thing' part of your story. Don't get me wrong, I believe you saw the wolf and that it attacked you. But... the thing at your window? Surely, you don't believe that it was a, what did you call it? Never mind, it couldn't be real, I mean, you would have found some evidence of the *'thing.'* You said you and your sister looked, but found nothing, right?"

Missy was doing a slow burn. She'd known he wouldn't believe her about the wolf-thing at her window before she even opened her mouth to speak.

"You could ask my sister Elisa if it was real—If I even knew how to contact her! But I haven't seen or talked to her in over ten years! She was always a loner, never seemed to need anybody. Right after high school she left town and then married some loser trucker, an alcoholic prick down in Texas. Last I heard from her, she was divorcing his sorry ass!

"I thought what we'd been through might have brought the two of us closer, but Elisa was already an enigma, withdrawn and isolated, following our father's death. And she became even more reclusive almost overnight after nearly shooting our mother," she remarked, looking at the front of Jake's house.

Jake suddenly made a choking sound.

Missy turned to look at him, "Seriously, are you okay?"

Jake was gob smacked. "I'm gonna be sick!" he gasped, trying desperately to open the door with his left hand.

He barely managed to get it open, leaned out and tossed up his lovely hospital lunch, along with the meds he'd taken earlier. Missy got out and rushed around to his side of the VW, careful not to step in the steaming miasma of puke, as she leaned into the vehicle and helped him out onto the gravel drive. He heaved, bent over, until nothing was left, then she handed him some tissues from her purse.

Jake wiped his mouth and spat on the ground. "I-I need to sit down—I can't believe this shit! Elisa *Starr* is your *sister*?? This is crazy!"

Missy frowned at him and asked, "'Starr' is not her last name, unless she changed it. And how do you *know* her?"

AS THEY WALKED UP TO his front door, he turned and looked at her for a moment, then clumsily dug his key out of his left pocket and opened the door. They walked inside, and Jake plopped down onto an ugly brown sofa.

Missy shivered, at least partially from the cold, and glanced at the pot-bellied stove thinking it could stand stoking.

"You got any wood for that thing, Bud? It's close to freezing in here!"

"Yeah, I managed to chop a few pieces before all this shit happened, they're out back by the cutting stump."

She nodded, opening the back door. She grabbed a couple pieces from the small stack of wood and brought them in, opening the barely warm stove door to toss them inside on top of the small glowing pile of embers. Then she returned to the couch and waited expectantly for Jake to continue his explanation.

He propped his right arm up on a grungy-looking sofa pillow, sighed and said, "Yeah, I know her, I'm the 'alcoholic prick' that she divorced over ten years ago!"

Missy looked stunned! She slowly sank down on the sofa, shaking her head, and demanded, "What the hell is going on here, Jake?? You're telling me you were married to my *sister*? For how long...? Do you know where she is?? I... I'm at a loss here. Is she okay?"

Jake felt his whole world had turned upside-down!

He put his left hand up defensively, "Missy, please, slow down a minute. We were only married for a little over a year. I haven't seen or talked to her since I left Texas more than ten years ago! I left town soon after our divorce was finalized. She was fine—or good as you can be after something as painful as we went through.

"I'm sorry that I can't be more help, but we've had no contact whatsoever since I left Texas! I moved back here to get my shit together. I've been clean and sober since I returned. I started writing again, it's kept me sane—or it did up until all this shit!"

Missy just stared in silence as he continued, "Anyway, no, I don't know if she is still in Texas or not, I suspect you would have heard something by now if she wasn't. But surely, you've tried over the years to find her, right? I mean—oh, I don't know what I mean!" he said miserably, shaking his head, his eyes pleading.

"I don't know what any of this means, but I don't really believe in coincidence. All of this must have happened for a reason, right?"

Missy was suddenly uncomfortable as his words echoed her thoughts earlier. And she *had* tried over the years to contact Elisa. She'd google-searched and even considered hiring a private investigator to try and find her. But Elisa was good at not being found. Even when they were kids playing hide and seek, if Elisa didn't want to be located, you'd never find her! And sitting here, next to her, was her sister's freaking ex-husband! Coincidence?

Maybe. But what if it wasn't? What if he'd done something, something terrible to her sister after getting the divorce? What if he had roughed her up in a drunken rage and hurt her or, God forbid, killed her and gotten away with it! It would be a convenient excuse to leave town and haul ass to somewhere two thousand miles away to hide, wouldn't it? She could be sitting next to a *murderer*! Missy, after all, *didn't* know jack-shit about Jake, except what he had told her. How much should she believe, after all, he's a writer, for God's sake! He was used to creating fiction, who's to say he hadn't just whipped up some bullshit souffle to feed her!

She was no longer uncomfortable—now she was scared!

She stood up quickly from the couch, "Jake, I'd like you to tell me the truth! Did you ever hurt or hit Elisa in anger, or when you had been drinking? No bullshit! We may be estranged, but she's my sister! If you ever laid a hand on her or seriously hurt her and I find out about it..." Missy left the rest of the threat unsaid, trembling with a mixture of anger and fear as conflicting emotions ran though her.

Jake shook his head, standing up somewhat unsteadily. "Missy, honestly, I messed up a lot back then. Long lonely nights on the road, missing Elisa... drinking a lot to deal with it! Yeah, I screwed up one time too many. And I was jealous of the way she dealt with my long absences by going out and hanging at local bars, knowing all the guys were after her! At least that's the way it seemed, but that's not the whole truth.

"The truth was everything I thought back then was filtered through an alcoholic haze. But I swear I never hurt her. At least, not physically. I loved her, but the alcohol was this big hairy bitch that came between us, broke us apart! Couldn't see it then, took years of hindsight before I realized there was always a third party in our relationship, and it wanted me all to itself."

Missy relaxed a little, thinking about what he'd said. It felt like he was telling the truth, but how could she be certain? No way to know. Give him the benefit of the doubt—or run like hell?

She saw genuine sorrow in his eyes, and maybe, regret? Hard to tell—either way she needed to leave.

"Jake, I've gotta' go, it's been a damned long day. You've got my number, if you need a ride into town, call me," she said as she picked her purse off the couch.

She stopped mid-stride in the doorway, "You best get some wood into that 'antique' stove there or you'll freeze tonight."

"Yeah, I'll get more in, there's more outside, don't worry about it. Thanks for reminding me," he replied.

She started to leave, then stopped. "You said you'd give me an autographed copy of your book. You happen to have one already signed? Cuz I don't think you'll be signing *anything* any time soon, unless you're ambidextrous!"

Jake gave her a strained smile, went to his bedroom, rustled around in the room a minute and came back out with a copy of "Finding Atlantis." He handed it to her as she reached for it, then held onto it while looking her in the eyes.

"I'm really grateful for all you've done for me. If I could tell you where Elisa is, I would in a heartbeat. If there's anything I can do for you, just name it! I'm not a terrible person, I've just got, uh, demons to fight, only most of mine came from a bottle!"

Missy gave him a quick tight smile, then it was gone. "Thanks for the book. I'm gonna find her, Jake, it's only a matter of how and when."

Jake slowly nodded as she turned and walked out to the VW. She said over her shoulder, "See ya 'round—and try to stay out of trouble!"

As Jake was closing the door after her, Jinx came flying around a corner and dashed into the house. The big cat's chief concession to domestication was his feline taste for being warm when it was cold outside. On frosty nights, he relished stretching out on Jake's couch or at the foot of Jake's bed, and he knew Jake would eventually feed him and also let him out when he needed to go.

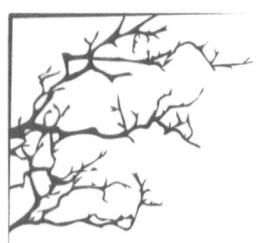

Chapter Seven

Jake sighed watching Missy pull out of his driveway, then picked up the remaining sodas she'd put down on the couch and took them to the fridge out back. He took one and sat down in the porch rocker, placing the can between his knees to open it with his left hand. The sun was setting, turning the overcast sky a beautiful shade of burnt orange, reminding him of sunsets back in Texas. The conversation about Elisa had stirred memories of their relationship and one incident that particularly still haunted him.

He watched the sunset, taking a sip of his soda. "Well, it ain't Pabst, but it'll do," he grumbled, staring into the gathering darkness beyond his porch. Yeah, that was part of the irony. He'd had a job driving a big rig delivering good old Pabst Blue Ribbon up and down Interstate 35, made a decent living too!

YEAH, GOOD OLD 2007. Good, that is, until he had started drinking more than he delivered. Until he'd picked up a lovely young brunette hitching a ride on the side of I-35. Until she was giving him the best blow job he'd had in memory. Until just as he came, one of his rear tires blew and he swerved over the center line at 80 mph. Until his semi-collided head-on into a family of four, sending all of them to the hospital's ICU and damn-near severing his junk entirely when the brunette's head broke the steering wheel along with most of her front teeth! Luckily, none of the family's injuries were life-threatening.

He'd never have picked up the woman if he'd been sober! The cops said his blood alcohol level was more than twice the legal limit. He'd had to take their word for it as he was unconscious after the head-on, and with all the empties lying in the cab, the case was cut and dried. His lawyer made a plea bargain—got him a huge fucking fine, ten years' probation and 400 hours of community service since it was his first offense.

After the doctor had gotten Jake's cock sewed back together in the ER, his soon to be ex-wife Elisa had come by briefly, looked at him and just laughed bitterly, saying, "That's the last fucking straw, Jake!" She flipped him off with both hands and walked out the door. She'd given him an ultimatum months before, "the alcohol or me, but not *both*!" following a previous drunken incident. His life would never be the same. After paying the brunette's hospital and dental bills and for part of the family's hospitalization, and with Elisa filing for divorce, he'd been tapped out.

"Way to fuck up your life!" Jake had thought morosely as he sat on a crappy pigeon-shit-coated bench outside the Greyhound bus station in Corpus Christi, Texas, in 100-degree heat in "air you could wear." He'd been skipping town after finishing community service and selling his rig to pay off his fine and all the medical bills. The bus was late, go figure. Didn't matter, it would be a long ride up to Oregon. The bus pulled up in a blue cloud of diesel fumes; they loaded his backpack full of jeans, tees and underwear. That was all he had to his name after paying off his lawyer.

He was heading for his boyhood home up in the Wallowa Mountains. His old man had left him the house in his will, as his mom, Syla, had passed when he was ten and he had no siblings.

Jake had joined the Marines as soon as he graduated. He'd met Elisa Starr on a blind date in his fourth year of serving in the Corps in Texas. One of his buds had told him about this beautiful raven-haired woman with eyes like emeralds, who was a good friend of his sister's. She worked as a beautician in a small shop in a strip mall. They'd double-dated off and on for about six months, by then he was smitten by her good looks and the sound of her laugh. Yeah, beautiful—and she damn well knew it!

They had married the following year. His four years were up, and he hadn't even considered re-enlisting. He'd had trouble finding work at first, drifting from one job to the next while Elisa became increasingly vexed 'til he finally spotted an ad in the paper for long haul delivery driver. He was hired on the spot. Really, thinking back on it, that had been the beginning of the end for them.

One tumultuous occasion stood out in his memory, even after all these years had passed.

Eleven years earlier, he'd been trying to get some shuteye in his truck at a rest stop about fifty miles from home after a grueling twelve-hour run. He was sleeping in his cab to try to save a few bucks when his cell rang, startling him awake. He looked at the time and number: 2:30 a.m. and it was Elisa calling. That alone was strange, as she never called after midnight!

He answered groggily on the third ring. "Hello, Elisa...? Hellooo... Elisa, that you?" No reply.

Then he heard moaning and groaning in the background.

"What the hell's going on?? Who's there...? *Elisa*—are you *there*??" he was almost shouting at the phone.

All he heard was, "Ohhhh, Hank, give it to me baby! Ohhh, yessss, do me harder!!"

The blood drained from his face and his fingers had a death grip on the phone. He screamed her name over and over—either she couldn't hear him or didn't give a shit or maybe both! Apparently, she had "butt-dialed" him and didn't realize he was listening in on her little tryst!

He could barely hear over all the grunting and moaning. Shaking with rage, feeling like his heart had been torn out and stomped on, he threw the damned phone out the window onto the highway, where it lay in pieces like roadkill. He fired up the big rig and roared out of the rest stop heading to Corpus as fast as his rig would safely allow. Jake pulled up in front of his building, parked his rig and sat in the cab seething, planning what he would do if he found them screwing.

Jake kept a nine mm Glock seventeen in his glove compartment while out on the road, and a concealed handgun license in his wallet. Lotta crazies out there!

Yeah, crazy like me right now! he thought, he took the gun out of its paddle holster and tucked it the back of his jeans. He jumped out of the cab and stalked toward his apartment.

He'd intended to slip in quietly and catch them in the act, but said, "Fuck that!" kicking the cheap entry door hard enough to send it flying inward against the wall.

Jake marched over to the closed bedroom door, stopped and listened intently. Hearing nothing, he swung the door inward. The room was dark except for the blue flickering images from the silent TV. It lit the room enough for him to see his wife asleep on the bed under the covers. Alone.

Jake stuck the Glock in the back of his jeans again and stalked over to the bed, swaying a little from the beer buzz. She was lying on her left side, pillow over her head, snoring lightly. He grabbed the pillow and threw it across the room. Elisa jerked awake—saw him standing over her breathing hard, fists clenched—and let out yelp of surprise and fright. She grabbed the sheet and pulled it over her naked breasts.

"Jake! What are you doing back this early? I didn't expect you to get in until noon." She sniffed the air. "Have you been drinking??" she asked shakily.

Jake roared, "Where *is he*??"

She fell back onto the bed, her face shocked and pale from the threat of potential violence in his voice.

He yelled again, "Where's the *cocksucker* hiding??"

Elisa looked at him indignantly, anger making her voice shake even more. "What the *hell* are you talking about?? *Who* the hell are you *talking* about?? Are you fuckin' *nuts*?? And how *dare* you *yell* at me like that!!" she screamed, tears streaming now.

Jake wasn't the least placated. "You fuckin' butt-dialed me at 2:30 a.m.! I heard every fucking moan and groan, Babe!" he yelled, spittle flying with vitriol.

"Oh Hank, give it to me, baby, do me *harder*!!" he mimicked a falsetto with a sneer, his eyes wild with jealousy and white-hot rage.

Elisa shook her head, a bitter smile forming beneath the tears streaming down her face. She picked up the remote and hit the DVR rewind button—images of a naked couple coupling on a large bed in hyper movement flew by. She got to a stopping point, pressed 'play' and turned up the volume.

Jake stared at the screen as the audio became clearer.

The woman in the scene cried out, "Oh Hank, give it to me baby, do me *harder*!! Yessss, baby, do me sooo good!!"

Jake's mouth dropped open with understanding, he felt the blood and jealous rage rush from his head like a receding tide. His stomach felt greasy, like he'd swallowed something nasty!

Now *she* was the one shaking with rage. She pointed a shaking finger at the screen and said in a low growl, "*There's* my mystery lover! You inconsiderate, drunk *asshole*!! I fell asleep watching the fucking Playgirl channel!" She took a step toward him—he retreated a step.

"Get the hell out of here, right the fuck *now*!! I mean it, don't try to come sneaking back or I'll file a restraining order on *your* sorry ass or worse!! *Leave! Now!*" she hissed at him, pointing toward the front door.

Jake felt like he'd just wandered into the twilight zone.

He stammered, "I'm sorry, Elisa, I... am an asshole!" turned and walked out of the apartment, pulling the broken door to behind him.

He'd walked steady and purposely back to his rig, his beer buzz long gone. He climbed up into the cab and replaced the Glock inside the glove compartment. This was now home. "Better get used to it, I guess," he muttered dejectedly to himself. "She'll forgive me in time, maybe." She would—*that* time.

JAKE TOOK ANOTHER SIP of his soda, recalling that Elisa liked to flirt with guys, but she hadn't really had any close female friends—except for maybe Ava, the sister of his Marine buddy who had introduced them.

Men had no problem with her "social skills," you didn't really need many when you were a beautiful woman. She preferred to read or watch old romantic movies at home in her spare time alone. She had never talked much about her past or that she even had a *mother*, let alone a sister. He'd never questioned her about her parents, either. Now, thinking back, it seemed a little strange to him that she never talked about her family at all! What had happened to cause her to basically erase her family from her life?

Elisa and Jake had been together for over a year, but she could have been a total stranger as far as his knowledge of her family was concerned. He'd been busy driving and drinking most of the time. She might have talked about her past, but he'd usually been drinking or drunk when they were together, so no way would he remember any conversation they had.

If he were brutally honest with himself, he'd married her mostly for her looks, not her personality. No crime—a lot of men did it, but surely nothing to be proud of. Not many marriages survived such a weak foundation. Theirs had crumbled in a very short time!

Jake had been in love with the idea of "being in love," when all was said and done. But nothing had been stronger than his love for that bitch, alcohol!

"WELL, THE PAST IS BEHIND me," Jake muttered, as he finished up his diet coke, tossing it in the small trash container by his chair. Then a thought struck him. Maybe he could look up Ava and see if she and Elisa had kept in touch or were still friends! *Ava might still have Elisa's phone number or know where she's living now.* Jake thought somberly.

Suddenly he saw a blur of movement out of the corner of his eye! He turned to look and was rewarded with twenty-five pounds of bobcat in his lap! Of course, Jinx landed directly on Jake's balls, causing a crushing wave of fresh pain and nausea!

Jake let out an *oomph* of air as the big cat gave out what passed for a purring sound and plopped down on his lap, staring at him with his amber-yellow eyes as if to say, *what can you do for me?* Or maybe, *where's my fucking food?* Jake recovered from the ball-bruising and using his left hand, lightly patted him on the head, to which Jinx responded by whipping his head around and nipping him on his thumb.

"Shit! You traitorous, fat fleabag!" Jake hissed, dumping the big cat off his lap onto the floor and inspecting his thumb for damage.

Seeing nothing but a couple of teeth dents, he shoved himself up out of the chair, opened the back door and went inside. Jinx trotted in behind him, padded over to his feeding bowl and stopped, looking up at Jake, then down at the empty bowl.

Jake frowned at him, "You're gonna have to earn your keep for the next month or so, seeing as I almost got my hand eaten off by one of your fellow feral forest fuckers last night!"

Try saying that three times! Jake thought, grinning slightly as he opened a bag of cat chow he kept by the back door. He poured about two cups into the dish and Jinx sniffed at it, gave him a look that said, *what's this shit?* then dug in like he hadn't eaten in a week.

Jake poured some water into a bowl next to the cat as it crunched its food. Then he grabbed his phone, sat in his recliner, got on Facebook and started perusing the various "Ava Farina" listings, until he found one about the right age. He looked at her profile and thought, maybe she's the right one. He knew, back then at least, Ava was single. But if she'd married, he'd play hell finding her. That was the bitch about locating women you only knew when they were single. Hardly any of them kept their own surname.

Facebook made it a little easier—sometimes. He looked for relatives, found a 'Chuck' listed as "brother" and felt a surge of hope. He posted on her timeline, asking her if she knew Elisa's current whereabouts or was in contact with her, texting Ava that, "Elisa's sister Missy is very worried about her and would very much like to know that she's okay." He left her both his and Missy's phone numbers.

He didn't know how much Elisa had bad-mouthed him after the divorce, so had no way to gauge if Ava held a grudge or not unless she contacted him or Missy. "Friending" her probably wouldn't work if she didn't want to hear from him. Besides, maybe Elisa didn't want to be found.

Jinx wandered in and curled up on an oval rug by Jake's chair, staring at him for a moment, then closed his eyes and fell into a feline coma of oblivion. Jake got off Facebook, rose and went to bathroom to pee.

He unzipped and had to remember to use his left hand. Unfortunately, he was used to aiming with his right, so of course he missed left and then over-corrected, missing the bowl entirely on the right! *Shit!* He finally got centered, finished and zipped up, got some paper towels and cleaned up the floor. *That'll take some practice,* he thought.

He walked back into his kitchen, opening the freezer to see what kind of frozen delicacy was awaiting his palate tonight. He chose teriyaki beef tips with broccoli and mushrooms, with a chocolate brownie that invariably came out looking like a piece of half-baked shit. *How appetizing!* Jake thought sourly.

He shoved it in the microwave and sat down in his recliner to wait for his food to nuke. The oven *dinged*, he got up, grabbed an oven pad and reached in. Balancing it on the unfamiliar hand, he almost made it to the counter before it tilted backward, splashing steaming hot teriyaki sauce onto the back of his hand!

Jake screamed, "*Fuuucck*!" dropping the whole dinner, which splattered on the kitchen floor. He raced over to the faucet, shaking off the steaming sauce while running cold water over his hand.

He turned off the water and inspected the hand. It was red, but no blisters. He looked down at the disgusting mess on the floor, the brownie still intact inside the plastic tray, as expected, looking like a soggy "teriyaki turd." Jinx appeared as if he'd materialized out of thin air, and started lapping up the still-warm sauce, eating small chunks of beef while purposely avoiding the broccoli. Jake managed to clean up the mess, using half a roll of paper towels.

"I hope you enjoyed that, cause I sure as hell didn't!" he said to the cat, as he dumped the remainder in the trash. He'd lost what little appetite he'd had. He grabbed a banana off the counter, peeling it with his teeth and opened an old jar of peanut butter by wedging it under his right armpit as he twisted the lid off.

He used his finger to scoop out a glop and spread it on the banana, then slowly ate, thinking about Missy again. If he could somehow get Elisa to contact Missy, it would go a long way in paying Missy back for all the hassle she'd endured. Plus, if he and Elisa could reconcile their estrangement, he *might* come out this shit smelling like a rose! Well, he'd have to wait and see if Ava would make contact.

In the meantime, he had his hand to take care of—it was, after all, his bread and butter. He finished off the banana and locked the front door, then went into his office-bedroom and sat down in front of his computer.

He pulled out the keyboard tray and experimented typing with one hand. That sucked! He didn't think he would be able to produce more than a page of dialog a day at this pace. He hadn't had to "hunt and peck" since he'd learned to type in school. He wrote laboriously for two hours until his hand cramped up.

He had realized it was after ten o'clock and decided that was enough for the evening, when Jinx's snarling growl emerged from the living room. Jake got up to see what the problem was. Jinx stood by the back door, his back arched, and every bit of fur bristled like he'd just gotten out of a dryer. Then Jake heard the *wailing* again, and it sounded close!

Jake stood looking at the cat and started to ask, "What's gotten into–" when suddenly, there was a *skritchh... skritchh... skritchh* at the back door! The hair on the back of his neck stood up, while Jinx hissed and ran under the kitchen table.

Jake's first thought was, *My gun! Fuck! It's still in Missy's tackle-box!* His back door was solid wood, didn't have a window in it, so he couldn't see what was outside, making the odd sound. Then he realized the back door *wasn't locked! Shit!* He quickly reached out to seat the deadbolt, then slid the security chain on. A loud *thump* shook the door in its frame, making him jump back! Something growled on the other side as the door was tested again.

Jake was scared shitless! After Missy relating her past experiences, this was becoming all too real! Looking frantically around for something to use as a weapon, he spied a can of bear mace called "Bear-B-Gone" on the counter. He'd never encountered a bear so never needed it. But it was better than nothing. He listened and thought he heard movement on the porch. A board squeaked as something heavy moved around just beyond the door. The bobcat was having none of this—he hissed, ran through Jake's bedroom and hid in the bathroom. *Should I open the door and spray this shit quickly at whatever it is out there? Or just leave it be?* he thought feverishly, trying to decide.

The security chain on the door was like those on motel doors everywhere, meant more as a deterrent than to keep someone or *something* determined enough from getting inside. It wouldn't take too much force to tear the slotted bracket from the door frame—that was the deadbolt's job. Jake was thinking, *If I released the deadbolt and opened the door just wide enough to spray this shit, would the chain alone hold back whoever or whatever was out there long enough for me to re-secure the deadbolt?"* Good fucking question!

But it was *not* gonna be answered—he had no intention of unlocking the door to find out who or what might be lurking on his back porch! He set the bear spray on the counter and pulled one of his kitchen chairs over, shoving it under the doorknob on a tilt to wedge it tight, then picked up the spray and backed up into the living room.

The two windows in the kitchen were small but still vulnerable. Nothing he could do to secure those. He listened intently for any sound. The attack on the door hadn't been repeated. Jake was breathing hard, trying not to freak out. He picked up his phone and retreated to his bedroom. Locking the door, he set the phone down on his desk and dialed 911. The phone dropped the signal twice before finally connecting.

After ringing five times, a dispassionate-sounding dispatcher answered, "Joseph 911, what is the nature of your emergency??"

Jake hesitated briefly, thinking of what to say, "I've, uh... got somebody, *or some-thing,* trying to break into my house!! Could you please send someone out? I-I think it may be some large animal!"

The dispatcher said, "Sir, please give me your address." Just as Jake gave him the address, he heard a *crash* from out back.

"Sir, that address is in the National Park," the dispatcher said calmly.

Jake gripped the phone impatiently, "Yeah, I know, I *live* here! Can you just get someone out here, my life is in danger! Please hurry!!"

"Sir, we can, but that address is in the jurisdiction of the National Park Service. They'll have someone close by who can respond quicker. Please hold while I get them on the line."

Jake heard a noise behind him and turned to look anxiously at the window near his bed but couldn't see anything. His palm was sweaty, and he lost his grip on the phone. It clattered to the hardwood floor, lying there like a wounded animal. After wiping his palm on his shirt, Jake scrambled to grab it again. The screen had a crack running across its face, but it still worked.

Thank you, God, he thought. As the line started ringing, he felt something bump against his leg! He gasped, whirled around and saw that Jinx had come out from hiding in the bathroom and was looking at him expectantly. The big cat paced by the bedroom door his fur still puffed-up.

"Shit! don't *do* that, Jinx, I nearly crapped myself! I'm scared enough for both of us."

The cat gave him a look that said, *fuck you, I want out of here, now!*

A familiar voice answered, "Park Ranger, this is Morning Star, how can I help you?"

Jake cringed—he hadn't mentally connected what the dispatcher had said about "Park Service" a few moments before. Of course, logically, it would be Missy, and she lived only a mile away.

"Missy, it's Jake! Someone or something is trying to break into my house! I-I think they're still out there! You've got my pistol! I have both doors locked, the only weapons I have are a can of fucking bear spray and a worthless chicken-shit bobcat!" Jinx gave him his, *now I'm* really *pissed-off!* stare.

Missy said, a little sarcastically, "I thought I asked you to try and stay out of trouble, Bud!"

Jake answered heatedly, "It's not *me* that's causing any trouble, damn it all! Some weird shit is going down here!" A *crash* came from the porch outside the bedroom. Jake whirled around, trying to see out the window, but it was too dark. *The light... I must've forgotten to turn on the fucking light!* he thought frantically.

"Hold on, Missy," he said, as he tucked the phone into his pocket, unlocked the bedroom door, grabbed the bear spray and ran into the kitchen. The light-switch was *on!*

He set the spray down, pulled his phone out, and said hurriedly, "Missy, my security light's not working! The switch is on, I just checked, it was working fine yesterday!"

Missy replied, "Okay, Jake, just stay calm, I'm on my way. And Jake—don't open your front door until I get there, I'll knock twice, got it?"

"Yeah, yeah, got it, just please hurry!" Jake said, as she hung up. His right hand was starting to throb like a bad tooth, he needed to take a pain pill but was afraid it would dull his senses and reflexes. His heart was racing, and a cold sweat had broken out on his face as he gripped the Bear-B-Gone tightly in his left hand. He pressed up against the front door while waiting for Missy to arrive.

Hearing a loud *thump... thump,* he looked up sharply at the ceiling! It sounded like someone was on the roof! There was no entry into the attic from outside the house.

Why would someone climb onto the roof?? Jake wondered, pacing in front of the door. *Fuck, if I had my Glock, I'd teach that fucker—yeah, right!* He couldn't hit shit with a pistol left-handed, and he damn well knew it.

Jinx let out a growl, staring up at the ceiling. Suddenly, Jake smelled smoke, turned to look at the pot-bellied stove and saw a dark cloud pouring from it! The flue of the stove extended through the ceiling and attic, on through the roof for ventilation and terminated about a foot above the roof ridgeline.

The fucker's sealed the flue closed! He's trying to smoke me out of the house!! Jake thought, terrified, as he started coughing from the thick wood smoke pouring into the living room. Jinx uttered an awful yowling noise, pacing the floor, looking for a way out. Jake set the phone down, ran to the kitchen and filled a plastic pitcher with water. Tucking an oven mitt under his arm, he sat the water on the floor, used the mitt to open the red-hot door to the stove, causing even more smoke to billow out. As he tossed the water onto the wood, the coals inside hissed like an angry snake! By now, the black clouds were so thick, he could barely see across the room.

I gotta get out, can't breathe! Jake thought frantically, making his way to the door, coughing and choking on the dense wood smoke. He was more afraid of dying in here than he was of what might be waiting for him outside! Tucking the bear spray under his right armpit, he fumbled with the deadbolt on the front door, got it unlatched and tore the door open, half-falling outside into the fresh air. Jinx shot by him and hauled ass up the nearest tree. Jake knelt on the gravel by his front step, filling his lungs with fresh air, coughing and hacking.

Something large leaped off the roof and landed about fifteen feet away with a *crunch*, where it crouched. A horrible snarling sound issued forth from the darkness just outside the weak circle of light cast by the porch light. Jake froze as something huge shambled toward him.

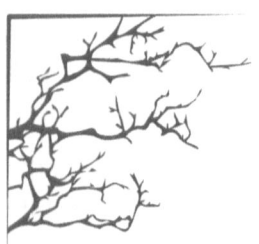

Chapter Eight

Just then, headlights briefly illuminated him, and he turned to watch as Missy's bus tore into his graveled drive, sped up the curves and jerked to a stop near the house. Jake heard a horrific growl and quickly turned back from Missy's vehicle to the spot where he'd *almost* seen the "whatever-it-was" a second ago, but it was gone! Missy jumped out of the bus, leaving the headlights on to bathe Jake and the front of his house in halogen light as she held her pistol at arm's length, shining her flashlight around between the trees out front. She could see nothing out of the ordinary.

"Are you all right, Jake? I told you to stay inside until I got here," she chided, walking over to him.

Still coughing from inhaled smoke, Jake nodded yes, slowly getting to his feet, as a large ball of fur raced past him. Jinx had come down from the tree and now sought shelter inside the house again.

"Shit, Missy, di-did you see it? Over there, by that big pine!" Jake rasped, spitting up some phlegm onto the gravel.

She came up beside him, noticing smoke still issuing from the doorway.

"All I saw was that big-ass cat run into your house. Uh, did you have a fire in there, Bud? Wait—first, let's get in the bus, Jake. We don't know who or what's out there!"

He didn't need to be told twice. He hurried over and got in the passenger seat, reaching over with his left hand to shut the door and lock it. Missy slowly backed up while sweeping her flashlight beam back and forth over the front yard again. Satisfied there wasn't an imminent threat, she holstered her weapon and jumped inside, also locking the door.

She turned to him and demanded, "What the hell is going on here, Jake? You said you had a prowler! Did *he* try to set fire to your house? I'm confused! You didn't say anything about a fire when I had you on the phone!"

Jake felt drained, as adrenaline ebbed from his system. He sat staring out the windshield of the bus for a moment, then in a strained voice he told her of the events leading up to his being outside when she arrived.

"I swear, someone or some-*thing* was trying to break in—even went so far as to smoke me out of the house! If you hadn't gotten here when you did... Don't you believe me?"

She stared at him for few seconds, then said firmly, "I believe you heard someone trying to break in, but I don't think it was an animal. A large animal most likely wouldn't have been able to get on your roof and then cover the exhaust vent. No animal is that clever or malicious—except for humans!"

Jake shook his head and swore, "I've never heard a human utter a sound like *that*! It was like... the sound a pissed-off bear or wolf would make! Almost the same as that damned wolverine that almost chewed my hand off! This is so fucked!! Why is all this shit happening to me? Who did I piss off to get this truckload of 'bad karma' dumped on me?"

Suddenly the bus shook, as something heavy landed on top of the roof, bowing it in where it landed. Jake jerked up straight and stared at Missy with wild eyes, as they both heard the muted snarling sound coming from above them!

"It's on top of us!! Quick, Missy get us the fuck outta here! Now!"

Missy said tersely through gritted teeth, "Okay, okay—I got this!"

She cranked the engine and threw the bus into reverse, twisting the wheel a full 180-degrees and accelerating as the back tires chewed gravel. Then she abruptly stomped hard on the brake—the bus jerked to a sudden halt, throwing whatever was on the roof off into the darkness of the night with a howl of frustration and pain!

Missy threw the gearshift back into drive and accelerated down the little gravel road toward the main highway. Jake turned his head, looked out the back windows of the bus, and nearly pissed his pants as he saw a big furry *something* in the taillight's red glow—racing through the dust cloud sent up by the bus, it was running on *two* legs and was catching up *fast!!* She glanced in the rearview mirror, grimacing.

"Whatever you do, don't stop!!" Jake almost screamed!

He watched in horror, as the *thing* sprang the few remaining feet between itself and the rear bumper of the bus, somehow attaching itself to the frame of the vehicle even as Missy swerved left and right, attempting to shake it off!

Missy hissed angrily, "Fucking 'cling-on!' There's nothing for it to hold onto! Why doesn't it fall off??" as she viciously twisted the wheel both directions, almost tipping the bus completely on its side.

She was quickly running out of road, coming to the intersection where the graveled road met the highway. If she slowed down for any traffic, the creature would surely take advantage and possibly get inside. The side doors *don't lock!* she remembered despairingly. She pulled out her service pistol and handed it to Jake.

"If it gets in, shoot the fucker, aim for mid-torso! Empty the clip in 'em if you have to!"

"I can't hit anything with my left hand unless it was right on top of me, in which case it may be a little too late!" Jake said worriedly, awkwardly turning in his seat to keep his eyes on the side doors. It was pitch black outside and he couldn't see anything through the windows.

Missy's face was a pale white in the glow of the dashboard lights as she said, "We're coming up to the highway! Pray there's no traffic—I'm not slowing down and giving that *thing* a chance get inside! Hang on, Jake!"

The end of the drive had a small upward slope where it met the highway. Jake held his breath as the bus ramped up the slope at forty miles per hour, causing it to go briefly airborne and come down hard in the middle of the highway, blowing out the front right tire. Missy struggled to keep control of the vehicle as it crossed the highway and onto the other side of the road, skidding dangerously close to a drainage ditch. As she braked hard, momentum shoved the bus over into the shallow trench about three feet deep, where it came to an abrupt halt, throwing them both hard against their seatbelts as the belts locked, saving them from further serious injury.

The bus was tilting at a forty-five-degree angle to the right. Jake screamed in agony as his injured right hand was caught between his body and the door. The window on his side shattered, safety glass showering over him. Missy had smacked her head against the driver's side window hard enough to see stars.

"Jake! Are you hurt bad?? Do you still have the gun?" Missy gasped out as she felt warmth trickling down her face. She reached up, feeling up above her left ear and felt a knot, and her hand came back bloody!

"Yeah, I've still got it. *Shit* that hurts!! Are you okay?" Jake groaned, as he freed his hand and passed the pistol back to her. He reached over and released Missy's seatbelt and then his own.

"Jake, can you open your door? We've got to get out of here! The side panel doors are blocked by the embankment!" Missy told him as the consequences of their situation began to sink in.

Jake said in a panicky voice "My door's jammed up against the embankment, too—what about yours, can you get it open?"

Missy unlocked the door, pulled on the door handle and pushed it. Fighting gravity, she managed to get it partially open before gasping, "I can't hold it, it's too damn heavy at this angle!"

She let the door slam back shut, her left arm shaking with muscle fatigue and adrenaline. As she massaged it, she quickly thought, *the only way out is through this door... also, the only way in!*

She told Jake, "We've gotta either climb out my door, or we'll have to stay here until someone drives by and helps. If we climb out, we could flag down someone, but if that *thing* is still out there..." she left the rest unsaid.

Jake, looking like he might puke, said, "What about your phone? Where is it, you can call 911, I fucking left mine at the house!"

Missy shook her head, instantly regretting it as her vision swam with little sparks of light, then replied, "I left it here on the console when I got to your place! I guess it's in the back somewhere. I can try and find it, gotta find the freaking flashlight first!" She twisted out of her seat, crawled over the console and felt around the floorboard until she located the flashlight.

She switched it on and looked around for her phone. She found it wedged under Jake's seat, turned it on. It only had one bar and the battery symbol was flashing. *That's just freakin' great!* She just hoped it would get a signal long enough to call.

Missy punched in 911 and waited... it rang three times, then was answered "911, what is the nature of your—" The line went dead. She tried again, this time the phone died after two rings. "It doesn't have enough juice. I haven't charged it in two days and the damned car charger is at home!" she said, crawling awkwardly back into the driver's seat.

"That's just great! Either way, we're screwed! We go outside and maybe get eaten or stay in here until help arrives. God knows how long before someone sees us and stops to investigate!" Jake complained miserably.

Missy turned and leaned toward him, arching an eyebrow, said angrily, "You know, Bud, for a big strong guy, you sure complain a lot! You want some cheese with that *whine*? Or maybe you have a better idea? If so, let's hear it, because saving *your* ass is becoming a full-time job and a pain in mine! You're a fucking *writer,* be creative! I can't think of everything!" she sat back, crossing her arms, staring out the tilted windshield, where the right headlight illuminated the three-foot wide drainage ditch, the left one shining up into the night sky.

Jake felt like he'd been bitch-slapped! "I'm sorry, Missy, you're right, I'm angry, scared and hurting! Maybe we should climb out and try to get back to my house, it's only about two hundred yards away.

"Maybe that thing got creamed on the highway or maybe it gave up—why is the fucking thing after *me,* anyway? This shit is driving me crazy!" Jake rambled on until he noticed the blood on Missy's hand. "I thought you said you were okay! Where are you bleeding from?"

Concerned, Jake reached over to turn her face toward him, but she slapped his hand away. "I'm alright, just bumped my head on the window when we bounced on the highway."

Jake said seriously, "I hope you're not bullshitting me, we're a long way from the hospital, and I'll need your help getting out of here, I don't think I can crawl out one-handed."

"Who said we were going anywhere? If that thing *is* still out there, it could ambush us as we're climbing out of here—we'd be defenseless! At least in here we can defend ourselves. If it tries to get in, I'll blast the crap out of it!" she barked, with a tight grimace.

Jake looked at her, "Well, I guess we'll just sit tight and wait for 'Joe Good Samaritan' to come along, someone's bound to drive by at some point."

Big raindrops suddenly began hitting the windshield haphazardly, then the rain picked up speed and intensity. The sky opened as tremendous sheets of water pounded down, making a deafening drumming noise on the roof of the bus and drenching Jake through the shattered window.

"Fucking great! If this keeps up, we're gonna' need bigger boat!" Jake's weak attempt at a joke fell flat as the deluge poured down around them.

Missy was becoming more anxious. "Jake, if this keeps up much longer, we're gonna have to make a decision. Either climb out of the bus or drown!"

Water began to rise in the ditch at an alarming rate and was already close to pouring in Jake's shattered window and into the bus.

Jake said uneasily, "Then let's get the hell out of here, we can make it back to my house, you've got the gun and flashlight and hopefully that thing will have left or died!"

Missy looked at him, then took a deep breath and let it out. "I hope we're making the right choice, Bud! But the alternative is looking pretty shitty." She pulled her purse over her shoulder, putting the gun and phone inside.

"You'll have to help me push the door open and hold it while I climb out. Then I'll help to pull you out!" Jake nodded, as she pulled the handle and shoved—it wouldn't budge! She shoved harder.

"It's stuck! The damn thing's jammed, or something's holding it shut! Help me push, Jake!"

Bracing his right arm on the steering column, he leaned over and shoved with his left against the door as hard as he could. The door didn't give an inch.

"It opened just fine a few minutes ago, there's no reason for it to be stuck!" Missy ran her flashlight's beam around the door frame and spotted the trouble. Her seat belt had not retracted fully and part of it was wedged between the door and the frame, jamming it shut.

"Jake, you push the door while I try to pull the seat belt out!" Jake pushed hard and she tugged, managing to dislodge it.

"Okay, let's try it again," she grunted.

As they both shoved, the door opened enough for Missy to barely squeeze through, slamming shut as soon as she was out.

The rain pounded down, showing no signs of letting up, and water began pouring in through the broken window in a rushing river of dirty muddy liquid. The car's right headlight was now submerged under the murky water, glowing like an alien moon.

Jake hollered, "Missy, can you get the door open from out there? Can you hear me? Please hurry!" as the water continued to rise rapidly inside the bus.

It was almost to his chest, and Jake began to panic! He could pull the handle on the door with one hand but had to use his shoulder to push against the door at the same time.

He pulled and shoved, pushing with his legs, and the door opened to a gap of about two feet—enough for him to wedge his shoulders between the door and frame. He was unexpectedly blinded by the intense light of Missy's flashlight as she reached out and grabbed his left hand, pulling him the rest of the way out of the bus and onto the muddy embankment. They both collapsed on the edge of the now-roaring ditch-turned-river, gasping for breath as the rain continued to inundate them.

Suddenly, a fierce snarling came from behind them! Missy swiftly swung the beam of light toward the source of it with her left hand, right hand bringing up her pistol, but razor-sharp claws swatted the pistol out of her hand! Her trigger finger was sprained or worse from the force of the blow that seemed to come out of nowhere!

Missy screamed as white-hot agony shot through her injured finger. Clutching it to her chest like a wounded animal, she rolled from the force of the blow. The flashlight she still held made a horror show of it all—catching brief images of the creature's terrible face illuminated almost stroboscopically in the frantic movements of the its beam—as Missy struggled frantically to find her weapon on the muddy embankment.

Jake froze helplessly in shock and terror, as the creature turned from Missy, leaning ominously over him. Its fetid breath washed over him in waves as its face came within inches of his own, its wolfish grin showing rows of sharp teeth dripping with long strings of saliva mixed with pouring rain.

Jake screamed with fear, promptly crapping his pants. The creature snorted and seemed almost amused as it paused to study him in the pouring rain.

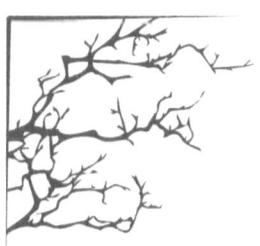

Chapter Nine

The monster reached out and seized Jake by the neck, claws digging into his throat and closing like a vise. Jake's eyes nearly bulged out of their sockets as he grabbed at the furry hand, desperately trying to dislodge it from his airway. Its jaws opened impossibly wide, preparing to tear Jake's throat out in one huge bite.

Just then a bright beam of light captured the beast briefly. Jake heard a muted *pop-pop* as the creature was jerked back by the bullets' impact, clutching at its arm and freeing Jake. It howled in pain, snarling as it stumbled, then plummeted into the roaring cascade of muddy water in the ditch and disappeared into the darkness.

Jake was coughing and gasping for breath. He looked over at Missy, the rain all but obscuring her as she held her pistol in her left hand, still aiming where the beast had been seconds ago.

She turned the beam on Jake. "I'm sorry, I couldn't find the damn gun, I think that *thing* may have broken the trigger finger on my gun hand! Lucky for you, I'm an ambidextrous shot!"

She made her way over to where he was kneeling in the rain and mud, holstered her weapon and leaned down to help Jake up.

Sniffing the air, she frowned, wrinkling her nose. "Hoo-boy! did that *thing* shit on you, Bud??"

Jake, now thoroughly embarrassed and humiliated, hoarsely said, "No, Missy, it didn't. I managed to do that all by myself, thank you very much!"

She pulled him to his feet, and Jake adjusted his muddy jeans and duck-waddled over by the back of the drowned mini-bus.

He turned and said, "I gotta wash out my pants, could you please turn your head? Keep an eye out for that fucker, you might not have killed it!"

"I know I hit it—it was only ten feet away. Anyway, even if I didn't, hopefully it drowned in that torrent!" As she turned away from him, the light went with her, throwing Jake into instant dark.

He fumbled with the button on his pants, "Ahh, Missy, maybe a *little* light, just shine it down by my feet."

Missy sighed, "I can't do that without looking where I'm shining it, Bud! You can't have it both ways! Hurry up! We're exposed out here in the open!"

Jake growled back angrily, "Excuse me? *I'm* the one *exposed* here!!" He wrestled his jeans and underwear one-handed down to his ankles, pulling his boots off similarly. He leaned against the back of the bus to steady himself as he pulled one foot, then the other out of his jeans, turning the mess inside out.

Carefully kneeling on the muddy bank, he hung the soiled clothing down into the rushing current, the water almost pulling them out of his grasp.

Missy, holding the light, couldn't keep herself from looking at his butt as he let the water wash away the crap from his soiled clothing.

She muttered "Nice ass." Then louder, seriously, "The sooner you can finish that up, Bud, the safer I'll feel! We need to try to get back to your house, quickly! There could be more of those things out here, for all we know!"

Jake lifted the jeans out of the rushing water, discarding the underwear. "I'm gonna need some help pulling my jeans up, one-handed is going to take some time!" He struggled to yank one side, then the other up around his knees while leaning against the bus with his back to her. Then managing with some difficulty to get his boots back on, he stuffed the strings inside without tying them.

Missy rolled her eyes and walked over beside him.

"Don't get any ideas, Bud!" she smirked, as she grabbed on to his belt-loop with her left hand and together, they tugged his jeans up over his hips. She fed the brass button through the loop, as he pulled it over, securing them.

Then stepping back, she said "The zipper's all yours," as she held the light on his crotch.

Jake said curtly "I don't need the light for that, thank you!"

She shrugged and turned away, sweeping the beam around them, up and across the embankment once more, just in case anything might be lurking in the water.

Jake zipped up and urged, "Let's get out of here. I'm damn sorry about your bus, I'll pay you whatever it takes to repair it. Right now, we need to get back to my place as quick as possible so we can call the cops and get your head and finger looked at!"

As they started out, Missy looked at him and said sarcastically, "Really? And what are you going to tell the cops? That the 'Wolf-Man' happened to be in the neighborhood and decided to drop by to chat and maybe borrow a 'cup of sugar,' then you pissed it off, and it tried to kill you? They'll laugh you all the way to the loony bin and give you a nice rubber room to keep you safe from the 'big bad wolf!' You know as well as I do, they'd never believe you! Hell, *I* wouldn't believe you if I hadn't seen the same damn thing when I was a teen and then again tonight!"

Jake limped along beside her, not arguing the point, as they crossed the highway and onto Jake's road. Missy kept swinging the light back and forth on either side of the road, frequently checking behind them as they anxiously made it to Jake's front porch. The front door was still wide open as they cautiously approached. Missy went first and cleared the living room, then the kitchen and bedroom while Jake bolted the door behind them. They both plopped down on the couch, looking half-drowned! Water puddled on the floor of the living room.

Jake went to his room and took off his filthy jeans. He put on a fresh pair then carried the soiled ones into the kitchen and dumped them in the washer. He grabbed a couple of dish towels and gave them to Missy who thanked him.

"We need to figure out what the hell is going on here and fast!" Jake growled.

"What do you suggest we do? No one will believe a word we say!" Missy finished wiping off the rain-smeared grime on her face and arms, wincing at the pain in her right index finger.

Jake sighed as he paced the floorboards, trying to reflect on their situation. "Is there anyone who lives around here that might possibly know what that *thing* is or... was?" Jake asked Missy.

Missy stared at floor for a moment, thinking about the *wolf-thing* that had appeared at her window, long ago in her past.

She looked up at Jake, saying quietly, "*Yeenaldlooshi,* Jake! A lot of our people believe that such creatures did or *do* exist*!* It's been passed down in our folklore for many generations. A lot of it may be bullshit, stories used to scare the little children. But there's always a grain of truth embedded in folklore that science can't explain. There have been documented cases of people who truly believed they could transform into another creature and back. It's called *therianthropy,* a form of shape-shifting."

Jake asked, "You seem to know quite a bit about the subject. Is there anybody else that has ever seen one of these things? I mean, besides us, that you know of?"

Missy looked at him and nodded. "Yeah, my sister Elisa. She was kind of obsessed about that *thing* after what happened to us. After Mama told us the story, Elisa started researching it in books and at the library, on the internet, anything she could get her hands on. I mean, we never talked about it again. It really freaked us out, Jake. But neither one of us was ever close to the other again after it happened."

Missy sighed, "We never really got over the trauma of that day, I guess. We each dealt with it in our own way. Mama told us over and over, 'Don't worry yourselves, mother time heals all wounded souls'—except it hasn't! Not for me anyway."

Jake looked at her sympathetically, then changed the subject. "Hey, we need to get your head and finger checked out, you might have a concussion! You can drive my 'Porsche," he added innocently, as he got the keys hanging on a hook by the front door.

She gave him curious look and cocked an eyebrow, "I hope your 'Porsche' is in better shape than my 'Cadillac,' if not, we're in deep shit, Bud."

Jake shrugged, "Well, it runs anyway. At least it did the last time I drove it."

Missy took the keys and looked at him. "Yeah? And when was that, Jake? Recently or what? I don't relish the idea of going out and getting inside, then finding out the damn thing won't start! We could call a cab, but it would probably take forever to get here."

Jake held out the keys. "Only one way to find out. I really hope that thing was the only one of its kind out there. Besides, you have a gun, I mean, what could go wrong?"

Missy gave him a doubtful look but got up as he unlocked the deadbolt and opened the door. The *creature* stood on the porch, its right shoulder covered in blood and muddy water dripping from its claws!

Jake nearly soiled his pants again! He screamed like a little girl and slammed the door, frantically twisting the deadbolt into place as he recoiled, tripped over the throw rug, and fell back onto the couch.

Missy raised her gun and fired four times rapidly through the wood door, deafening in close quarters! With both their ears ringing, she yelled, "Take *that*, you furry bastard!" Then she peeked through the drapes to look out on the porch area. Nothing there—the monster was gone again!

Jake cried, "Did you hit it? Is it still alive? It looked like you only wounded it before! Shit! Now what are we supposed to do? You know what they say about wounded animals, it just pisses them off and makes them unpredictable!"

Missy turned from the window and bit out, "Jake, please shut the hell up! It's not out there! I think we'd better sit tight until sun-up. I don't think it moves around in daylight." *At least I hope it doesn't!* she thought, as she walked over to the couch and sat down, re-holstering her gun awkwardly with her left hand.

"Sorry about your front door," she offered, looking at the four neat holes punched through in a tight one-inch grouping. "You needed a peephole anyway, now you've got four!"

Jake just shook his head and mumbled, "Some payback for your bus, I suppose, well... what do we do in the meantime? If there's no one we can call for help, then we're stuck here for a while. Unless you want to try to make it to my truck?"

Missy looked thoughtful for a moment. "You got an ice pack I can put on my finger? It hurts like a bitch!"

"I keep a couple in the freezer, I'll get you both." He got up, opened the freezer, took out two frozen gel ice packs and gave them to her.

"If you give me your shirt and pants, I'll throw them in the dryer, they'll be dry in no time." He told her. An eyebrow went up as she mulled over the idea of being without her clothes for half an hour. "Yeah, well, do you have a robe I can borrow? I'm not sitting here in my underwear and giving you a free show, Bud!" she said.

Jake smiled wickedly "I can't think of anything with a better view at the moment...but yeah, I'll go get it." He gave it to her, and she went into his bathroom to disrobe. She emerged and handed him her shirt and pants. She sat back down on the couch and picked up both ice bags.

She thanked him for the robe and put one on the damaged finger with a sharp hiss of pain, then pressed the other one against the raised bump on the side of her head.

Jake grabbed a couch pillow and placed it under her head to give it some support, then sat down near her.

"Before you sit down, could you please charge my phone?" she asked nicely. He grunted and got up, taking it from her and plugging it into his charger.

"You got anything to eat in there? I shouldn't be hungry, but I feel ravenous! Must be the adrenaline wearing off," Missy asked, as she curled up on the couch.

Just then a blur of fur leaped onto the couch. Jinx had come out of hiding in the bathroom. He sat down between them and glared at Missy as if to say, *Who the fuck are* you? *And why are you sitting in my spot?*

Missy stared back until Jinx decided to ignore her, jumped back off the couch and went to inspect his food bowl, hoping for some stray morsel of kibble left inside it. Disappointed, he sulked and began cleaning himself.

Jake said, "Okay, I've got a teriyaki beef tips dinner or turkey with potato and green beans, also I make a mean peanut butter and banana sandwich, but one-handed, it will be a little slow."

Missy yawned, "Whatever is easiest for you, I can help if need be, between us we at least have two working hands, anyway."

Jake hesitated, thinking about the disaster he'd had earlier with the frozen dinner, and decided to take the easy route. "Peanut butter and banana it *is*, then. Do you like potato chips on yours?" he asked her.

Missy made a face. "Potato chips? On peanut butter? Yuck! Who did you inherit your taste-buds from? Sounds like something a five-year old would like!" Then she thought better of it and added, "Sorry, didn't mean to criticize, now *I'm* the one tired and hurting. You could put a dead frog on it, and I'd eat it right now!"

Jake smiled, "One peanut butter and banana-toad sandwich coming right up!" He took the jar of peanut butter over to the couch, "You unscrew the lid, I'll hold the jar."

She got the lid loose with her left hand and he took it back into the kitchen, where he slowly spread it on two slices of bread. He peeled back the banana skin, carefully sliced the banana up, placed it on one side of bread, then pressed the other slice to it. He slapped it on a plate, took it and a glass of water to her and sat back down on the couch as she slowly ate.

Thirty minutes later, the buzzer on the dryer went off.

Her phone chimed. She frowned and asked Jake to get it. When he handed it to her, she didn't recognize the number. The text read, "Missy, u r in *grave danger*!"

"Well, tell me something I *don't* know! Who the hell is this? It doesn't make any sense, nobody knows where I am right now, how would they *know* I'm in danger?" she said, showing the text to Jake. There was no name, only the number she couldn't identify.

Jake took it and looked for himself. He shook his head.

"It's someone who knows your name, obviously they know your phone number, too," he handed the phone back to her. "You don't recognize the number?" he asked as he put the peanut butter up, then returned to sit down beside her on the couch.

"No, I don't! They could be using a burner phone or maybe that 'people finder' app for all I know!" she said as she set the phone on her lap and typed out a text, "Who are you? How did you get my number?" And finally, "Why would I be in danger?"

She hit send, not really expecting a reply. They both sat watching the phone screen as the seconds, then a couple minutes ticked off... nothing. Slowly, ten minutes passed. She punched in the phone number and put it on speaker.

After five rings, an automated voice informed her, "This person's mailbox has not been set up, please try your call again later."

"Chicken-shit asshole!" Missy spat out, as she angrily disconnected the phone and handed it to Jake to continue charging.

"There's only four people that I know of who have my number! My mother... well, the nursing home staff, Elisa *used* to have it, my supervisor Ben, and... you." She frowned, trying to think if she had missed anybody.

"Oh, and I gave it to that nurse at the hospital as an emergency contact in case they couldn't reach you. That makes five," she finished.

Jake looked at her, a bit puzzled.

"You know... what's her name? You called her Nurse 'Wretched,' I think." Missy said.

Jake nodded, "Yeah, it was Brittany or Bethany, something... Beverly! That's it! So, it's just a process of elimination, right?"

Missy agreed. Using Jake's phone, she looked up the hospital number, called and asked for the third-floor nurses' station.

A woman answered, "Third north nursing, this is Stacy, how may I help you?"

Missy told her about giving her number to Nurse Beverly during Jake's stay there. Could she please talk to Beverly? It was important!

Stacy said, "I'm sorry, Beverly is off today, can I take a message? I'll see that she gets it when she comes back on shift tomorrow."

Missy sighed, "Look, is there any chance you could give me her phone number, I really need to ask her a really important question ASAP!"

There was momentary silence, then Stacy said "I'm sorry, we can't give out the nurses' personal numbers. For security reasons, you see. I'm sorry I can't be of more help to you! Would you like to leave a message anyway?"

Missy, disappointed, said, "No, I guess not, thanks anyway. Oh, do you happen to know what shift she works tomorrow?"

Stacy paused, "Ahhh... looks like she works the morning shift, eleven to seven tomorrow!" Missy thanked her and hung up.

She retrieved her dry clothes from Jake's dryer, folded and laid them over a wooden chair in the spare bedroom.

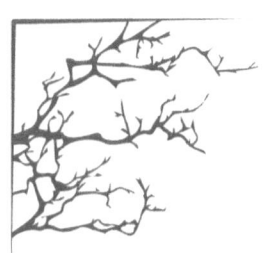

Chapter Ten

T he pain was excruciating! Luckily, it had leaped off the front porch a mere second before the pistol slugs punched through the front door. Blood seeped from the wound in its shoulder as it jumped over a pile of cut logs behind the house, barely avoiding a fall as it tripped over a rusting lawnmower on the other side of the pile. It stopped at the edge of the forest where the trees crowded together as it caught its fetid breath. It had almost killed the man—if the woman had not interfered, he would be dead by now! The shoulder wound was superficial, of no real concern, it would heal.

Already the bleeding had stopped. The flesh around the groove the bullet had cut was beginning to knit itself back together, the blood vessels, sinew and nerves seeking out their counterparts, reconnecting at astonishing speed. The healing process was extremely painful, and the accelerated recovery took a toll on its strength! It would need fuel to complete the job.

Its eyesight was incredibly keen, as was its sense of smell. The forest was very dark, but it might as well have been daylight as far as the creature was concerned. It sniffed the air, catching the scent of an unfortunate rabbit huddling under a shrub nearby. It saw the rabbit and pounced—the rabbit squealed a high-pitched cry of pain and despair as it was neatly bitten in half.

Blood and gore flew in all directions as its teeth tore through the rabbit's fur and flesh with a nasty slurping sound. Meat, fur, organs and bone were devoured, gulped down in large chunks, as blood covered its face and body in coagulating clots, until finally there was no trace left of the hare. It belched loudly, feeling a shiver of exhilarating power ripple through its muscles as the regenerated tissue continued its metamorphosis from torn flesh to new skin. It knew it would need more time to heal before attempting to kill the man again. It could feel the light of the coming sunrise before it was even visible in the east. "Soon," the creature thought, as it loped off deep into surrounding forest to heal... and plan.

SUNLIGHT STREAMED THROUGH the window slats of the bedroom window, dust motes floating lazily in the air, as Missy awoke with a start. Disoriented, she looked around the unfamiliar room, realizing she must be in Jake's spare bedroom. She vaguely remembered getting off the couch at some point in the early morning at Jake's insistence, then slipping under the covers and immediately falling asleep.

She threw back the bedclothes only to discover that she was naked! Crap! She didn't remember disrobing before climbing under the covers—had she? She looked around the room, found her clothes folded where she'd left them, her purse on the floor by the bed.

Her gun belt and holstered gun were hanging on the doorknob of the closed bedroom door. She yawned, stretched and was immediately rewarded with fresh agony, as a jagged bolt of pain shot through her injured finger! She dressed slowly, careful not to bump the digit. She opened the door to the auspicious smell of freshly brewed coffee. Jake was in the kitchen pouring himself a cup, the toaster *dinged,* and he pulled out a couple waffles as she walked in and sat at the small dining table.

"Did you undress me last night after I went to sleep? Cause I sure as hell don't remember taking off your robe before crawling into bed," she demanded, with a cocked eyebrow.

Jake looked at her innocently, "Good morning to you, too! Not that the idea hadn't crossed my mind, but no, I didn't take any liberties with your clothing or you personally, if that's what you're inferring."

Missy shook her head and snorted. "Guess you missed your chance, Bud! Anyway, I appreciate the bed, that couch is pretty lumpy!"

"You're welcome, but we need to get you to the hospital to see about your head and finger. Think you can drive okay? Or you can drive, and I'll shift, I think your hand is in a little better shape than mine. My truck is a standard shift," Jake offered, handing her a cup of coffee and a waffle with syrup.

She took the cup, added some sugar from a dispenser on the table and replied smugly, "I was raised on a standard shift, an old Ford Pinto—a 'fire-bomb' on wheels. We called it 'the bean'—my dad bought it a couple of years before he passed. I've been driving since I was fourteen. I drove that car everywhere!"

She wolfed down the waffle, finished her coffee and rinsed the cup and plate in the sink, placed it back on the counter. "Let's go, I need to make some phone calls after the hospital trip, you ready?"

Jake nodded as he gulped down the remaining coffee. "I sure hope you're right about that *thing's* aversion to sunlight, I got on my last clean pair of underwear."

Missy gave him a tight grin, "Ahh, TMI—maybe you need to take some *Imodium.* before we leave, just to be safe!"

Jake muttered, "That's not gonna—oh, never mind, let's go!"

He handed her the keys, took a deep breath and let it out, then unlocked the front door, opened it and looked out. The rain had stopped overnight, leaving the air smelling crisp and clean.

They both glanced down at the cement porch, looking for traces of blood. There was nothing but puddles of rainwater, reflecting the azure blue of the morning sky. Jake quickly shut the door behind them. They walked in tandem out to Jake's pickup, looking around warily as they got to the vehicle. They inspected both inside the cab and the bed of the Ford F-150 before climbing in and locking the doors. Missy inserted the key in the ignition—it wouldn't start!

"Shit! Jake, when's the last time you started this thing?"

Jake smiled, "Remember, put it in neutral first, then you can start it."

Now Missy felt her cheeks redden, as she recalled that. She did as he said, and the truck roared to life. She engaged the clutch and with some small jerking motions, backed the truck up and headed down the graveled lane to where it joined the highway.

They pulled onto the highway and saw her bus lying in the ditch looking like a drowned animal covered with a muddy veneer of chocolate sludge.

"My poor bus! I need to take a picture of it for my insurance, Jake," she said, as she pulled his truck parallel, put it in neutral and set the parking brake.

She dug her phone out of her purse, opened the door and went over to the passenger side. She took three or four pictures, climbed back inside and they accelerated up the road.

"I can't tell you how sorry I am for all this shit!" Jake repeated, grimacing as they hit a pothole that jarred his right hand. "I've gotta figure out why that thing is trying to kill me! I mean, what the hell did I do to deserve all this? I've never intentionally hurt anyone in my life that I can remember!" he exclaimed woefully, staring out the window at the beautiful tree-lined landscape.

Missy glanced over at him, asking hesitantly, "Jake, do you recall ever having 'blackouts' when you drank?"

He scowled at her and snarled, "How the hell would I know? If I was *that* drunk, I'd never remember it, now would I? That's why they call them 'blackouts,' right? I'm sure I had my share. Elisa could probably tell you better, but, oh, wait— she's not here!"

Missy cringed, as his words made her feel foolish. *Of course, he wouldn't remember.*

"There's a friend of my mother's, he's a psychologist and a shaman, he's on the tribal council. He specializes in regressive hypnotherapy. His name is Mika 'Laughing-Bird' Boucher, or just 'Birdie' to his friends. He might be able to give you some insight, help you recover memories from your past," she told him, as she swerved to avoid some mangled crimson-crusted road-flounder in her lane.

Jake grunted, "I don't know anything about hypnotherapy, but I'd piss on a spark plug if it would help me figure out why that *thing* wants to chew my balls off and eat me for dinner!"

Missy shuddered at the image he'd put in her mind. "I'll give Birdie a call after I get finished at the ER. And maybe I can talk to Nurse 'Wretch,'-uh, Beverly while we're there," she added, as they drove past the Joseph city limits sign.

"You honestly think he can shed some light on this nightmare? I've had a shitload of bad luck lately, if you haven't noticed!" Jake replied, as they pulled into the emergency room parking area.

Missy killed the engine, turned to Jake, "Maybe a shitload of bad karma somewhere in your past is catching up. If so, better to find an answer sooner than later."

She opened the truck door and got out, waited for Jake, and they walked inside. The cold air inside gave Missy goose-pimples as she strode up to the receptionist.

The woman remarked, "Back again so soon? How can I help you—today?"

Missy told her she'd been in an auto accident and injured her finger and hit her head on the car window. Which was almost the truth. She *had* been in an accident and she *had* hurt her finger. She just conveniently left out the "monster" part.

The receptionist stared over her reading glasses at Missy. Frowning, she said, "Please fill out this information sheet and have a seat, someone will be with you shortly."

Missy thanked her, took the clipboard in her left hand and sat down to fill it out, then remembered her injured finger was on her writing hand. Jake was no help, as his was wrapped up like a mummy. Crap! She got back up and returned to the window.

"I'm sorry, but I can't fill this out," she pointed to the swollen finger.

The woman sighed. "Just give me your name, date of birth, address, social and a phone number you can be reached at, I'll fill in the rest."

Missy gave her the information, sat down next to Jake and waited. After twenty minutes, a nurse came out of the triage area, pushing a wheelchair. Missy got into the chair, motioning Jake to follow. The nurse pushed her into a cubicle, Jake sat in the visitor's chair while they got her onto the hospital bed. A short female doctor came in on the heels of the nurse.

She announced, "Hello, I'm Doctor Kelton! Ms. Morning Star, we're going to do an x-ray of your hand—how long ago did this injury occur?"

Missy looked at Jake, shrugged and said, "I'm guessing around two o'clock this morning, right, Jake?"

Jake mumbled, "Sounds about right," fidgeting in the chair.

The doctor looked at Jake, noticing the bruising around his neck where the creature had tried to throttle him. It was turning interesting shades of black and purple. The doctor looked at Missy's chart, then turned to him.

"Did you receive those bruises from the same accident, Mr. ...?"

"Anderson, Jake Anderson," Jake quickly replied. He hadn't even thought about the damned marks left on his neck from his near strangulation. *Yeah, Doc, a fucking werewolf was a little too happy to see me and...*

"It, ah, was from the seat belt. It got tangled around my neck when the car went in the drainage ditch," Jake improvised unconvincingly. "It looks worse than it feels!" he added weakly.

"Uhh-huhh..." the doctor replied skeptically.

She turned back to Missy, examining the bump on her left temple, asking, "Any headaches, double-vision, nausea?"

Missy shook her head no as the doctor pulled a pen light from her pocket and shined it in each eye. She made notes in the chart, then finally told her, "No signs of concussion. We should do a CT scan, but that's up to you!"

Missy answered, "I don't think it's necessary, right now all I'm concerned with is my finger."

Just then an x-ray tech rolled a portable machine in to the side of her bed, placed her hand on an image recording plate, took three pictures at different angles, thanked her and left.

Doctor Kelton said, "I'll be back with the results shortly." She stepped out and walked into the next bay to see the next patient.

Missy's phone *dinged* in her purse. She dug it out and looked at the text. It read, "U R pissing me off! Thot U were *smart* person! U stay away from Jake! *B Smart*!"

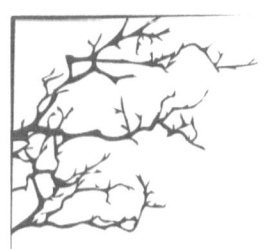

Chapter Eleven

Missy stared at the screen, getting angrier by the second. "Whoever keeps sending this shit is just playing mind games!"

She typed furiously, "Who the fuck *is* this?? Why are you trying to frighten me? What do you *want* from me??"

She pressed send and waited, her phone *dinged* as the text appeared, "U been warned!!! U stay away from him!!"

"I'm going to show this text to the police, you ass-wipe!" Missy responded, bluffing, for the moment, anyway. She showed the text to Jake.

He replied, "You think they'll buy it?"

Missy shook her head angrily. "I don't know, maybe—but I'm not going to let some shithead psycho try to frighten me into playing their sick mind games, either way!

"I could take it to the cops and tell them someone is threatening me, *that* much is clear from the texts. But I sure as hell couldn't explain that freaking *thing* that's been after us—not us, *you*! It wants *your* ass, Bud! I'm just an in-the-way 'appetizer.' Apparently, you're the main course!"

Jake looked dismayed, "You know, if I didn't know better, which I don't, I'd say you were 'throwing me to the *wolves*,' no fucking pun intended! I didn't *ask* you to pull my ass out of the lake, did I? Though I'm grateful that you did. I'm sorry you're involved in this nightmare! If you hadn't tried to help me, you wouldn't be involved in this mess!"

He stood up to leave; her voice stopped him. "Jake—stop! I'm sorry. I didn't mean to exclude myself from the situation. I'm just angry and frustrated that somebody out there *knows* something about what's been happening here! They're either warning me off or taunting me, I don't know which, but either one pisses me off!"

Jake seemed mollified and sat back down. There was an awkward silence, then he changed the subject, "Do you think Nurse '*Wretched*' is available to answer your questions? It's 11:15 a.m. According to that nurse you talked to, Beverly should be here working her shift."

Doctor Kelton came back in carrying an x-ray, clipped it to observation screen, and pointed, "You're in luck! You've got a bad sprain, but it's not broken! I wish I could change your mind about getting the CT scan of your head. If not, I recommend you ice it three times a day, take two ibuprofen for the pain and swelling, and call me in the morning!"

She chuckled at her lame joke. "Anyway, we'll bandage the finger for you to keep it from further injury." She looked at Jake and said knowingly, "Sorry, can't do much for your neck, you gotta be more careful with those 'seat belts'!"

Missy asked, "Doctor, do you know if I could talk to a Nurse Beverly on the third floor? She was Jake's nurse while he was here. We-I need to ask her some questions."

The doctor smiled, "Just dial the operator, ask for third north nursing and they'll connect you. Really, call me if you have any questions. If you're having any vision problems or headaches, call immediately. Goodbye!" She turned and left the room.

Missy got Jake to dial the operator and hand her the phone, and she requested third north. The phone rang several times, then a voice answered, "Third north nursing, may I help you?"

"Yes, this is Melissa Morning Star. I talked to a Nurse Stacy yesterday and told her that I needed to speak to Nurse 'Wre'-uh, Beverly if she's available. She said Beverly worked the eleven to seven today. May I speak to her please?"

The charge nurse replied, "Oh, I'm sorry, she isn't in today. She called in sick. Can someone else help you?"

Disappointed, Missy answered, "No, no, that's okay. Do you know when her next shift is?"

"Ahh, let's see, looks like she's scheduled to work the three to eleven tomorrow. Would you like to leave a message?"

Missy thought for a second, "No, thank you for your help," and hung up.

"Well, guess you could call your boss or your mother next," Jake reflected as he stood up, stretched, rubbing his lower back where the crappy chair had done a number on his lower lumbar.

She sighed, "It won't do a lot of good to call my mother, she's in the tribal nursing center. She has early-stage dementia and had a stroke six months ago. I doubt seriously that she remembers what she did five minutes ago. S-she's been sliding downhill mentally for the last couple of years. It breaks my heart that Elisa hasn't called or contacted her all these years. It's like Mama and I don't even exist!" A dual trail of tears rolled down her cheek as she swiped them away.

"Anyway, Mama wouldn't know how to text, even if she *had* a smart phone!" she continued, as Jake passed her a tissue from a box sitting on a shelf. Missy blew her nose and thanked him, wadding up the tissue and tossing it toward a trash can, missing it by a foot.

A petite young nurse came in, to splint and wrap the swollen finger several times with an ace bandage. She finished up by putting two butterfly clasps on to secure it, adding, "Ice it three times a day, twenty minutes at a time and take ibuprofen for the any pain. If it isn't better in two weeks, call Doctor Kelton and let her know. Try not to aggravate it by slamming it in a car door or doing any push-ups for a while!" she admonished with a grin.

Missy thanked her and got up off the bed. "I just thought of something, how are you going to be able to get home, Jake? I mean... I can drive myself home, but how will you manage to get home from there? You can't shift with your right hand!" she observed, as she put her shoes on and collected her purse.

Shit! Jake hadn't thought about that. He paused a minute, then said, "Look, it's mostly my fault your bus is trashed, you drive me home and just take the pickup until you can get your bus fixed. I'll pay for it all!"

She answered, "Well, you can call 'Johnny Six-Fingers' Garage and have them tow it to his shop. He's the best in town, he did a lot of the restoration on the bus."

Jake looked at her, "Never heard of him. Funny last name, why's he called that?" he asked, as Missy signed off on the release form at the receiving desk the best she could left-handed.

She replied, "He was born with an extra pinkie finger on his right hand," as they left the ER, heading for Jake's truck.

He smiled, "That must come in 'handy!' Get it—'hand-y'?"

Missy just rolled her eyes but smiled as they got into the truck.

"I think I'm gonna call Ben and see if he can get someone to cover for me for a day or so. Give me time to sort through this mess, plus I need to find out if he gave my number out to anyone else that I can't think of right now," she explained, as they pulled out of the hospital parking lot for the second time in two days.

Jake thought, *I really don't want to be stuck at home with no wheels... no escape if that monster comes back!* For a big guy, Jake wasn't all that brave and courageous unless he had to be. He just really didn't want to be by himself now!

But no way was he going to admit that he was scared to go back to his house in the 'hundred-acre woods,' where that *thing* could be waiting, biding its time, just waiting to... *Shit!* Well, he *did* have Jinx—big help!

"Say, Missy, why don't you ... I've been thinking that since we're both crippled-up some, that maybe we should, like, uh, stick together or something?" Jake rambled. "We could run by your place and you could pick up anything you might need for the next day or so. You could stay in my extra room and I—that *thing* could come back! What I mean, aww, crap!

"I *really* don't want to be there by myself with only one freaking hand to defend myself, if that hairy fucker decides I'm its meal *du jour*! I'd like to at least have a fighting chance!" Jake said, hating the whine in his voice.

Missy replied, a little sarcastically, "Jake, let me get this straight—you want *me* to protect *you*?" Then she chuckled, "That's sweet! But I'd need to talk to Ben before I can make any decision; someone needs to be able to cover my shift at the Park. I've got some vacation time coming, and I have to use it or lose it before the end of the year!" She came to the turnoff for her cabin, slowed down and turned onto her drive.

She parked and they walked up to her front door. Missy unlocked the door and they went inside. Jake sat in the old recliner while Missy opened the drapes over the two small windows on either side of the front door, letting sunshine inside.

"I only run the generator at night, one of these days I'll get connected to the grid. It's a Ranger cabin, so no frills. Only thing I pay for is the gasoline and the upkeep," she explained, filling a small pan with water. "Coffee or tea?"

She glanced at Jake's blank expression. "The coffee's instant, I don't drink it often, besides its cheaper!"

Jake replied, "Ah, tea is fine." She dropped two teabags into the water and lit the stove. Then sitting down on her bed, she dug her phone out of her purse and called her supervisor, Ben Dover.

BEN HAD BEEN A SMALL, skinny kid growing up and unfortunately, had one of those last names that drew every anal retentive in school to it like "flies on shit," making his life a living hell until he could graduate and get a job. Alas, he escaped from school only to find out the 'real world' was just a larger, meaner version of the status quo. So, he quickly changed the pronunciation to "Duh-ver" instead. Didn't matter, people always mispronounced it. He could still see and hear the evil, giggling kid behind those benign smiles when they routinely hailed him on the street to say hello or in the store buying groceries.

"Hey, it's Ben Dover—and kiss my ass! Ha-ha, etc...

So, Ben had started lifting weights and working out religiously until he'd put on forty pounds of muscle when he finally reached his adult height of six-foot three in his eighteenth year. He considered himself average-looking, with hazel eyes, a roman nose that was slightly crooked from being broken years ago, and sandy blond collar-length hair. He currently weighed in at an even two-hundred-thirty pounds of pure muscle!

Now, when he happened to meet any of the jerks who had picked on him in school addressed him, it was "Mr. Dover" or just "Ben," which was fine with him. No more fucking "bend-over" jokes—not if they knew what was good for them! Ben wasn't a bully, but he was damned if he would take any shit off anybody anymore!

BEN ANSWERED THE PHONE on the second ring: "Hello, Missy, what can I do ya for?"

Missy gave him a version of the events of the last twenty-four hours (*sans* most of the truth!*) She told him she'd had an accident, hurt her head and hand, and needed to get her bus into the shop. She didn't mention Jake. Could she requisition some of her vacation time to take care of herself and her vehicle?

Ben replied in a rush, "Sweet Jesus, Missy! *Sure,* ya can—are you okay? Is there anything I can do in the meantime for ya? I'll get Bob to cover for you, he's always whining about not getting enough overtime."

Missy responded, "Thanks, Ben, I owe you one. I just need a couple days to get myself together, and my bus fixed! I'll see you then. Oh, by the way, you haven't given out my phone number to anyone recently, have you?"

Ben exclaimed, "No, I haven't, you know that's against Park policy!"

She thanked him again, hung up and sighed, "I wish I could tell him what's really been happening, he's a good friend and a better boss!

"But he'd never believe this shit!" Jake replied. "I wouldn't have believed it either, if that *thing* hadn't tried to strangle the shit out of me!"

Missy cocked an eyebrow, giving him an evil grin, "Well, Bud, seems to me, if I recall right, that's *exactly* what happened!"

Jake felt his face redden, snapped back, "You're about as funny as a broken leg, Ranger Morning Star! Ha-ha! Got any more astute observations? Sure you can't possibly find anything else to embarrass me??

Missy looked thoughtful, then winked. "Not at the moment, but give me an hour or two, I'm sure I'll think of something!" She poured some tea and handed it to him with her left hand, poured herself a cup and took a chair beside him.

They were quiet for a while as they drank their tea. Missy was thinking, *does he really expect me to stay at "Camp Werewolf" and protect him? Do I trust him—did Elisa? Or does he just want to get in my pants? He is handsome, sorta cute in a pathetic, accident-prone sort of way! On the other hand, he's a walking, talking calamity waiting to happen! Do I really want to get sucked up into that vortex? Actually, I'm already there!*

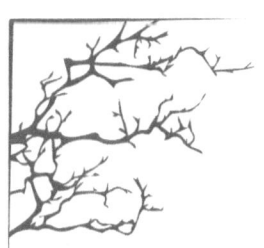

Chapter Twelve

Missy finally said, "Look Jake, I don't know if it's such a good idea for me to stay at your place. I... I mean, say that *thing* does come back, how..." her phone *dinged* with an incoming text.

She dug the phone out and looked at it, frowning as she didn't recognize the number, but there was a name attached. "Ava Farina?" she puzzled. "I don't know any Ava Farina!" That got Jake's attention fast.

"Ah, Missy I sent her a message on Facebook, she's a long-time friend of Elisa's, maybe her only close friend. I was hoping she might still be in contact with Elisa or at least know where she's living."

Missy gave Jake a questioning look, then opened the text and read out loud, "Melissa, my name is Ava Farina. I'm an old friend of your sister. Jake Anderson has contacted me, asking if I know of her whereabouts. I thought it best to contact you instead of Jake. I think it might be better if you could call me at the number on your phone, ASAP. Ava F."

Missy looked up angrily, "Shit Jake! Why didn't you tell me earlier about this Ava person—and where do you get off, giving someone else my phone number without my permission?"

Jake explained defensively, "Look, I had no way of knowing if Elisa had told you about her! I didn't even know you *existed* until you pulled me out of the lake and all the other shit that's happened! I thought of it after you'd left—then posted that to her, thinking it might give you a lead on where your *precious sister* was! I'm fucking sorry I had to give her your number. I also gave her mine, but I figured she wouldn't contact me until she talked to you first! She wasn't *my* friend!" Jake stood up and stalked out the door, slamming it shut behind him.

Missy felt her anger ebbing away. She *did* want to know where Elisa was, didn't she? She heard the truck door open and slam shut, looked out the window and saw him sitting in the driver's seat, sulking.

She thought, *Jake was only trying to help me, so why am I so pissed-off? Maybe because he's opened old wounds that I had long thought healed! That wasn't Jake's fault. Funny, how the universe intertwines our lives. Twisting them apart, then the lines of time reconnecting them when you least expect it! I mean—fishing a stranger out of the lake, only to find out he's your sister's ex? What are the odds? Then again, what were the odds of both Jake and me being terrorized by some wolf-like creature at different junctures in time? I don't believe in coincidence!*

Missy sighed as she heard the pickup door open and shut and the crunch of feet on gravel as Jake made his way back inside.

Still looking upset and embarrassed, he said, "I... ah, don't have the keys. Can't drive anyway! Could you just drive me back to my place? I promise, I won't bother you anymore. But I'd like my pistol back, if you don't mind!"

Missy got up and walked over to where her tackle box sat. She opened it, folded back several trays of assorted lures and produced his pistol. She pulled out the clip, then ejected the bullet from the chamber and reloaded it in the clip, handing the Glock to him butt-first. Jake thanked her and stuffed the gun into the front of his jeans, lacking any better way to carry it.

Missy smirked, "I hope I don't hit any potholes on the way back—be a damn shame to change yourself from a rooster to a hen, Bud!" The jest was lost on Jake.

"Seriously Jake, I need to call this Ava back and see what, if anything, she knows of Elisa's whereabouts as soon as possible. Look, I'm sorry I jumped your ass about the phone number, I'm a little OCD about who I give it out to. But since you now have your gun back, you should be safe enough in your house." *Yeah, if he doesn't shoot his balls off first!* She thought grimly.

Jake looked disappointed but replied, "Yeah, well... I guess so. We'd better get going. I'll need to call and make arrangements to get your bus towed to the shop before dark."

Missy drove Jake back to his house. He had taken the pistol out of his jeans and placed it on the seat between them. Jake stared at the old house uneasily as they pulled to a stop. The place didn't *look* any different physically, yet Jake felt an aura of danger surrounding it now like an invisible dome. Maybe it was his imagination—but hadn't he closed the front door before they'd left earlier?? It was standing wide open.

Shit! That thing could be inside! Jake thought miserably to himself. "Damn it, Missy, I *know* I shut the door and locked the bottom part before we left! I didn't lock the deadbolt, but I hardly ever do, it's so remote out here. I don't get many visitors."

Missy observed, "Well, Bud, looks like you got one today! Let's go see who it is. I'd better jack a round in your gun for you, please be careful where you point it!"

Jake nodded okay, all the while staring anxiously at the open door. *Won't you step into my parlor, said the spider to the fly!*

Something was waiting, but it wasn't a spider. They got out of the truck and quietly pushed its doors closed. Missy took the lead, with Jake following close behind. She motioned for him to stop before they reached the doorway. She took a deep breath and shouted, "Whoever is in there, come out with your hands, paws, whatever you got, up! This is a Park Ranger speaking, I'm armed. You have ten seconds to respond!"

Ten seconds went by... no response. Missy looked at Jake, he just gave her a "now what?" look. Missy took another deep breath and stepped fully into the doorway, her weapon extended in both hands, quickly sweeping the entry area left and right and saw—Jinx!

He was sitting on the couch, quietly cleaning a paw when they stepped fully into the room. They both let out sigh of relief upon seeing the big cat. He damn well wouldn't be sitting there if that *thing* was anywhere around. *But then, how did he get in?* they both were wondering.

Missy asked, "Do you think he's learned how to open a door?"

Jake shook his head, "I don't think so, at least I've never seen him do it. I had a regular cat once a long time ago, he'd jump and twist the knob with both paws and open a door! No, either the door wasn't fully closed, or... someone let him in."

Missy replied tersely, "I need to clear the rest of the house! Stay here, Jake!" She carefully went through all rooms, finding no one to shoot. Damn!

Missy calmly holstered her weapon and walked back into the living area. "Well, there's no sign anyone's been here, but you'd better check on your valuables just to be on the safe side, Jake."

He agreed and started in his bedroom. He came out minutes later and exclaimed angrily, "My laptop, my fucking laptop is missing! Why would they take that?"

Missy asked, "Was there anything on it of importance?"

Jake paced the room and thought about it. "The only thing on it was the new story I was writing. No one would want it for *that*! Uh, I mean... it's not even close to being finished. It only has value to me."

Missy sat on the couch beside Jinx. "Do you want to call the cops and report it? After all, there was a break-in and we don't know if the person responsible might not still be around here." Jake didn't answer but walked over to the front door and bent down to inspect the keeper on the door frame.

"It's been jimmied! Look, there's scratch marks around the striker plate, and it's bent a little. I bet the damned lower latch won't close lock now!" He closed the door. Sure enough, the latch wouldn't lock into place. "At least the deadbolt still works," he reported, as he threw the bolt and pulled on the door, testing it.

"As far as calling the cops, I'm not sure it would do any good. I guess they could dust for prints or something. But I doubt the asshole who did it left a 'calling card' of any kind."

Missy mumbled something about *no coincidences,* then continued, "Was anything else missing? Anything out of the ordinary?"

Jake thought about it for a minute, then headed back into his bedroom. He came back out several moments later.

"There *is* something missing! I had a small picture of Elisa and me. I keep it in a drawer in my desk. I'd just gotten out of the service when it was taken. We'd been at a carnival that day. They had one of those photo booths, you know, where you get five pictures for a buck. Anyway, we made a couple of goofy faced pictures and then one of us just smiling, our heads together. That's the only one I kept."

Missy thought she spied tears forming in his eyes, but it might have been the light. "So, you're saying they stole your laptop and a photograph. Which one was more important to you?"

Jake paced the floor and stopped, staring wistfully out the window before speaking.

"Good question! I used to think it was Elisa. Now I know better. We never really communicated. The whole relationship was doomed from the start! We never started a conversation that didn't end up in an argument!" He sighed and plopped down on the couch, pissing Jinx off, as the startled cat fell from the couch, landing indignantly on its ass before giving him a hiss, then running into the kitchen to recover his dignity.

"My laptop can be replaced. I have my novel backed up to the 'cloud.' I'm not going to be able to write much any time soon, anyway," he grumbled, holding up his right hand. "But why take the picture? That doesn't make fucking sense, it only has sentimental value!"

"I don't know, Jake, but something very strange is going on—something connecting both of us to the past and present! Are you going to report the break-in or not? If not, then I'm gonna call this Ava back and see what she has to say about Elisa, if anything!" Missy was looking at her phone, waiting for Jake to answer.

"I think I will call 'em. Look, if this is any way connected to that fucking freak of nature that's trying to kill me, then at some point, if it's not dead already, it's gonna try again—and next time I may not be so lucky! Maybe I just tell the cops enough of the truth, say some maniac has been trying to kill me, and has broken in, stolen my laptop. Maybe they can get a fingerprint or some DNA and find out who or *what* is behind all this!"

Missy shook her head in frustration. "Jake, you know damn well this is *all* connected to that *thing* somehow! Do you really think that creature is going to leave any viable fingerprints? And God knows what the DNA would show! I really doubt the cops will be of any help in locating that...*monstrosity!*"

Jake blew out a breath of frustration, "You're probably right. Hey! We could track my laptop with GPS if the asshole turns it on and uses it for any length of time, right? The IP address will show wherever its used!"

Missy replied, "That's presuming whoever took it even uses it. If they're smart, they'll wipe the drive first or just sell it on e-bay! If you have everything on it backed up to the cloud, just buy another laptop. Getting the cops involved is just going to cause more problems. Do what you want, but I'm calling this friend of Elisa's. Can you please call Johnny Six-Finger's

Garage and arrange for them to tow my bus in for me?" She dug a business card out of her wallet and handed it to Jake.

He looked at the card and grunted as he pulled out his cracked phone, "I hope he's got a big shovel for all the mud that's gonna be inside it!"

Missy frowned at him but refrained from making a nasty comment. She got up, walked into the kitchen for a little privacy and called the number on her phone.

It rang four times before a woman answered breathlessly, "Hello? Who is... this?"

"This is Melissa Morning Star, Elisa's sister. Is this Ava Farina?"

"Yes, it is. Excuse me, I... just... finished my... exercises, I'm a little... out of breath."

"That's okay, I'll give you a minute." *Sounds more like coitus-interruptus to me!* Missy thought, giving her some time to recover.

"Whew... thanks, I'm sure you want to know about Elisa, right?"

"Yes, yes, I do! Have you heard from her anytime recently or talked to her?" After a long pause, Missy was beginning to think she'd lost the connection when Ava spoke.

"Ah... Melissa... I-I don't know how to say this—I'm so sorry, but Elisa is *dead*!"

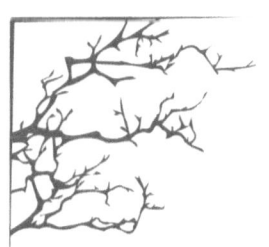

Chapter Thirteen

Missy felt the blood drain from her head and almost dropped her phone as the words sank in. "S-She's... dead?? A-Are you sure?? How? When?"

"Yes, I'm pretty sure! I didn't know she *had* any family, I-I mean, she never mentioned that she had a sister! She never talked about family. As to how it happened, it was a boating accident, like, about a mile offshore Mustang Island, no, closer to Port Aransas, at night.

"She was out on a chartered fishing boat when a storm blew in. She apparently fell overboard! They threw a lifesaver out to her, but they think the boat propeller hit... ah, well, there was blood in the water, like, a lot of it! And they think, well... there were sharks and... anyway, sadly, they never found any trace of her."

Missy was stunned. "My God! Did they even search for her after it was daylight?"

Ava replied, crying, "Yeah, they did. The Coast Guard searched a grid area of, like, 4,000 square miles for two days... nothing! I'm so sorry, I would have tried to contact you, if I'd known she even *had* a sister."

Ava sobbed, then blew her nose and went on, "This happened about six months ago. I—we'd been close, up until about a month before she... was lost! She'd been, like, obsessing about her ex-husband, Jake Anderson."

Ava continued, "All I know is he was a no-good long-haul trucker, a jealous drunk and a wife-rapist! She should have, like, cut off his balls with a dull knife and dumped his sorry ass long before she did! Dumped him, she *did*. I don't know about his balls! God rest her soul!"

Missy glanced angrily over at Jake, who was still on the phone with Johnnie's Garage, as if she were really seeing him for the first time. She suddenly felt very queasy. *Wife-rapist*??

"Did you just say that he'd *raped* her??!" Missy snarled into the phone, holding it so tight that her knuckles whitened.

Defensive now, Ava persisted, "*I* didn't say it! I'm just, like, telling you what Elisa told me a few years back. Elisa said he was drunk as a skunk one night after coming home from a month on the road. Said he'd been drinking heavy all night and he wanted some 'nookie.' She *didn't*!! She told him she was 'on the rag.' Jake got belligerent, pushed her onto the bed—pinned her arms down, and raped her twice! Then he passed out. Elisa told me next day, he didn't remember a fuckin' thing when she confronted him about it! Said he had 'blackouts' all the time and didn't remember *half* the things he'd said or done to her when he was like that!"

Ava continued, "Anyway, for the last couple of months of her life, she was obsessed about finding a way to make Jake pay for the way he had treated her. I think she blamed him for how her life had gone since the divorce. She got involved with some Native Indian cult bullshit! Was always online, researching some seriously weird stuff! She never explained when I asked her about it, except to mumble some strange phrase over and over like a fucking mantra! I think she was really losing it toward the end—it's so sad!"

Missy asked warily, "Do you remember what the phrase was, that she kept repeating?"

Ava thought about it for a minute. "You know, it sounded like something that Ricky Ricardo character from the old '*I love Lucy*' show would say. Something... like, 'You know Lucy?' or 'You knew Lucy?' I remember asking her, 'What the fuck does that mean?' She just got all cryptic on me, saying shit like, 'Best not said, better off dead!' It scared me!

"I didn't know what to say to her anymore. The last week before... it happened, she wouldn't answer or return any of my calls. Then two days before the accident, she sent me a text that said, 'I love you, you're my BFF! I'm going to make things better! Talk to you soon, gotta take care of some shit first!'

"I showed it to the cops when they were investigating, but I think they passed it off as the rant of a mentally-ill person or possibly a-a suicide note. I really miss her, Melissa! I'm, like, so sorry that you had to find out about her death this way!"

Missy felt icicles of anxiety and fear gripping her heart as she pondered what to say and do next. "I appreciate your help in clearing up the mystery of my sister's whereabouts, Ava. I'm sure you were a good friend to her. She didn't have *any* that I was aware of. We-we lost contact a long time ago. Do you know if she left anything behind, maybe a laptop or her phone? What did they do with her belongings?"

"I think the police went through her apartment... afterwards. She didn't have a lot of possessions that I'm aware of. I'm not sure about a laptop, but her phone was missing and presumably went in the water with her. They probably gave her clothes to Goodwill. The only thing I have is a selfie picture of us that's a couple years old! I could email you a copy of it, if you'd like," Ava offered.

Missy said, "That would be nice—the only photo I have of her was from back in high school."

Ava sent her the photo. "Well, I gotta go pick-up my son from school. If I can help in any way, please let know! I—I hope you will have some closure now, but I guess we never truly want to close the door on the ones we love, do we? Good-bye, Melissa, and God bless!" she said, disconnecting.

Missy walked slowly back into living area as Jake finished up his conversation with Johnny Six-Fingers, "Okay, Johnny, yeah I appreciate it! Thanks again." He looked up from the couch at Missy.

"Johnny said he'll be out to get the—what's the matter? You look pissed! What did Ava tell you?" he demanded, as she stood glaring down at him.

"First off, you asshole, my sister is either dead or missing, I'm not sure which! Second, Ava said you *raped* my sister! Is that true—or don't you *remember*??" she angrily accused, as she advanced toward him, her left hand clenched dangerously close to her side-arm.

Jake's face paled and he jumped off the couch, holding up his hands, palms out. "Whoa, whoa, whoa—Elisa's *dead*?" He was hyperventilating as he backed away. "How the fuck did she die?? When?? I *never* raped her! I-I swear on my life!"

Missy advanced until she was a foot in front of him. "You have some explaining to do, Bud! And it better be the fucking truth!" she barked, shoving him in the chest.

Missy was pissed, but at least she hadn't shot his balls off... *yet!* Breathing hard, she moved two steps back out of his discomfort zone and began telling him what Ava had imparted over the phone. When she finished, Jake looked shell-shocked. He collapsed on the couch like he'd been punched.

"I *never* forced myself on her, Missy! I swear to you, I-I never could have done that!"

Missy hotly snarled, "Who are you trying to convince, Jake—me or *yourself!*"

Jake shook his head in frustration, "You don't fucking understand, I-I... could never *perform* when I drank! It made me... impotent! There's no way I *could* have raped her! You fucking *get* that—right?" he implored.

"So, you're telling me that you can actually remember everything you said and did when you were drinking? C'mon, give me a break! What about the blackouts Ava mentioned? Look... I'm willing to give you the benefit of the doubt, *if* you're willing to talk to 'Birdie,'" she demanded.

Jake saw no other way of convincing her of his innocence. *It's just my word against Elisa's, and Missy's going to be biased toward her sister, no matter what I say!* "Alright, if that's what it takes to convince you I'm telling the truth, give him a call," he conceded.

"I need to go see my mother first, this news is going to hurt her terribly! But she has a right to know. She's worried herself sick over the years, wondering what's become of my sister." She gathered her purse and the keys to Jake's truck.

"Ah, Johnny will be out to tow your bus into town, around 4:00 p.m.," he told her.

She checked the time—it was a little after 3:00. "Okay, I should be back before he gets out here, he's almost always late! I'll give Birdie a call before I get back and see when we can meet." She left the house and drove off in his pickup, spewing gravel as she accelerated down the road.

Fifteen minutes later, Missy rolled into the entrance of the Pleasant Valley Nursing Center. She had some trepidation about giving her mother second-hand information that was sketchy at best. After all, she hadn't talked to the cops herself yet to get any details of the accident report.

Shouldn't I wait and get the facts before I tell her for sure her daughter's dead? What if Elisa's still alive? They never found a body, so it's still possible, right? These thoughts swirled around like water circling a drain. All of this, before she had even gotten out of the truck. She sat thinking and staring out the windshield.

Silence except for the ticking sound from the cooling engine, and the north wind lightly rocking the truck with the occasional gust. Missy finally got out and walked up to the front door. There was a keypad by the door for entry.

She entered the code, opening the door and walking slowly past the elderly people, mostly women, in varying states of mobility and alertness. Many were in wheelchairs, some shuffled around the room on walkers, with the haunted look of the forgotten in their eyes. Others simply stared out the window forlornly—perhaps reliving treasured memories before time cruelly stole them away.

Fucking depressing! Missy thought as she made her way around the building's hub to her mother's wing. *I hope I don't live long enough to have to end up here!* Then suddenly felt ashamed, thinking, *Elisa won't have to worry about that now, will she?*

Saddened at the thought, she sighed as she came to her mother's room. She mentally prepared herself before knocking and entering. It was a semi-private, but at present no one occupied the first bed. Her mother was sitting up in a chair facing the window, which opened to the mountains that rose majestically around them.

"Mother, it's Melissa. How's my favorite person in the world doing today?" she asked as she leaned over, gently kissing her cheek.

Mother smelled like lavender. *Good! So at least they've bathed her today.* Her mother slowly turned her head and looked carefully at her daughter, her eyes unfocused.

"Who ahh you? Why ahh you heahh, it time fah ma baff?" she asked, her words slurring as a string of saliva slowly stretched from the corner of her mouth to her chin, dangling like a spider lowering itself from its web.

Fucking stroke! Fucking dementia! Missy silently raged to herself, using a tissue to wipe away the drool. "I'm Missy, Mama. Your daughter."

Her mother's eyes suddenly lost their thousand-yard stare, focusing in on her like a laser. "Misshy, you in dangehh! You neee wassh out, itt comm bac! Itt comm fah mann, you neee shtay awaaay!"

Missy's jaw dropped open like an unhinged door. *It couldn't be... the texts! Could it be the unknown person was—her mother?! But how?? She didn't have a smart phone, and she wouldn't even know what a 'text' was.*

Missy squatted down to eye level and asked, "Mama, did someone loan you a phone recently??" Her mother didn't respond.

"Mama, did someone—"

"*Yeenaldlooshi!*" her mother suddenly cried out.

Missy jerked back as if she'd been slapped!

"Elly knowss, ish dangehhh! Staa awaay, Misshy!" her mother continued, but stopped abruptly.

Missy was speechless, as her mother's face went blank as stone, and in a heartbeat, the vacant stare was back. *What the hell was that all about? How could she know anything about the creature that attacked us?*

"Mama, what is it that Elisa knows?"

Should she tell her about Elisa's death? Would she even understand or comprehend if she told her? Missy decided to probe around the edges.

"Mama, have you talked to or seen Elisa lately? Has she called or come to see you? She doesn't talk to me anymore."

Her mother continued staring out the window at the distant mountains. If she heard Missy, she gave no indication.

"I need to know if you've talked to ... Elly! Please, I've got to know if you've seen her!" she almost begged.

A single tear leaked out and ran down her mother's face as she continued staring out the window.

"Ellyssh ish gonn!" she slurred slowly, turning to look sadly at Missy. Her mother's pained anguish was so palpable, it filled the room.

Missy sat down beside her, taking her mother's hand in hers, "I know, Mama, everything will be alright." She didn't know what else to say. She laid her head against her mother's shoulder and sighed.

Anything I tell her will just make it worse! Is she just missing Elisa or does she somehow know? Doesn't matter, I'm not going to make it any harder on her.

Missy kissed her, told her she loved her. She said she would be back in a few days. She left her as she'd found her, staring out the window, sitting still as a statue and just as alone. As she walked by the nursing hub, one of the nurses called out to her. She turned around and said, "Yes?"

The nurse inquired, "You're Mrs. Morning Star's daughter, aren't you?"

"Yes, I am, what can I do for you?" Missy replied solemnly.

"Well, we were wondering if this is yours or your mother's?" She held out a shiny red iPhone. Missy stared at the phone as if it were a snake that might bite.

"I-I've never seen it before, where did you get it?" she asked tensely.

The nurse smiled, "Housekeeping found it in your mother's bathroom trash can. We didn't know why anyone would throw away such an expensive phone on purpose. We asked your mother about it, but as you know, she doesn't always respond. We've questioned the staff, and no one claimed ownership, so we thought it might belong to you. We turned it on and were going to check for the owner, but it's password protected."

Missy took the phone and examined it closely. It had a red screen protector, but there was nothing out of the ordinary about it. *Except, why was it found in Mama's room!*

Missy thought for a moment then told her, "I've been getting some, ah... very weird texts lately from someone who has my number. I'm wondering if I might borrow this to see if it has any relevance to these texts?"

"Well, as I said, it's password protected. Unless you have some way of bypassing that, I don't see how it would be of any help locating the owner. But as no one here claims it, I don't see any harm in letting you try to find the owner! Besides, we all love solving a good mystery, right?" the nurse finished, with a wink.

Missy agreed, thanking her, and stuffed the mystery phone into her purse. She walked back out past all the ancient souls gathered in the common area with nowhere to go and nowhere to be. On the way out of the building she thought sadly, "*All the lonely people,*" *McCartney got that right!*

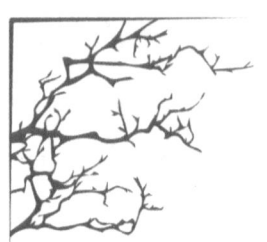

Chapter Fourteen

From the truck, Missy called Dr. Boucher's office and got his receptionist. Missy said, "Hello, this is Melissa Morning Star, do you know if Birdie can squeeze me in today or tomorrow? I need to schedule a visit with him ASAP!"

"Let me see what's on the menu for today... he has a five o'clock opening today or a one o'clock tomorrow. Which would you prefer?"

Missy thought about it. "How about the one o'clock tomorrow, I've got a, umm... 'friend' that needs some help. His name is Jake Anderson," she said.

Melanie answered, "Got you down for 1:00 p.m. See you soon," and hung up.

Missy thought, *another benefit was Birdie is a computer geek. Hopefully, he can hack this freaking phone and find out who it belongs to.* She looked at the time, 4:10 p.m., and made her way back down the highway toward Jake's house.

SHE NOTICED JOHNNY'S tow truck in the process of pulling her poor mud-filled bus out of the ditch and up onto the highway. Johnny waved as she slowed to make the turn to Jake's. She pulled into the drive and parked the truck. She sat there for a moment, then got out, walked up to the door and knocked. No answer. Missy peeked through one of the four new "peepholes" she'd blasted through his door. *Shit! Where is he now?*

Something snapped behind her! She let out a startled "Eeep!" as she whipped around. Awkwardly drawing her weapon from her purse at the same time, she brought it up in a blur of motion, her finger squeezing back on the trigger as she lined the sights up on—Jake.

He jumped backward holding his hands up. "It's just me! Don't shoot!!

She blew out a strained breath of relief. "Don't *ever* sneak up on an anxious woman with a gun! What the hell were you thinking??! I just about ended your writing career, Bud!" she scolded, as the adrenaline faded a bit.

"I didn't hear you drive up. I was out back, I found some interesting tracks you might want to see!" he announced, lowering his arms.

"Yeah? Well, I've got something interesting, too!" she responded. Putting her gun back into her purse, she pulled out the mystery phone and showed it to him. "They found this in Mama's bathroom trash can! No one knows where it came from. Mama doesn't have one, at least not to my knowledge. I asked the nurse if I could borrow it."

Jake looked it over, turned it on, but that's as far as he got. "This thing is password protected," he observed.

"No shit?" she replied sarcastically. "Anyway, I was just about to tell you, I called Birdie's office, got you an appointment for tomorrow at 1:00 p.m."

"That's great!" he mumbled unenthusiastically.

She continued, "He's known as a real computer geek, I thought if anyone can hack the password, it's him!"

"Whose phone do you think it is?" he asked.

"'Not sure, but I'm gonna try to find out!" she said confidently, as she took the phone back, stuffing it in her purse.

"In the meantime, come take a look at these tracks I found." He led her into the backyard and pointed to some shallow imprints in the soil close to the side of the house.

The prints were large and strangely- shaped. They were wider at the top with four pad-shaped indentions in the soil, a larger one just below those and in the center. But about eight inches back, a heel mark. The front part of the print seemed canine, but the back section looked *human*! The tracks led away from the house in the direction of the surrounding forest.

"I think it's hiding out there in the forest, we should try to track it down—finish the fucker off!" Jake asserted, looking out into the gathering shadows as the late afternoon sun began to wane.

Missy gave him a look. "You in a hurry to die, Jake? Forget about it! I suspect it hasn't forgotten where you live. I'm not risking my ass trying to hunt down a wounded animal or whatever it is! It'll be dark in less than an hour. I suggest you either fortify your house now, or I could take you to a motel for the night!"

Jake knew she was right, yet if they could find that thing before dark and kill it, he might not have to go through another horror-show tonight, which he might not survive!

"I refuse to be a prisoner in my own house! I'm just waiting around to be executed by a monstrosity that by all known laws of science shouldn't even exist in the first place!" Jake ranted, pacing back and forth.

"Calm down, Jake, *whatever* that thing is, it's alive and if it's alive, it can be killed! You need to decide what you're gonna do for the rest of the night," she reminded him, as they walked back inside. Jake just agreed as he sat down on the couch.

"Listen, Mama was semi-lucid today, she said to me almost the *exact* same words that are in the texts to my phone! Telling me 'I'm in danger!' I don't know how or why the phone was found in her room. Mama doesn't even know what a smart phone is, let alone knowing how to *text*!"

"Who do you think the phone belongs to, then?" Jake asked.

Missy thought, *good question!* "Well, I can't think of anyone else who's been there to see Mama lately. I'm pretty sure all visitors have to sign in for security reasons."

"How about you? Do you sign in when you visit her?" Jake asked, walking to the kitchen to refill Jinx's dishes.

"Well, no, I don't. They all know me by sight, or most of them do. I suppose the ones working the graveyard shift don't. I never go up there that late."

Jake poured out some cat chow, filling the bowl. Then he topped off the big cat's water dish. He checked the time: 5:25 p.m.

"You forgot to call Nurse 'Wretched'! She should be working by now."

"I don't think she's behind the texts. It's someone who knows me, it says "Missy" in the first text they sent. Nurse 'Wretched' only knows me from when I was up in your room, remember? I wrote my number and left it with you. She might have gotten the number somehow, but she didn't have my *name*! Besides, what good would it do to ask her? All she has to say is no. My money's on someone close to me. Someone who's involved in all this and knows what that *thing* out there is, and why it's after you!"

"Okay, 'Columbo,' how many people know you go by 'Missy?' I'm thinking probably most of the old-timers in town. That's a lot of people! Whoever is writing the texts obviously knows you and is trying to warn you away. Maybe your 'shrink' friend 'Birdie' will be able to crack the password encryption on that phone tomorrow. If so, end of mystery, but not the end of that *thing*!" Jake proclaimed, as he opened the fridge, grabbing a diet soda.

"I don't think we're gonna a name associated with it—it's probably a burner phone with some unfamiliar number, but it's worth a shot!" she answered, snagging the soda he'd just set on the counter and taking a gulp.

"Anyway, have you decided where you're gonna stay tonight?" she asked, between sips of soda.

"I guess there's no way I could bribe you to stay here in my extra room, is there?" Jake grinned, hopefully.

She thought for a moment, then smiled back. "Pizza!"

He did a 'double-take.' "Pizza *what*?"

"Pepperoni, mushrooms, olives, with extra sauce, extra-large, I'm starved! I haven't eaten since your 'continental breakfast' this morning."

"*That's* all it takes to get you to stay?" he inquired doubtfully.

"That and a salad, with bread sticks—oh, and chocolate ice cream for dessert!" she added.

He grinned. "You *know* the pizza will be cold and the ice cream half-melted by the time it gets here, right?"

"That's what microwaves are for—and the ice cream will be fine!" she said, her stomach growling.

Jake nodded, looked up the Pizza Palace in Joseph and gave them their order and the address. He added that if someone could stop and buy a gallon of chocolate ice cream, there would be a nice tip in it.

The guy told him, "No worries, dude! We'll have it all delivered in like, forty-five to an hour!"

Jake thanked him and hung up. He walked to the living room window and looked out at the last of the hazy sunlight lancing through the pines as the sun began to hide itself behind the mountains.

"I really should go and get a few things from my place, if I'm staying the night," Missy told him, as she gathered up her purse and the keys to his truck.

Jake looked uneasy but nodded. "Hurry back, don't want to be late for the cold pizza."

"Shouldn't take me more than half an hour. Save me a slice, and no ice cream diving before I get back! You also need to put a fresh bandage on that hand. If it gets infected, you could lose it! Then 'Mr. Happy' would miss his close friend!" she finished with a wicked grin, glancing pointedly toward his crotch. Then she got into his truck and tore off down the graveled lane to the highway.

Jake blushed and shut the front door, locking it. He went into his bathroom and gingerly unwrapped the ace bandage from his hand. The skin was an angry red around the sutures in it. He applied some antibiotic cream on both sides, then carefully wrapped it with a fresh bandage, grimacing as he pulled it tight and secured it with the little metal clip. *Time for a pain pill,* he thought as he walked to the nightstand in his adjoining bedroom. He shook out a pill, went to the kitchen and washed it down with a couple swallows of water.

MISSY TURNED OFF ONTO her drive. As she got closer, she saw a truck with the park ranger emblem on its side parked next to her cabin, and her boss, Ben Dover, sitting in the driver's seat, talking on the phone. She pulled up alongside of him and parked.

What is Ben doing here? she wondered as she got out, walked up to the truck window. Ben saw her and ended the conversation, rolled down his window.

"Hey Missy, just stopped by to see how you're doing! How's your head?"

Missy smiled, "Could be worse—got a mild concussion and a sprained index finger, my bus got the worst of it, a shitload of mud inside. Called Johnny's and had him tow it to his shop. Jake'll be paying for it."

Ben frowned, "Jake?? You talkin' about Jake Anderson, that so-called 'writer?'"

Missy then told him it was Jake whom she'd rescued out of the lake.

Ben's face darkened, "My daddy sold his daddy that 150 acres of land he's sittin' on, over forty years ago. His old man never finished paying the amount agreed on. The S.O.B. up and died, still owing $20,000 to my dad! Technically, part of it's still *my land*!"

"Did you approach Jake about paying off the debt?" Missy asked.

"'Wouldn't do any good, my dad and his *just shook on it!* Back then a man's word stood for something. There wasn't any paperwork signed, not that I could ever find," he said bitterly.

"I asked Jake about paying off the rest of the money years ago, he just told me to prove his old man *hadn't* paid it off, then he might consider it! He doesn't have anything to prove his old man *did* pay it! So, basically, it's my word against his, and it burns my ass that he's sitting on land that isn't all rightfully his!"

Missy didn't know how to reply. Apparently, she'd opened an old can of worms, so she quickly changed the subject. "Uh, was Bob okay taking my shift for a couple days?"

Ben was still simmering, "Yeah, he needs the overtime. That girl of his turns eighteen come January, and she wants to go to Stanford. I just wished him good luck! If she makes it in, he'll need every dime he can spare.

"Well, I gotta go, was just making the rounds, thought I'd check in on ya," he said, starting the engine, staring at Jake's truck. "That Anderson's truck?"

"Yeah, well, I sorta requisitioned it while mine is in the shop. Thanks for checking on me," she replied quickly, wanting to end the conversation before he could ask any more awkward questions.

He just grunted, "Yer welcome, let me know if you need anything," put the truck in reverse and slowly backed up, staring at her strangely, then drove back toward the highway.

Missy blew out a sigh of relief, walking up to her front door. She was inserting the key in the lock when she noticed the door was ajar. *That's not good!* she thought, as the hairs on the back of her neck stood up! With her mother's words echoing "Youu *in dangehh, Misshy,*" she drew her weapon from her purse and slowly pushed open the door.

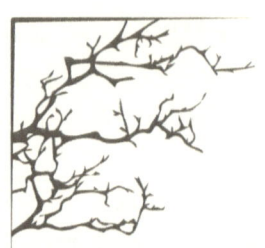

Chapter Fifteen

The headlights ricocheted off the tree-lined drive as his '98 Ford Focus, with its ancient shocks, bounced its way up to the house, clanking and clattering. The twenty-year-old driver was Pete Chandler, or 'Pizza Pete' as he was known at the store. He'd been called back to the Pizza Palace after his shift was technically over to make this run out by the lake. He'd been in the middle of taking a class from an online college, trying to get his B. S. in Botany, when he got the text.

"Pizza-shit car!" he thought, as he killed the engine. *"It's a fucking wonder any pizza I deliver survives intact!"* He grabbed the box out of the insulated warming bag, opening it. Sure enough, some pepperoni was stuck to lid—and it was cold, breadsticks, too! *"Shit! There goes my tip!"*

He exited the car by reaching out the window, pulling the outer door-release handle to open the door. The inside handle had broken off years ago. He grabbed the plastic bag containing both the boxed salad and ice cream that was probably melted from the passenger side! He trudged up to the front door, admiring the fancy 'peepholes' in it, and knocked loudly.

Jake went to the door—first looking to see who or *what* was on the other side! On the thresh-hold, holding their dinner, stood a young man in a red shirt and cap with "Pizza Palace" on both. Pete was average height, when he wasn't slouching. He had shaggy, shoulder-length blond hair that often partially fell over blue-gray eyes the color of a winter sky, giving him a slight semblance to a blond sheepdog. He carried a few extra pounds due to his sedentary job but wasn't fat.

Pete stood there with the box of cold pizza in one hand, the other holding the bag of melting ice cream, and delivered his spiel, "Pizza Palace, delivered hot to your door; if it's cold, we'll make more!"

Jake opened the door and said, "The pizza or the ice cream?" The joke went over the kid's head.

Jake took the pizza and the bag from him, setting it on the couch. He opened the box, touched a piece with his finger. Cold. He turned to the kid, "Do I get a discount—half the toppings are stuck to the lid, and it's cold?!"

Pete just shifted from foot to foot, looking uncomfortable. "Um, it was *hot* when I put it in the car, Mister! One of my car windows won't roll all the way up, and my old 'beater' out there will barely hit 50 mph, so it took me awhile to get out here!"

Jake looked out at the pathetic excuse for a car and felt sorry for the young man. "Okay, kid, what's the damage?"

"Ah, that'll be $30.00 for the pizza, breadsticks, salad and ice cream."

Jake had stuffed all his cash into his left pocket for convenience. He counted out two twenties, gave it to him, telling him, "Save your money and get some decent wheels, you'll get better tips!"

Pete, smiling, thought, *Yeah, I'll go right out and buy me a Mercedes-Benz, asshole!* But he took the money, "Thanks, mister, enjoy the pie." Pocketing the cash, he headed back to his "pizza-shit" car. He cranked the engine, reversed and headed back toward the highway and town.

Jake was about to close the door when Jinx zipped past him from out of the dark, startling him, and headed straight for the cat chow. "Wondered when you'd show up." *He's never late for pizza*, Jake thought.

Jake took the pizza and placed it in the oven, turning it on low. He put the salad in the fridge and the ice cream into the freezer and looked at the time, Missy had been gone for an hour. *Wonder what's taking so long? Women! They tell you thirty minutes and two hours later, there you are, still waiting around with your thumb up your ass.* Jinx finished his food, jumped up on the couch and curled up in a ball, promptly falling asleep.

MISSY WAS LOSING THE afternoon light—it was almost dark inside the cabin. After finding the door ajar, she didn't want to go in without being able to see her surroundings. So, she stepped around to the back and cranked up the generator. It roared to life as she made her way back to the front door—now she could at least see. She stepped in, gun at the ready, seeing nothing out of the ordinary. She checked the bathroom, nothing touched or out of place. She holstered the gun.

Did I just forget to lock the door earlier? No, I distinctly remember locking it! Nobody else has a key. She went over and closely inspected the striker plate in the door frame.

Yes! There were fresh scratches and grooves cut into the surface of the plate. Someone had jimmied her door, just like Jakes! But who and why? She thought of Ben sitting in his car when she had pulled up. *No way Ben would have broken in... would he? For what reason? Too many strange things happening in the last thirty-six hours.*

She was mentally exhausted. *I need to relax,* she thought, remembering she had a bottle of Merlot in her solar-powered refrigerator. She got a wine glass out of a small cabinet and opened the fridge to find—*a* severed *baby's head covered in blood, bulging eyes staring out at her from the top shelf!!*

Missy screamed, slammed the door shut, dropping the glass, which shattered on the floor as she scuttled away like a crab on a hot skillet! *Was that damn thing real? What kind of sick fuck put that in my fridge??* She was hyperventilating! Taking several deep breaths, she managed to calm her heart rate down to a mere 100 beats per minute. Her hands were shaking badly, as she pulled her phone out of her purse, dropped it, scooped it back up and walked shakily back to the refrigerator.

She stood there for what seemed like an eternity. Finally, she shakily reached out toward the handle but paused, suddenly terrified if she opened it, something inside might leap out at her like an evil jack-in-the-box! She selected the camera app on the phone, gathered her courage and yanked the door open with a jerk.

She made herself look closer—it wasn't a *baby's* head at all! It looked like, like... a freaking rabbit's head?? Minus the ears, which appeared to have been chewed off entirely!

She quickly snapped a couple pictures, then slammed the door and made it to the sink before throwing up. After a few dry heaves, she ran some water, rinsing out her mouth.

Missy finally calmed down enough to decide that the head in her fridge had to go. *No way am I leaving that thing in there!* She got a pair of BBQ tongs and a pair of rubber gloves from a utensil drawer, grabbed a small trash bag and steeling herself, she opened the refrigerator door. She picked up the grisly head with the tongs and dropped it in the bag. There was a repulsive *plop* as the bloody remains slid to the bottom. Gore puddled at the bottom of the refrigerator. She'd deal with that next.

She filled a five-gallon bucket with hot water and some bleach. After she donned the rubber gloves, she opened the fridge door. With paper towels, she thoroughly scrubbed the shelves clean of the poor rabbit's blood, bumping her injured finger twice, and cursing the asshole who did this. *Probably cleaner than it's been since I bought it!* she thought, as she dumped reddish-colored water down the drain, then discarded the paper towels and rubber gloves she'd used into the trash.

She sealed up the bag, picked up her flashlight and opened the door. Walking to her garbage bin out back, she took off the padlock that kept animals from foraging inside. She lifted the lid, dumping the bag inside and relocked the hasp. Then she returned inside, locking the door behind her.

She sat down in her recliner and glanced at the clock: 7:00 p.m. *Shit! Jake! I forgot I told him I'd be back in thirty minutes.* It had been almost an hour and a half since she'd left his house. She looked up his number and dialed.

He answered on the second ring. "Well, hello, I was beginning to wonder if you—"

"Jake, listen!" she interrupted. "I'll be there shortly. I-I had a bit of a nasty surprise when I got here. Ben was here earlier, but—listen, I'll explain when I get there." Then she abruptly hung up. She gathered her toothbrush, makeup, and some other things, threw them into a backpack. She paused, then grabbed her bathrobe. *No one to blame but myself, if I wake up naked!*

SHE GRABBED HER FLASHLIGHT and backpack, locking the front door behind her. *For whatever good it would do, since someone already defeated the flimsy latch to get in. I'll have to install a deadbolt, like ASAP!* she thought. Turning on the flashlight, she went around back and turned off the generator. It chugged to a halt.

She checked her surroundings quickly with the beam of light, then examined the bed of Jake's truck and its interior before climbing in and locking the doors. She turned the key in the ignition, the engine coughed and idled for a moment and sputtered to a halt. She tried again, the starter turning over and over, but the engine wouldn't catch.

Shit! Why won't it start? She turned on the headlights, illuminating her equipment shed in stark relief. *Okay, so it's not the battery.* She turned off the headlights, then switching on the interior lights she opened the glove compartment searching for a manual. Nothing but a bunch of old receipts, a couple CDs, a tire pressure gauge and an old crumpled box of unopened rubbers that had expired in 2015. *Not getting any, eh, Bud?* she smirked to herself. She finally gave up and called Jake.

"Hello! I thought you were on the way?" he asked, an echo sounding like he was in the toilet.

"I've got another little problem—your damn truck won't *start*! The battery's fine, the headlights and the starter work, but the damned engine won't catch!" she explained, growing more agitated.

Jake was silent for a moment. "Um, what does the fuel gauge read with the key in the *on* position?"

She turned the key, looked at the fuel gauge. "It's sitting on *'empty,'* it's not moving! When was the last time you put gas in, Jake?

"Well, it's been a month or two back, I guess," he replied.

"Are you telling me you only fill up *once* every couple of months?" she asked incredulously.

"Yeah, but that's for both tanks! I don't go to town often, so I don't use much gas!"

There was a pregnant pause, "Soooo, you're saying there's *another* gas tank?"

"Yep! Did you switch tanks? There's a toggle under the dash below the steering column. I had it installed when I put the extra tank in, cost a pretty penny but better than running out of gas!" he replied, sounding smug.

Missy rolled her eyes, felt under the dash. Sure enough, there was a toggle switch. She flipped it, "Okay, I flipped the switch, now what?" she barked impatiently.

"Well, just crank the engine until it catches. The switch opens a valve from the extra tank to the engine, cranking it will help prime the—"

"I *know* what it operates—*you* just better hope it *works*. I'm not walking in the fucking dark, Bud!" she interrupted before he could begin to explain some technical car bullshit. She cranked the engine, letting the starter do its thing. Finally, the engine sputtered and caught as the fuel from the other tank reached it.

"Be there shortly!" she growled tersely. She threw the truck into reverse, gunned the engine, shifted into first and roared down her lane to the highway spewing gravel in her wake.

IT WATCHED HER LEAVE from the rooftop of her cabin as she pulled onto the highway. Its shoulder was still healing. She'd been warned. Still, she chose to stay close to the man instead of minding her own business! If she gets hurt or dies, it will be of her own doing. Had the woman not interfered, the man would surely have drowned in the lake. She had intervened again, twice now thwarting its plan to destroy the man! Fate could not possibly smile upon either of them so favorably again! Soon ...

MISSY PULLED TO A STOP in front of Jake's house. Retrieving her backpack and flashlight from the back seat, she walked up to Jake's front door, looking into the new and improved peepholes she'd made in it. Two eyes stared back. Startled, she jumped back, as Jake quickly opened the door, looking nervously to the left and right, then motioned her in. She stalked inside, tossing her backpack on the couch and startling Jinx, who gave her an indignant look before leaping off and wandering into the kitchen to check around his empty food bowl for stray kibble.

Jake closed the door, locking it. "Sorry I didn't tell you about the dual tanks on the truck, I hardly ever pay attention to the gas gauge. Nobody else ever drives it, so I didn't think about it."

Missy just shook her head and waved it off. She related her conversation with Ben. Jake looked uncomfortable when she brought up the subject of the remaining money Ben claimed was owed to him.

"Anyway, he left, and I started inside. *My* front door had been jimmied, just like yours! I cleared the cabin. Nothing had been touched as far as I could see." She paced as she talked. "I was jumpy, so I decided to have a glass of wine. I opened the fridge and there was a fucking *rabbit's head* covered in blood, staring out at me from the top shelf!"

Jake didn't say a word.

She continued, "I thought at first it was a *human* baby's head! It freaked me out and I slammed the fridge door, made me puke! After I recovered some, I threw it in a trash bag and tossed it in the container outside, cleaned up the fridge and called you!"

Jake was silent for a moment. "It sounds like something out of the 'Godfather' to me. You thinking it's the same person who broke in here and stole my laptop? That seems like a warning, Missy."

"I don't know, I'm just thankful it was in the refrigerator instead of under the covers of my bed!" She shuddered at the thought. "If it's the same person as the sender of the texts, then we have a seriously disturbed individual stalking *both* of us!"

"I don't think that *freak* and the person texting you are the same individuals. But I could be wrong," he replied, going into the kitchen and turning off the stove. "You still have an appetite left, after all that crap?" he asked, pulling the pizza box out of the oven, putting it on the counter, and getting Jinx's immediate attention.

"Yeah, I'm hungry, did you get ice cream?" She wearily sat down at the kitchen table.

"It's in the freezer, it was beginning to melt when the pizza guy brought it." Jake put a couple slices on paper plates, got the salad out of the fridge and placed both on the table. With some difficulty, he opened two cans of soda, giving her one.

"All he brought was ranch dressing, I forgot to ask you for a preference. I hardly ever eat salads, so I don't keep any on hand," he commented, as he tried to open the little dressing packet by putting it between his teeth and pulling on it. *Splurp!* The dressing squirted out in a sloppy stream onto his face and tabletop, making a mess.

Missy laughed, "Looks like you had a food-porn moment, Bud!"

Jake felt his cheeks redden as he wiped his face with a napkin. "You watch porn, do you?" he asked innocently, as he sat and took a bite of pizza.

Now *her* face flushed, as she chewed on her slice. "I've seen enough to know most men are all about 'optics' when it comes to sex. Most women want romance and tenderness before, during and after sex," she stated without missing a beat, smiling at him as she bit into a seven-inch bread stick.

Jake nearly choked on a bite of pizza, gulping down some of his soda to push the offending piece past his airway.

Changing the subject, he asked, "Do you really think your friend 'Birdie' can... what, hypnotize me into recovering any memories from my past?"

She took a sip of soda. "Nothing's for certain Jake, but he's supposed to be very good at regression therapy. I'd really like to know if Ava was telling the truth about Elisa's accusations or not. It's possible she's just a little prejudiced against you and exaggerated what *she* was told, so there's that!" She asserted with a tight smile.

"I'll tell you right now, I'm not real comfortable staying here overnight! Between that *thing* out there targeting you here and whoever broke in at my place, I'm not feeling very safe anywhere right now! So, that said, what kind of ice cream did you order?"

"Um, I ordered chocolate, I hope that's okay." As they finished, he cleared off the plates of remaining pizza crust into the trash, giving Jinx a few bites.

Jake took the ice cream out of the freezer, scooped out large helpings into two bowls on the table. Jinx stared at him from the floor, his look inferring, *that's right, just fucking ignore* me, *thank you very little!*

Jake sighed and scooped out a small portion into the cat's food dish. Jinx got up, stalked over to the bowl, licked once, shook his head twice and gave Jake a glare that said, *this tastes like shit—and it's cold!* The big cat turned and jumped back on the couch, still shaking his head trying to rid himself of the taste.

"Finicky fuck, he'll lap it up once it melts and warms to room temperature!" Jake said, chuckling as he sat back down at the table.

Missy took a bite, made a face and grabbed her napkin and spit out her mouthful, exclaiming, "That tastes like *shit*! What brand did you get??"

Jake dipped his spoon into the ice cream, tasting it, and immediately followed suit, looking over at Jinx, who just sat there looking smug, *I told you so.*

Jake apologized, "I'm sorry about that, but you're right—it does taste a bit freezer-burned!"

He got up and went to the freezer, got out the tub of ice cream and looked at the expiration date. It read, "Best used by 7/20/18!" He turned the carton around and looked at the brand name, "Happy Cowz." *More like 'Crappy Cowz!,'* he thought, with the nasty aftertaste lingering in his mouth.

"That stuff expired three months ago! Pecker-head pizza guy that bought it obviously didn't even bother checking the expiration date!" Jake huffed, as he picked up his phone to call the Pizza Palace.

"Come on, Jake, cut him a break! You *do* remember what it was like to be young, right? Did you always check the expiration date on the things you bought? He was probably in a hurry to get the pizza delivered before it got cold," she chided, as she dumped the remaining "ice crap" in the sink, washed the bowls out and put them up in the cabinet.

"That's not the point! The point is, I tipped him $15.00 for a supposedly 'hot' pizza and edible ice cream!" he barked, dialing the Pizza Palace.

The guy who answered was apologetic as Jake told him about the pizza and mainly, the ice cream. "Sorry about that Mr. Anderson, I'd be glad to make you another pie, but if I do, Pete's the only one I got that can bring it and it'll probably be cold again before he gets there! One of the power windows on that old car of his won't roll up anymore."

Jake told him, "I'd like either a new tub of ice cream or my money back, forget the pizza!"

The man said he'd send Pete right away to get some fresh ice cream and bring it out pronto, adding there would be a 'freebie' pizza waiting in his name, and next time, he'd deliver it himself! Jake thanked him and hung up.

"You're being kinda hard-core about the ice cream, Jake, I've sorta lost my appetite for it."

Jake nodded in frustrated agreement. "Well, how would you like to play a game? I've got a couple stored away."

"What have you got?" she asked, sitting sat back down at the table.

He got up and went into his bedroom closet. "I've got chess, Scrabble, cards and monopoly, although I tend to cheat at Monopoly, so better pick one of the others," he called out.

"Scrabble would be fine. I haven't played in years!"

He brought the game out and set it up on the table.

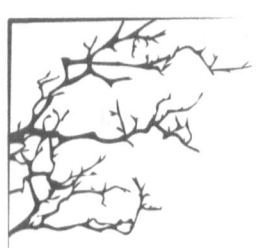

Chapter Sixteen

"Pizza Pete" grumbled to himself as he made his way out of the parking lot of the local 'stop n rob' convenience store with another tub of ice cream sitting in the passenger seat.

"How was I supposed to know the fucking stuff was out-of-date?" He pulled onto the highway and headed down the road toward the park, cranking up the stereo with blown woofers, the shitty speakers barely worked. His manager had texted him about the damned ice cream right when he was fixing to score with his girlfriend!

He accelerated up to 50 mph, which was as fast as the crappy car would go, his shaggy blond hair whipping around his face, the cold mountain air pouring through the window that wouldn't roll up. The steering wheel shimmied in his hands and the valves knocked like they desperately wanted out of the poorly maintained engine, blue smoke pouring out of the exhaust pipe like a locomotive. He saw the turnoff for Jake's drive coming up, slowed down and turned onto the graveled lane, bottoming out the oil pan against the gravel. *Shit, I hate this car!* He traveled the 100 yards up to the house and killed the engine.

"I don't think '*fraggled*' is a real word! Use it in a sentence." Missy disputed, as Jake placed his tiles on the board.

He smiled, "The woman was sooo hot, that he 'fraggled' her right on the spot! See? I'm also a poet."

Missy cocked an eyebrow and said sarcastically, "You're *something*, all right! What's your definition of '*fraggled*', Bud?"

Jake looked mock-offended, then cocked his head toward the living room. "It's, ah, I... think I just heard our ice cream arrive!"

"Talk about saved by the bell," Missy added, as he got up and looked out the window in the living room.

"Yeah, he's here," Jake opened the door before Pizza Pete could knock. "Hey, kid, come on in."

Pete thought, *that's the last thing I want to do.* But he just shrugged and, holding the bag of ice cream, stepped inside as Jake shut the door behind him.

"Sorry to drag you back out here, but the ice cream you brought expired three months ago and tastes like it! Come in here, please."

Pete swiped his hair back out of his eyes and followed Jake into the kitchen, nodding to Missy as he passed the table. Jake opened the freezer, pulled out the "crappy cowz" and placed it on the counter. He took a spoon and worked the top off the tub, using his right forearm to support it. He dug out a spoonful, holding it out to Pete, who stared at the spoon like it was holding a giant spider instead of ice cream.

Jake ordered, "Have a taste, it won't hurt you." Pete stepped forward and tentatively opened his mouth.

Jake slid the spoon smoothly between Pete's open lips. Pete's eyes got big and he leaned over the sink and spat the gob of "crappy cowz" into it. Then he turned on the water, cupping his hand to catch some, brought it to his mouth, swished and spit.

"That tastes like shit!" he declared, his mouth dripping water on the floor. Both Jake and Missy had to laugh.

"I just wanted you to know I wasn't bullshitting about the stuff. Did your boss make you pay for the new batch?" Jake asked him.

"Uh, yeah, he told me to either pay for that, or another pizza if you wanted it," Pete replied, tucking his hair behind his ear again and shuffling his feet, eager to get the fuck out.

Jake dug out his wallet and handed him a ten spot. "This will cover your loss. Next time, you'll check the expiration dates, right?"

"Yes, sir! I'm real sorry about that. Well, I-I gotta get back to the store, got other orders to deliver, have a good night!" he prevaricated, turning to leave the house. He dropped his keys outside somewhere between the house and his car. *Crap! I need a fucking flashlight.* He felt in his pocket, but he'd left his phone in the car. He went to the car and grabbed his phone. *Whoa... something stinks! Must have left a half-eaten burger in here,* he thought. Turning on the phone's flashlight, he quickly found his keys.

Shit! I hope Sheena's still awake when I get back. Thinking of her luscious body waiting for him gave him haste. He jumped in the car, cranking the engine, threw it in reverse and bounced down the road. *Phew! Something really stunk, like rotted meat!*

He was halfway to the highway when he glanced in the rearview mirror and saw—to his horror—burning yellow eyes staring back at him! A long wide mouth framed by a row of razor-sharp teeth dripped saliva from its terrible mouth, the obvious source of the smell. A savage growl preceded a clawed appendage as it whipped forward to rip out his throat.

"THIS ONE TASTES PRETTY good! Sure you don't want some?" Jake offered Missy a bite from the new tub of ice cream.

"Sorry, but I'll pass. You want to finish the game?" she asked.

Jake sat back down at the table with his bowl. "Guess I lose a turn—I was just testing your vocabulary proficiency."

Missy smiled, "I majored in English Comp in college, with a minor in bullshitsu!"

"Bullshitsu, what's that?" Jake said, playing along.

"Ancient martial art used to deflect bullshit when you hear it!" she explained as she drew five new tiles. *Crap! All consonants. Aha!* She made the word "Cyst" for a triple-word score of 27.

Jake was just about to play the letter "*Q*" to make "Quirk" when they heard a loud *Crummpp* from not that far away.

"What the hell was that?" Jake looked at Missy and they hurriedly got up and looked out the living room window. An orange glow flickered through the shrubs and trees lining Jake's drive to the highway—a fire!

"I think it's that kid's car!" Jake ran into his kitchen, grabbed a fire extinguisher he kept by the stove and headed for the front door with Missy in tow. "You gotta drive—I don't know what happened, but we sure don't want it to spread!"

They rushed out the door and jumped into his truck.

PETE FREAKED OUT AS the *thing's* claws raked the side of his head, missing his throat only because of a fortunate bounce of the worn-out shocks. He lost control of the car, swerving head-on into a large pine. Amazingly, the air bag still functioned, deploying immediately, stopping his forward motion.

The same could *not* be said for the creature, who wore no restraint—it flew past Pete like a missile, rocketing through the windshield! It bounced off the crumpled hood, hit the tree then disappeared into the darkness, just as the car engine caught fire from the busted fuel line with a loud *wooomph!*

Pete groaned in pain, the right side of his head feeling hot and wet. He desperately hit for the release button for his seatbelt, as heat and smoke from the burning engine poured inside the mangled car through its shattered windshield. The belt released and he frantically reached outside for the door handle, managing to pull it open wide enough to roll out onto the graveled road. He smelled gas from the ruptured fuel line.

Fuck! it's gonna blow any minute! He tried to stand, but his right leg wasn't having any of it. The harsh glare of headlights blinded him as Jake's truck slid to a halt ten feet away.

Both jumped out of the truck, Missy carrying the fire extinguisher as Jake reached the injured boy first. With his good hand, he grabbed Pete under his right arm and pulled him to his feet, half dragging him away from the burning vehicle.

Missy pulled the safety pin on the extinguisher and aimed it at the flaming engine, spraying out a cloud of white powder, putting out the fire just as the extinguisher sputtered and died. She joined Jake, who had opened the tailgate on the truck and had Pete sitting up on the bed.

"What the hell happened... uh, what's your name, kid?" Jake asked him.

"It ... it's P-P-Pete! Pete Ch-chandler!" the terrified boy managed to say. "I—I was just driving do-down the road, I smelled something really bad in the car! Some—something in t-t-the back seat—it was *hor-horrible!* I—it tried to kill me! I lost control and hit that tree ..."

Then, shaking badly, he broke down, sobbing uncontrollably. Missy and Jake exchanged a knowing look.

Missy put an arm around the kid's heaving shoulders, hugging him as she whispered urgently to Jake, "We need to either take him back to the house to check his injuries or get him to the hospital!"

Jake assessed the situation, which had escalated—now a third person was involved with the creature.

"No hospital, unless it's absolutely necessary! We'll have to report the accident to the cops, no way around that, I guess, unless we can think of something else. Don't know how he's going to explain the big-ass hole in the windshield, though! Let's get him to the house," he said tersely.

They helped Pete into the cab of the truck, Jake climbed in beside him, closing the door. Missy turned the truck around and drove them back to Jake's, checking the rear-view mirror, thinking angrily as she did, *that fucking thing needs to die!*

IT LAY STUNNED IN THE shrubs that encircled the big tree. It had watched the boy escape the burning vehicle, its rage burning hot as the fire itself! It grew even angrier as the man and woman came to the boy's rescue. It had planned on killing the boy, leaving his eviscerated body on the man's doorstep as a message to him and a final warning to the woman. It had broken its left shoulder on the bole of a tree after being ejected through the windshield. Another four inches to the left, and its head would have burst like an overripe pumpkin! The shoulder would take a little longer to heal than the bullet wound had. No more diversions. Next time, it would kill them both!

THEY HELPED PETE OUT of the truck and into the house, locking the door behind them. They sat him down at the kitchen table. Missy inspected the wounds on the side of his head, while Jake went and gathered alcohol, peroxide, triple antibiotic and bandages. The claw gashes were bleeding profusely, but they were not deep. It didn't look like he would need stitches.

"Did you hit your head on anything?" Missy asked, as she carefully cleaned the wounds with peroxide.

Pete grimaced and shook his head slowly. "No ma'am, the air-bag kept me from hitting the steering wheel—wha-what the hell *was* that *thing*? Why was it in my freaking car?"

Missy looked at Jake. *What exactly and how much do we tell him?* "We-we don't really know for sure, Pete. But it's attacked us—Jake, once before today. It may be a hybrid of a wolf or something like that. All we know for sure is it's intelligent, and it's *dangerous!*"

Jake interjected, "That *thing* is trying to kill me—why, I don't have a clue, and I think anyone around me right now could become collateral damage!"

"Why haven't you called the cops? I mean, they're the ones who should be trying to catch or kill it, right?" Pete hissed, wincing as Missy applied the triple antibiotic on the shallow lesions in his scalp.

"First of all, I seriously doubt the cops are going to believe that there's a freaking 'werewolf,' or whatever it is, trying to kill me! Think about it, Pete! They'll just nod and laugh, then haul me straight to the loony-bin! That's not an option! We're kinda on our own... or at least *I* am anyway.

"I'll deal with this fucking *thing*. I've gotta figure out a way to kill *it*, before it kills *me* or someone else!" Jake exclaimed defiantly, as he sat facing the boy at the table.

"You'd better call the cops and report your accident. You can tell 'em that you swerved into the tree to avoid hitting a deer or maybe a bear, just not the truth!"

Pete looked at them nervously and nodded. "What about the gigantic hole in the windshield, how do I explain *that?*"

Damn good question! Jake thought to himself.

Missy offered, "What if we tear out the rest of the windshield, make it look like the crash caused it?

"That won't do it, it's safety-glass. It doesn't crumble when it's impacted like the side windows do. It has a sheet of plastic inside it to hold it together in the event of an impact, inside or out! The cops could tell if something punched through it either from inside or outside, the hole in the glass would have an entry and exit—just like a bullet wound," Jake instructed, getting up and pacing.

"What if it was melted? We could pour gas on the inside and torch the rest of the car along with the windshield!" Missy suggested.

"That won't work either. Gasoline burns at about 1500 degrees Fahrenheit. That safety-glass won't melt until the temperature hits 3000 degrees! Besides, they can tell if a fire started in a different area, at a different time," Jake elaborated.

"Well, '*Professor*,' that about exhausts all *my* ideas. You got anything better?" Missy challenged.

"I'm thinking. Do you suppose Johnny Six-fingers would come out and tow that car to the junkyard, no questions asked?" Jake asked.

Missy arched an eyebrow, "It's possible."

Pete looked up in surprise. "What do I tell my insurance company happened to it? I'm only paying 'liability,' I don't have 'collision.' Gotta have collision for them to cover hitting a tree! *Shit*! I'm so screwed! That's the only wheels I've got, Mister, I'm gonna lose my fucking job—and my place to live—all because you pissed off some freaking monster that decided to hitch a ride in my back seat! This isn't my fault!" Pete moaned miserably.

Jake tried to calm him, "Listen, if Johnny tows it to the junkyard, you just tell your insurance company it was totaled. Which, for all purposes, it was. Then tell them to cancel the policy. That way, the cops won't be involved."

Jake sighed. "I'll buy you a reasonably priced *used* replacement. It's the least I can do for all the trouble I've caused you."

Pete perked up. "Really, mister? You mean it? Th-thanks! I'd really appreciate that."

Jake just nodded. "The key words here are '*reasonably priced*,' you understand? That, and you promise not to sue me for damages!"

Pete readily agreed.

Missy just crossed her arms and shook her head, smiling. "Looks like you might have found a new calling in the 'used car' business, Bud! Two cars wrecked in two days!"

Jake didn't look happy. "Kinda seems that way, doesn't it?"

Missy called Johnny's Garage, explaining what they needed done.

"No problem! I'll be out to get it tomorrow morning, I closed the shop an hour ago. Say about 9:00 a.m. tomorrow?"

Missy indicated that would be fine. She turned to Pete, "I can give you a ride home if you'd like or Jake would be happy to call you a cab—*right*, Jake?

Jake grumbled something unintelligible, then said, "Sure, sure."

Pete thought about it, as Missy finished bandaging his head. "I guess a cab would be fine, I really appreciate it Mister ... um—?"

"It's Anderson, Pete, Jake Anderson. Give Missy your phone number and address so I can find you tomorrow to go look at cars." Jake called Lyft, gave them directions.

"They'll be here in twenty minutes or so. I've got a 1:00 o'clock appointment, so probably be mid-afternoon."

Pete cheerfully gave her his information. "We can go to Trader Jim's—he's got the best deals around!"

Jake just mumbled, "Whatever," then went into the kitchen. "You want some ice cream while you wait?"

Pete thought, *no fucking way!* but quickly replied, "Ah, no thanks, Mr. Anderson, my stomach don't feel too good right now."

They sat around the table in uneasy silence until headlights showed through the curtains in the living room, signaling Pete's ride had come.

They walked him out to the waiting car, Jake told him he'd be in touch the next day.

Pete thanked him, got in, and the car took off down the road.

Missy and Jake returned inside, locking the door, and sat back down on the sofa. Jinx woke, giving Missy a pissed look, but quickly settled back into catatonic cat sleep.

Jake glanced at the clock; it was 10:30 p.m. "Well, looks like it's going to be a long day tomorrow. I don't know about you, but I need a little stress relief. Back in a minute." He got up and went into his bedroom.

Missy gave him a questioning look. She heard him rummaging around in there, then he reappeared holding what appeared to be a cigarette between his left thumb and forefinger. Missy saw it was hand-rolled. A joint?

Jake asked, "Do you smoke?"

"Only when I'm hot! No, really, I haven't since high school," she answered with a slight smirk.

Jake produced a lighter and fired up the joint. "Since I don't drink anymore, I find it helps calm me down when I'm stressed, plus it enhances my creative process," he squeaked out, holding in the smoke, then exhaling a blue cloud of skunky-smelling smoke up toward the ceiling.

"You want some?" he asked holding the joint out to her.

"I don't know if that's a good idea, one of us should probably stay sober tonight," she replied. Jake started to withdraw the proffered hand.

Missy thought, *what the fuck, this day's been shot to hell and back since I woke up this morning,* reached over and plucked the smoldering joint from him and took too large a toke. She tried holding it but collapsed into a fit of coughing.

Jake laughed, "Take it easy, you can't just 'hoover' this stuff down, it's not like the shit you got in high school. The potency is ten times higher!"

She coughed again with eyes watering, "*Now* you tell me, asshole! I'll take one more toke, then that's it for me," she puffed hesitantly on it, then handed it back to him. He took three more hits, then extinguished it.

He got up and walked over to the window, parted the drapes and gazed out into the once-benign darkness that surrounded them.

"Maybe it's dead," he stated hopefully. *And maybe it's out there just waiting for the right moment to rip out my—not going there!* He closed the drapes and turned. He sat back down on the couch, smiling at Missy.

"Have you ever been married, Missy?"

She was lightly stroking Jinx's head, which the big cat seemed to tolerate. "Nope! Came close once, but he wouldn't commit to the relationship. Doesn't matter, that was a long time ago. Why do you ask?" she answered slowly, staring at him intently as her emerald eyes turned slightly glassy from the herb.

"Just curious, I would've thought someone as beautiful as you would be taken by now." *Shit! What am I saying? Must be the weed!* he thought, feeling his face flush at his words. "What I meant was—I-I don't know what I meant!"

Missy just grinned at him. Flustered, Jake asked, "Uh, would you like some of that ice cream Pete brought now? It's pretty good."

"I could go for another slice of pizza with maybe a small scoop of ice cream on top!" she said all in a rush. *Got the munchies already,* Jake thought. *But chocolate on pizza? Yuck!*

"Ah, right! You sure you don't want some pickles to go on top?" he asked with a straight face.

"You got any?" she responded, then realized he was kidding. "I'm serious! I've always loved pickles and ice cream, they go good together!" she said, defending her taste.

Jake snorted. "Yeah, but on top of pizza? Well, to each their own." He got up and went to the kitchen, put a couple slices in the microwave then got the ice cream out. He found a half-eaten jar of dill pickles in the fridge door. He pulled a slice of pizza out, put it on a plate, placed a scoop of "Crappy Cowz" on it, and inserted the small pickle horizontally in the ice cream, making a sorta pickle n' ice cream sandwich and took it to her on the couch.

She cocked an eyebrow, "Is that a pickle in my ice cream or are you just happy to see me?"

"Well, it's your stomach, enjoy!" he said, as he sat back beside her on the sofa, his plate of pizza in his lap. She took a bite of the pickle, then the ice cream and a large bite of pizza, smiling blissfully as she chewed.

Jake shook his head and they ate in silence. Jinx's eyes popped open as if he'd been zapped with a cattle prod. *Human food!* He sat staring at Jake until he pulled a pepperoni off and offered it. The big cat snagged it and jumped off the couch, taking his "kill" to eat privately.

They finished up their snacks, Jake cleaned the dishes. "I guess when you get up in the morning, you'll need to call a locksmith out to install a deadbolt on your door. You have to feel safe in your home." *Unlike me!* Jake thought wryly.

"Yeah, that—and buy a shotgun!" she said with a yawn. "I'm serious! Well, I'm turning in, does Mr. Jinx sleep with you?" she asked, rising from the couch.

"He sleeps pretty much wherever he wants, so if you don't want a twenty-five-pound furball on top of you tonight, you better close your bedroom door." Jake replied, turning off the lights as they went to their separate rooms, wishing each other a goodnight.

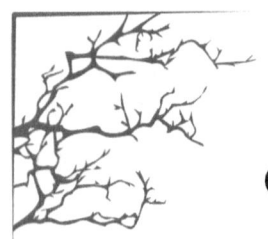

Chapter Seventeen

Tuesday, October 30^{*th*}

Jake awoke with a start as something heavy jumped on his bed. He opened a bleary eye and peeked out from under the pillow surrounding his head and face like a cocoon, to see a furry cat's asshole staring back at him from three inches away. Jinx farted a noxious cloud that smelled like pepperoni and ice cream.

Jake quickly covered his face and shoved the cat off the bed. The bed-pounce was Jinx's customary way of telling him, *get the fuck up, feed me and let me out!* Jake glanced at the clock on the bed-stand: 8:30 a.m. Groaning, he got up and stumbled his way to the bathroom, relieving his bladder mostly into the toilet.

"All right, we'll go, you flatulent ole fleabag!" he growled as he quickly tidied the bathroom floor, then put on a pair of sweats, opening his bedroom door and walking into the kitchen to the smell of coffee brewing.

He'd had a disturbing dream—*something had been chasing him through the forest. It was almost on top of him when he tripped and fell slowly to the ground. Turning to look up at the approaching monstrosity, it wasn't a monster's face he saw—it was Elisa's! Elisa with wickedly sharp teeth and claws reaching for his throat...* And then fur-face had jumped on his bed, thankfully, waking him.

Missy was sitting at the table, a cup of steaming coffee in her hand. She was fully dressed, staring off into space when he walked in.

"Good morning, you sleep okay? Oh, thanks for making coffee!" he said, as he fed Jinx and let him out the back door.

She turned her head, looking at him as if she hadn't heard a word. "Say w-what... I'm sorry, I was just replaying a strange dream I had last night."

Jake sat down at the table with his coffee "You, too? I had a nightmare myself, woke up with the cat's ass in my face! But that wasn't the nightmare.

Something was chasing me through the forest. I tripped over something, falling. I looked up expecting to see that creature's face, but I saw *Elisa's* face instead! She had all the nice accessories, the teeth and claws, etc.—It was horrible! I was glad Jinx woke me when he did," he finished, taking a couple of pain pills and chasing them down with coffee.

Missy's color drained from her face as she recalled her dream, "Mine took place in my childhood backyard. Elisa had kicked the ball into the woods, I ran to get it and when I picked it up, standing a few feet away, was the wolf-*thing*, not the actual wolf! I screamed and threw the ball at it, turned and ran back toward Elisa. Only it wasn't Elisa anymore. It was another *creature* like the one chasing me, but smaller. It had her face, sorta, and *she/it* was pointing Dad's rifle at me saying, 'I warned you not to go into forest, Missy!' Then she shot me—that's when I woke up in a cold sweat."

"Holy shit! Pretty strange coincidence, both of us having dreams with her in them, at the same time! And both starring her as the monster??" Jake shuddered, put his coffee down and went to the fridge, pulling out frozen waffles. "Maybe your friend Birdie could interpret what those dreams mean or represent, what do you think?" he asked, popping the waffles in the toaster.

"Possibly, but we won't know until you see him, Bud! Something very strange and dangerous is happening, and it involves both of us! We need to figure out a way to stop it, before it kills you—or both of us! We've been lucky, but the next time, our luck could run out. We've got to *kill it,* so there won't be a next time!"

Jake agreed, plating the waffles and placing them on the table with a bottle of syrup. They ate in silence, both pondering the imagery of their separate dreams and what they might mean for each of them in the coming days.

Missy's phone chimed, signaling an incoming text. She got her phone, checking the message sent. "It's from Johnny, says he'll be here in about ten minutes to haul off the car. He expects to be paid before towing it away," she informed Jake, as she returned to the table to finish the last couple bites of her cold waffle.

"Yeah, I figured as much," he took out his wallet to check his fast depleting supply of cash. He thought about his upcoming meeting with the psychologist and the more expensive one later with Pete. "I forgot to ask, how much does Johnny charge for the tow?"

"I think he said anything over five miles is $200," she replied, wincing.

Shit! That'll be $400 total, with Missy's bus yesterday. He assumed he still had to pay for the doctor visit this afternoon, plus whatever vehicle he managed to purchase for the kid! "I'm gonna need to hit an ATM before we go to the doctor's office later," he announced, clearing the dishes off the table and putting them in the sink.

Missy ignored him, looking up a locksmith on Google and dialing.

"Lenny's Locks, how can I help ya?" a man answered.

"Yes, I need a deadbolt installed on my front door."

"Ah, how soon ya need it?" he inquired.

"Like yesterday! I really need it done ASAP. I had a break-in and I live alone. Is there any way I can get it done today?" she asked, beseechingly.

"Well, I can get someone out in the next hour, where do you live?'

She gave him directions to her cabin.

"Okay, I'll get a guy out by 9:30—that work for ya?"

She agreed, hanging up, then looked at the time. "I'll have to meet him there in fifteen minutes to let him in. Johnny should be out there by now. Get your ass in gear, Bud, if you're goin' with me!" she informed Jake, grabbing the backpack of her belongings from his guest room.

"Soon as I get him lined out, we'll head into town to get you some cash and me a shotgun!" she explained, watching Jake from the living room, as he limped quickly into his room to dress. He came out in jeans and a flannel shirt. Grabbing his coat, he followed her out the door, locking it behind him.

They got in the truck, she turned around in the drive and headed down the tree-lined road, spotting Johnny's tow-truck up ahead. He already had the car on the lift, ready to tow.

She slowed down and lowered her window. Stopping, she asked Johnny, "We're heading into town in a few, can Jake pay you now for the tow?"

Johnny Six-fingers smiled, showing teeth that looked like they hadn't seen a toothbrush in ages. "Yes, ma'am, that'd be just fine. Sure did a number on that old beater!" he observed, as he waited on Jake to pull out his wallet.

"How much did you say for the tow?" Jake asked him.

"Well, since you're out past the five-mile limit, the price is $200.00 but seeing as Missy here has her car in my shop already, I'll only charge $100.00," he told Jake with his palm out and a smile that would bring dollar-signs to any dentist's eyes.

Jake counted out five twenties and handed it out the window to him.

"Thanks, appreciate your business," he said, stuffing the bills into his grease-covered overalls. Jake saw that he did indeed have six fingers on his right hand. "I should have your bus ready by the weekend, Missy! So long," he climbed into the tow-truck and slowly pulled out onto the highway.

Turning into Missy's drive, they saw an old maroon pickup sitting in front of her house, with "Lenny's Lock and Keys" painted on the side. Missy pulled up beside it, parking. An older man of about sixty with thinning gray hair and a sharp beak of a nose climbed out of the truck to meet them.

"Hello there, name's Kenny. You the one needs a deadbolt put in?" He stuck out a calloused hand.

Missy shook hands and introduced herself and Jake. "Mr., ah, Kenny, I need it installed on the entry door. About how long and how much for the installation?" she asked.

He scratched his stubbled chin. "Takes about an hour usually, and it'll cost $75.00 for the lock, with labor. That sound fair to you?"

"That's fine. I need to run some errands in town, probably take me an hour to get back," she told him, opening her front door for him. "If you want some water, help yourself."

He thanked her and got his toolbox out of the truck, placing it by the front door.

"Oh, if you need power, you have to start the generator out back," she added, climbing back inside Jake's truck. She backed up and headed for the highway.

Jake was frowning, "You trust that guy inside your place? You don't know him from Adam!" he said with a snort.

"I didn't know you from 'Adam' either when I first stayed the night at your place, Bud! You gotta trust someone sometimes to get to know them. Besides, I go with my gut feeling when I first meet someone. I'm rarely wrong," she retorted.

They drove in silence the rest of the way into town. She pulled up to the hardware store on main street and parked. "I won't be long, you comin' in?"

"You're serious about getting a shotgun?" he queried.

"You bet your ass!" she barked, getting out of the truck.

They both went inside and wandered their way to the gun area. All the long guns were lined up like soldiers at attention on a rack behind the counter. A heavy-set man with beefy shoulders wide as a linebacker's came over to wait on them.

"'Morning, somethin' particular you're lookin' for?"

Missy was examining the shotguns on the rack behind him. "Yeah, do you have a Remington 1187 super-mag 'Defender' in 12-gauge?"

The big man's eyebrows rose, along with a smile, "You know your hardware, I take it. You goin' after bear or moose?"

"Something like that!" she replied tersely.

He looked at her, grunted and searched the rack until he found the shotgun she'd requested. He pulled back the action until it locked open, exposing the breech, a safety procedure, then placed the weapon on the glass counter in front of her.

"Here she is, three-and-a-half-inch magnum, holds seven in the mag, one in the pipe, eighteen-and-a-half-inch barrel," the guy said proudly.

Missy picked up the shotgun and felt the heft. "Yeah, about eight pounds, nice! You have some ammo in 00' buck? Oh, and a box of deer slugs," she asked the man.

He went to another shelf and produced two boxes with five shells per box, setting them on the counter. "If you haven't killed it with ten shots, you either need glasses or give up hunting!"

Jake chuckled. Missy didn't. She asked, "How much for the gun and ammo?"

He tried to sell her a case for the gun, but she wasn't interested. He went in the back and came out with a gun that was new in the box. The other, he explained, was a "demo" model.

"Well, the gun is four hundred, and I'll throw in some extra ammo for free. Anything else I can get you? How about some tinted shooter's glasses?"

She declined, "Just the gun and ammo, thanks!" She handed him her credit card and he moved to the register to complete the transaction.

Jake asked, "You really think you'll need that much firepower?"

She hissed back, "Better to have too much than too little, Bud! My nine mm didn't do much damage, and I *know* I hit the fucker!"

"Okay! Okay! Just asking is all," he replied defensively.

The salesman finished up the transaction, putting the boxes of shells in a paper bag, adding an extra box of shells, and thanking her for her purchase.

They left the store and climbed back into Jake's truck, and she placed the shotgun on the back seat. She stopped by an ATM where he withdrew a huge stack of twenties, rolling the bills up and rubber-banding them, as they wouldn't fit in his wallet, then stuffing the roll into his left pocket.

Missy watched all of this with wry amusement. "You plannin' on blowing that wad today?" she asked.

Jake considered the double enténdre, decided best to ignore it. "Ah, better to have too much than too little," he shot back, parroting her.

Missy smiled *touché* and drove out onto the highway and back toward her place. They arrived a few minutes later to find Kenny just finishing up his work. There was a shiny new Schlage deadbolt installed, with two three-inch-long steel screws securing the striker plate to the frame.

Kenny observed proudly, "Someone'd have to break down the door to get in now!"

Probably bullshit! she thought, as he handed her the new set of keys. She locked and unlocked the door several times before nodding her approval, then paid the locksmith, and he loaded his tools back into the truck.

"Thanks again, Miss Morning Star, you have a good day," and he took off for town.

She decided she was going to be prepared for the worst and hope for the best! Jake retrieved the boxed shotgun from his truck, handing it to her, then brought her the sack of shells. She took the shotgun out of the box and wiped off the excess oil on it.

"Let's see how this sucker shoots!" She loaded three rounds into the magazine, chambered a round and engaged the safety.

They walked out back of her cabin where there was a clearing between the trees that she obviously used as a shooting range. Numerous destroyed paper targets were taped to a four-by-eight sheet of plywood that was mounted between two trees about five feet high. A box with several unused rolled-up human silhouette paper targets and a stapler lay nearby.

Missy handed Jake the shotgun, took one of the targets over to the board and stapled it to the board. Satisfied, she returned and took the shotgun from Jake. The target was ten yards away.

Flicking off the safety, she shouldered the gun, aimed for center mass and, using the middle finger of her right hand, pulled the trigger twice in rapid succession. *Boom-Boom!* The sound was deafening in the quiet surroundings, the semi-auto recoiled hard into her shoulder with the magnum rounds, almost knocking her off her feet! The combined sixteen .33 caliber pellets tore through the silhouette target from neck to stomach, traveling at 1600 fps—any one of them would have been lethal. If she'd been ten feet away instead of thirty, it would have cut someone nearly in two.

"*Shit*! That hurt!" she hissed, rubbing her shoulder, her ears ringing. *I should have remembered to get a recoil pad. Should've gotten earplugs, too!*

She put the safety on and turned to hand the gun to Jake who was just taking his finger out of his left ear. He'd forgotten about his right hand being incapacitated and had tried unsuccessfully to stick that index finger in his right ear, painfully reminding him of his injury. He was shaking his head, trying to get rid of the high-pitched ringing.

"Sorry, Jake! I should have gotten us something to use as earplugs—my bad!"

"Maybe you should have gotten that thing in a twenty gauge instead of twelve!" he muttered, as they walked up to the target to inspect the damage pattern on it.

"Nope! Believe me when it comes to that *thing* out there, bigger is better!" she proclaimed. *Even if it kicks like a mule!* she thought, absently rubbing her shoulder again.

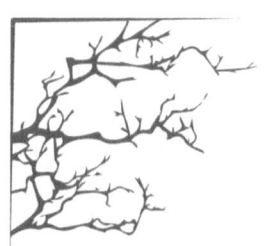

Chapter Eighteen

"You wanna get something to eat before we go see Birdie? I'm craving a burger at the 'R and R' drive-in!" Missy announced as she and Jake walked back to the truck.

"Sounds good to me, gotta have some of their famous sweet potato tots with it, though," he replied, climbing in the truck.

She locked the new deadbolt on her cabin door, placed the shotgun in the empty gun rack across the back window of the truck, the small boxes of shells in the console, then got in.

SHE DROVE THEM BACK into town, pulled up to the "R and R" and parked. Black cats and witches on brooms decorated the front door, and two carved pumpkins stood guard on either side like evil grinning sentries.

They sat down, and both ordered the "Rex with cheese" and large sweet potato tots.

"It's been awhile since I've been in here," Jake noted. "I don't eat out very often, so this is a treat."

"Does that mean you're paying for lunch?" Missy grinned.

Jake smiled, "I guess so, as long as I can have dessert."

Their order arrived, and they hungrily chowed down. They both had ice cream for dessert to top it off. Jake paid for the lunch and left a decent tip. He checked the time: 12:30 p.m.

"Looks like we'll be a little early for the appointment," he informed her, as they got into the truck.

Missy looked at him, "Don't worry, I hear Birdie isn't big on clock watching, except when he's billing for his services! He's not cheap, but I hear he's a good psychologist."

"Ah, you didn't tell me how much an hour he charges before you made the appointment, Missy, so how much damage to my wallet can I expect for this session?" he groused, with a frown.

"Probably $150 an hour, but don't hold me to that. If you can't afford it, tell me now and I'll call and cancel the appointment. Birdie will understand. But you really should've told me if you couldn't afford the therapy," she said frankly, backing out of the parking spot.

"I'm not trying to be chintzy, it's just all of the sudden expenses, between the repair to your vehicle and the potential cost of replacing Pete's car and now this doctor visit, are gonna put a dent in my savings! I live off my royalty checks from month to month, and they aren't as much as you'd think!" Jake explained defensively.

Missy gave him a tight smile and replied, "Sorry about all your bad luck, Bud! But that's one of the reasons you're going to see Birdie, to try to discern if it's indeed 'bad luck' or maybe something entirely unrelated."

She drove down Main Street, coming to an older brick building wedged between a laundromat and a pawn shop, where she pulled in and parked.

THE WOODEN FRAME DOOR had a glass window with plain gold lettering on it that simply read: "Mika L.B. Boucher, Psychologist." They opened the front door to Birdie's office, a little bell connected to top of the door chimed as they walked inside announced them.

The female receptionist looked up and smiled, "Welcome to Dr. Boucher's office. Do you have an appointment?"

Jake looked nervously at Missy, then replied, "Yes, I'm Jake Anderson, I have a one o'clock appointment."

The woman checked her computer. "Have a seat, Mr. Anderson, and please fill out these forms. Do you have insurance, or will it be self-pay?" She handed him a clipboard with what looked like a lot of pages to fill out.

"It'll be self-pay," he said tersely, and sat down in a comfortable chair beside Missy. It took him close to twenty minutes to fill out the forms with his left hand, most of it illegible, even though there were only two pages.

Under "Reason for Visit": he was tempted to write, *"Monster trying to kill me!"* but thought better of it and instead inserted, "Want to recover memories."

He handed the clipboard back to the receptionist, who said, "The Doctor will be with you shortly," then focused on her PC.

The inner door opened, and Dr. Mika "Birdie" Boucher appeared. He was tall, looked to be in his mid-thirties, with long raven hair streaked with silver, woven into a ponytail that fell midway between his shoulders. His face was angular with sharp edges, defining high cheekbones that stood out prominently, and anchored by a long hawk-like nose. He was dressed in an expensive suit and tie. Missy and Jake noticed his left arm was in a sling. His dark-brown eyes took in them both, crinkling as he smiled in recognition.

"Well, hello, Missy, it's been a long time! How's your mother doing? I heard about the stroke. I'm sorry to say I haven't seen her since she entered the nursing facility, I've been pretty busy," he said, shaking hands awkwardly with both her and Jake.

Noticing their injuries, he added humorously, "Looks like all three of us tried to arm wrestle a grizzly—and lost!" as he led them back to his office and shut the door. "May I ask what happened to you both?" He pointed to both of their hands.

Jake sat in a comfortable recliner and told him about the wolverine attack, then Missy, seated next to him, said she'd injured the finger when her bus hit the ditch, omitting any mention of the *creature*, of course!

"What can I do for you, Jake. I see in the chart that you're here to try to recover some memories, is that correct?"

Jake fidgeted in the chair, then sighed, "Yeah, Dr. Boucher, that's about it."

"Missy, I'll have to ask you to please wait out front. I'll need to speak with Jake privately during the session, if you don't mind," he informed her, sitting down in a high-backed chair behind a beautiful antique mahogany desk.

Jake threw a quick look at Missy, then spoke, "Doctor, if it's all the same to you, I'd like her to stay, she—she's got a vested interest in my reason for being here."

Birdie raised an eyebrow. "It's your session, Mr. Anderson, whatever you'd prefer. Well, then, shall we begin? I want you to recline in your chair, are you comfortable? Good, we'll start now. I want you to relax, Jake, tell me the how far back in the past would you like to regress?"

Jake thought about it. "I guess ten—no, eleven years back, and to be honest with you, I was drinking pretty heavily back then! I don't remember a lot, I-I guess I had what you call 'blackouts.' The thing is, Doctor—I was married to Missy's sister Elisa. I didn't even know Elisa *had* a sister until Missy and I, uh... met recently.

"Anyway, some-one, *he wanted badly to say some-*thing, has been trying to cause me bodily harm the last couple days. Missy saved my ass two times from this... person, after I was attacked by the wolverine. And then we recently found out Elisa is presumed dead!"

Missy spoke up, trying to clarify. "Birdie, my sister never kept in touch over the years since she left here. Elisa's only friend we finally located told me that Elisa had said... that Jake had r-raped her at least once during one or more of those blackouts before they divorced! From what the friend said, Elisa was acting very strange before she disappeared. Now it's presumed that she died in a boating accident, although her body was never found! Elisa supposedly accused him of sexual assault during a 'blackout,' according to her friend.

"I need to know if Jake can recall if he really raped her, or if it was just Elisa making up shit to get back at him for some perceived wrong! If it's the former, then he and I have a big problem. If it's the latter... I owe him an apology," she said, staring directly at Jake.

Missy was fighting an inner battle—should she tell Birdie about the creature? The boy Pete, also? Birdie's a tribal Shaman, surely, he'd believe them! She made her choice. "Jake, we need to tell him the truth!"

Jake looked at her nervously, "He won't believe us, Missy!"

She shook her head. "He's the only one who *might*, and we have to tell *someone!*" Birdie was looking very puzzled.

"Birdie, have you ever heard the word *Yeenaldlooshi*?" she quietly asked.

Birdie sat with his elbows on the desk, hands steepled against his lips. He smiled. *Yeenaldlooshi*! It's been awhile since I've heard that word." He leaned forward over his desk "'He who goes on all fours.' That's the old Navajo translation—a supernatural apparition used to scare little children. Tell me, where did you hear the word?" he asked, his face now serious.

"My mother told my sister and me about it. Listen, Birdie, I swear this *creature* or *thing* is real!" She told him briefly of the time long ago, of the wolf-like *thing* Elisa and she had seen leering and capering just outside their bedroom window.

She related her rescue of Jake from the water following the wolverine's attack, then the assaults on her bus and at Jake's house. And finally, about Pete's narrow escape from the creature. She told him her mother's words of warning at the nursing center and finding the mystery cell phone in her mother's bathroom.

Then she described the texts trying to warn her away. She pulled out her phone and showed him the texts, then took the phone found in her mother's room from her purse, handing it to Birdie.

"It's not my mother's, but no one claimed ownership. It's also password protected. I was wondering if you could somehow hack the password, so we can locate the owner?"

Birdie frowned, taking the phone and examining it minutely, as if it were some alien artifact, rather than the expensive personal government tracking device it was.

"Interesting! I might be able to crack the password, but it may take a while. Can you leave it with me for a day or so? Right now, I need to address Jake's reason for being here today. I'll talk to you about this matter further after he's off the clock," he offered with a tight smile. Missy agreed.

Birdie turned to Jake and began quietly, "Relax, close your eyes, take deep breaths and slowly count backward from 100 while imagining you're gradually walking down a spiral staircase, with every step you descend, getting more relaxed. Tell me when you've reached the bottom step," he instructed.

Jake felt himself slowly relaxing as he continued the countdown in his mind. He found himself on the bottom step of his imaginary stairway. "I'm there," he said softly.

Missy was fascinated—she'd never seen anyone put into a trance state before. She was suddenly anxious, not sure if she wanted to hear, or know, the unbiased truth as it poured out from Jake's hidden thoughts and memories of the past as if he'd been given a dose of truth serum.

Birdie told Jake in a soothing voice: "Jake, I want you to travel backward in time, can you do that for me?"

Jake answered, "yes," his eyes closed, his breathing slow and regular.

"Good. I want you to go back to the first time you had a prominent argument or fight with your wife Elisa. What were the circumstances surrounding the event and how did you react to it?"

Jake spoke without hesitation, "It's a month since I left the service. We're arguing over money. I've been looking for work but haven't found any. She starts screaming at me to find a job or we will lose the apartment."

"How do you react to that?" Birdie asked.

"I'm leaving the apartment—I'm angry! I'm going to the liquor store. I get a fifth of whiskey, I'm driving back to the apartment. I park and drink most of the bottle. I'm furious and frustrated with the job hunt and her constant criticism!"

"What are you doing next after drinking the whiskey?" Birdie coaxed.

"I'm pretty drunk, I stumble out of the car, dropping the bottle, breaking it. Now I'm weaving my way back to the apartment, I'm really pissed!" Jake's eyes were still closed but his breathing had increased.

Missy's apprehension grew as he continued.

"I kick open the door, it's not locked. Elisa's on the bed, crying. She's looking at me, screaming at me, calling me a lazy fucking asshole! I yell that she's a harping fucking bitch!" Jake said, obviously agitated.

Missy cringed inwardly, afraid of what was coming.

"How do you respond to her verbal abuse?" Birdie asked quietly.

Jake's respiration increased as he answered, "I'm screaming back at her, telling her it's not my fault! The economy's tanking and it's *my* fault I can't find work?? I turn and punch a hole in the wall. Then I do it again! Then I slide to floor, my hands are bleeding, and I'm crying because I scared her and I'm feeling sorry for myself. I'm sick, I'm puking on the floor! The taste is horrible... the room is spinning, I think I'm gonna pass out!"

Birdie instructed him, "Jake you are no longer in the apartment, you're moving forward in time, relaxing as you move forward. You will become calm and peaceful, and you will remember everything that's important to you. Now you'll awaken refreshed when I count to three, ready? One, two, three!"

Jake opened his eyes, tears streaming down his cheek. He blinked a few times and sat up in the recliner. Birdie gave him a tissue from a box on his table.

"I'm really embarrassed, those were *not* pleasant memories—it was like vomiting up the past! Speaking of, my mouth has a terrible taste in it! Do you have any water, Doc?" Missy sat still, not saying a word.

Birdie smiled, went over to a small minifridge, brought out a bottle of cold water and handed it to him. "The taste is mostly 'psychosomatic,' it will fade in a minute or two. Drink some and we will proceed from there."

Jake drained half the bottle in a couple gulps. "So, did I pass the 'truth test,' Doc?" he asked contritely.

Birdie said briskly, "There is no *truth test,* no right or wrong, it's merely a look into your past as *you* remember it. A sort of '*video*' of events of that occurred at that place in time."

Missy interrupted, "But that's only one event, there's no way he can remember every argument or fight they ever had. How is it proof he... did or didn't abuse her in the time they were together?" *She didn't want to use the* "r" *word.*

Birdie cleared his throat, "There is definitely emotional and verbal abuse occurring that is apparent in the narrative provided by Jake, with both parties mutually involved. Jake's anger manifests itself and is acted out physically, by punching the wall instead of your sister. Does that mean that he was not capable of sexual abuse? No. But alcohol can be the mitigating factor. In some males, alcohol will stimulate sexual arousal, at the same time, it can reduce or completely eradicate the ability to produce and or maintain an erection. Commonly referred to as '*brewer's droop,*' this makes it all but impossible for penetration to occur.

"Rape is about control and power and sexual gratification. It's an amalgam of stored rage, lack of respect for others, a selfish lack of empathy in its purest form. A loss of self-control. All the reasons for it have been debated endlessly since mankind came down from the trees. I would say, given that he lashed out at the wall instead of Elisa, there is high degree of certainty that he had enough control over his emotions to realize that striking *her* was wrong, deflecting his anger to an inanimate object such as a wall.

I can do another regression to explore the sexual aspect of the interactions in his past, but not today. I'm sorry, but time's up," he finished, glancing at the expensive watch on his wrist.

Missy wasn't satisfied, but it would have to do, for now!

Birdie's face turned serious. "You both really think this... 'creature,' for lack of a better word, is real?"

Jake exchanged a glance with Missy, "Look, Doc, whatever this thing is, it's for real! Real claws, real teeth and real dangerous! My freaking life is in danger, so is Missy's by association! Is there anything in that Indian legend that tells you how to kill this thing or appease it—preferably before it kills me or Missy?" Jake asked heatedly.

Birdie nodded, "I know some of the legend, but that all flies out the window if this is creature is truly 'supernatural,' as you say. There's always a grain of truth to myth and folklore, I suppose. Buried in the tales are a truth that is usually based on factual experience of something that couldn't be explained away at the time it manifested itself. Very interesting! I'll do some research and get back to you soon," he finished.

"That's it? We're no closer to finding out the truth of my so-called 'blackouts' than when I came in! In the meantime, that damned *thing* is still out there trying to kill me! How do I deal with that? What a waste of time and money. I'm fucking outta here!" Jake exclaimed heatedly, as he angrily stood and stalked to the door, slamming it behind him.

Birdie looked at Missy. "He'll need to have another regression session before I can help him any further."

Missy apologized, "I'm sorry, Birdie, we've both been under a lot of stress the past few days. Jake's just a little high-strung, as you've noticed. He'll give you a call and set up another appointment once we can sort this out. If you *can* hack into that phone and find out the owner's name, please call me as soon as possible," she said, getting up and shaking his hand.

As she closed his office door, Birdie dialed a number and, when it was answered, snapped, "We've got a problem!"

MISSY EXITED BIRDIE'S office in time to see Jake getting his receipt from the receptionist. He looked a bit embarrassed as he stuffed the paper into his left pocket.

"Sorry about walking out like that, but he really didn't give me or you much insight into whether or not anything pertinent happened during those blackouts. I'm just frustrated, I thought maybe he could get to the core of it all today!" he told her, as they left Birdie's office and climbed into the truck.

"I understand, Jake, but you can't expect to get 'instant results' from just one visit! I told Birdie you'll call and make another appointment. You can't make an omelet without breaking some eggs, Bud!"

Jake sulked on his side of the truck. "I guess I need to call that kid and tell him we'll pick him up to go to Trader Jim's. What time is it?" he glanced at the display on the dash: 2:15 p.m.

Missy looked up Pete's number, handing the phone to Jake. He placed it on his knee and slowly tapped out a text telling him they were ready to go to the car dealer. Pete texted back, informing Jake he was ready and waiting for them.

Missy exclaimed, "Shit! I forgot to ask Birdie about those creepy dreams we had. Guess it'll have to wait 'til the next appointment." *If there is a next appointment!* she thought grimly, as they headed toward Pete's.

THEY ARRIVED IN FRONT of his house a few minutes later. It was an older A-frame building with its green paint shedding flakes off the side, badly in need of a new coat. Pete was waiting, sitting on a stepped porch out front. He waved as they pulled up and walked out the truck.

Jake rolled down his window, "Climb in, kid—just push that shit in the back seat over and buckle up!"

Pete opened the door on the crew-cab and saw a small mountain of trash piled on the back seat and looking ready to "avalanche" at any second, with the overflow on the carpeted floor. "You sure must eat a lot of junk food, Mr. Anderson! How do you stay in shape?" he observed wryly.

"By jerking off a lot! You got any more wise-ass questions? Or can we go try to find you a freaking car that isn't actually held together with duct tape and bailing wire!" Jake replied sarcastically. "Freaking smart-ass kid!" he grumbled.

Pete shoved the mountain of burger wrappers, grease-stained cardboard and the like off the seat into a pile already growing behind the driver's seat and climbed in.

THEY DROVE OUT TO TRADER Jim's car lot, parked and climbed out, looking over the small sea of different makes, models and colors. There were maybe sixty cars on the lot in varying states of dilapidation and neglect. Some looked better than others, at least on the outside.

They walked over to the small dealer shack in the middle of the graveled lot. A small cardboard sign on the door said, "Back in five, I'm on the pot!" The shack didn't look big enough to contain a restroom. Jake tried the door—locked! So, he walked around the back and saw a portable outhouse with the sliding lock in "Occupied" position.

Jake walked back to the front of the building. Missy was sitting on one of the three wooden steps that served as stairs to the entrance.

"He's in a port-o-shitter out back," Jake told them, pointing with his thumb to the rear of the shack. "Pete, you might as well take a look around—please try to keep your price range to under $2,000."

Pete didn't look happy, but nodded and started wandering the lot, looking at various prices, hoping not to get stuck with another "pizza-shit" car. Missy watched Pete as he looked at prices soaped onto the windshields and peered through windows at the interior condition of the vehicles.

"Good luck finding anything that doesn't run on 'squirrel power' for that amount of coin!" a female voice from behind Jake said sarcastically. He turned and saw a pretty woman of about twenty standing five feet away.

She smiled, extending her left hand, noting the bandage on his right. "Hi, I'm Jenny! Sorry to keep you waiting, is there anything you're particularly interested in? Besides keeping in your price range, I mean."

Jake introduced Missy and himself. He told Jenny that he didn't have a personal interest in whatever vehicle the kid chose, just that it ran better than the last one.

"Well, I'm not exactly sure what we have out there in your price range, I don't really work here, I'm just baby-sitting the lot for my father today while he runs some errands," she explained gesturing for them to follow her down a row of cars, vans, and pickups.

Pete was heading back toward them, looking excited. "Hey, Mr. Anderson, I found one over here for $2,200.00 with T+T+L! It's a Honda CR-V 2000 model, I can't read the odometer to see the mileage, the doors are locked!" he exclaimed hopefully, brushing hair from his eyes with one hand.

Jenny said she'd get the keys and meet them at the car. They walked to the last row of vehicles and Pete pointed out the one he'd chosen. It was a faded maroon color with black trim. The front panel on the driver's side had a few dents, the tires were a bit worn, but other than that, the body integrity seemed intact. Jake and Missy walked around the car, looking for defects, but finding nothing else, they waited as Jenny made her way to them.

"Here you are, took me a minute to find them," she said, opening the doors with a *chirp* from the key fob. Pete got in the driver's seat, starting the engine, and looked at the odometer: 156,501 miles.

He popped the hood latch and got out to open it. With the hood up, they all looked at the engine compartment. There was some road tar and dirt on the engine, but no apparent oil leaks. They looked underneath the chassis for any dripping fluids or damage. Seeing none, Jake had Pete turn off the engine. Together, they inspected the belts and checked the oil, which was clear. The air filter was new. Pete closed the hood and they examined the vehicle's interior. The front seats had some wear, the back seats were fine. They opened the back hatch and inspected the spare tire. It was decent enough.

Jake started to try to barter down the price. He and Jenny negotiated until she paused and blew out a sigh of relief as her father drove into the lot, parking in front of the shack.

"I'll go get my Dad, he's a lot better at this than I am. I'll tell him your offer. Nice to meet ya," she told them, obviously relieved at not having to haggle over the price.

Jake conferred with Missy and Pete while Jenny explained Jake's offer to her father. Her dad nodded, walked over and introduced himself as Trader Jim, the owner.

"Jenny told me about your offer of $1900.00. I think that's doable, let's go to my office and fill out the paperwork. Are you financing? Paying by cash or credit card?"

Jake told him "credit card," as they entered the small building, with Trader Jim leading the way. Pete happily filled out forms—while Jake withdrew his wallet with a sigh, pulled out his credit card and reluctantly paid for the car.

"That should about do it, thanks for your business. Remember there's only a ninety-day warranty on the engine. If you need more coverage, you'll have to get it elsewhere. Other than that, you're good to go," Trader Jim smiled and, giving Pete the keys, shook hands with all three as they got up to leave.

"Thanks, Mr. Anderson, I really appreciate what you did for me. Those new wheels are so dope!" Pete exclaimed, pumping Jake's left hand and grinning ear to ear.

"I, er, you're welcome, I think? I hope it gets you where you need to go. But you might want to consider finding a different line of work. That delivery job'll be hell on the maintenance of the car, ultimately taking a huge chunk out of your wallet in repairs. Main thing is to change the oil at least twice a year! Good luck, Pete, and be careful," Jake suggested. Missy gave Pete a quick hug, then they walked back to his truck.

They watched as Pete got in his new-used Honda and drove off, grinning and waving to them out the window.

Missy pulled out behind him. "Well, that was pretty decent of you, Jake—he looked just like a kid at Christmas! I hope he has better luck with it than the last one."

Jake grunted in agreement. "He seems like a good kid, sometimes you just need a little help when life bites you in the ass! Speaking of bites, what would you like for dinner? My treat! Spending all this money makes a guy hungry."

"AND POOR!" SHE TEASED, as she drove them back into the center of town. She stopped at the local supermarket. "I'll make us something tasty to eat, least I can do if you're buying."

"Just nothing with broccoli, okay?" he warned her, as she climbed out of the truck. "It gives me really bad farts!"

She rolled her eyes but didn't reply as she entered the market. In the meantime, Jake called Birdie's office and made an appointment for the next Thursday. A pickup pulled into the open slot on Jake's right. He looked over and saw "Park Ranger" on the side. *Fuck! Just what I need!* he thought with a grimace, as Ben Dover climbed out of truck, scowling at him. Ben just stood there, hands on hips, staring in at him through the window.

Jake could read Ben's lips as he mouthed the word "motherfucker," then turned and headed into the store, glancing back, still pouring out colorful metaphors directed at Jake.

Jake grumbled to himself, "Hey, Ben Dover, kiss my ass!" though he wouldn't dare say it to Ben's face. The big guy could crush him like a bug, and he knew it.

Missy came back out twenty minutes later carrying a couple bags of groceries. She opened the back door and a small landslide of fast-food refuse toppled out onto the pavement.

"You really have to clean up back here! It's a pig sty!" She gathered up the small mound of trash and tossed it back inside, then placed her bags on the seat, slamming the door shut.

"Did you see Ben in there?" Jake asked casually, as she left the parking lot.

"Matter of fact, I did. He passed right by and didn't even notice me. He was grousing about something, looked very pissed! This have anything to do with that land deal with your dad he thinks he got screwed on?" she asked, as she pulled onto the highway.

Jake didn't answer right away. "What did you get to make for dinner?" he asked, changing the subject.

"I got chicken breasts, spaghetti, salad makings, garlic French loaf. I make a wicked chicken parmesan! I can almost taste it now," she replied, licking her lips. Jake smiled guiltily as he watched her moisten her lips, thinking, *I know what I'd like to have for dessert!*

THE DARK-COLORED SUV pulled up in front of Mika "Birdie" Boucher's office and parked. The lone occupant watched as the receptionist came out carrying her bulky purse and locked the door—never glancing at the car sitting near the front door as she walked to her vehicle parked fifty feet away. When the receptionist had driven half a block away, the driver of the SUV climbed out, looking both ways before taking out a key and slipping it into the lock, opening the door just enough to slide in, then quickly shut and relocked it.

Birdie's office door opened, he stepped out into the waiting area. "You should have waited until dark! Someone could have seen you come in. This whole thing is becoming too dangerous, especially for *me!*" he chided, motioning the visitor into his office. He waited as the person sat down before closing and locking the door. He then walked to his chair and sat down. "As I told you on the phone, we've got a prob-"

"*We* don't have a problem! *You* do! I'm paying you a hell of a lot of money to get this done!" his guest hissed angrily.

"If *you* hadn't dropped this fucking phone in her room, there wouldn't *be* any problem!" Birdie snapped back, holding up the phone Missy had given him earlier.

"They found it in her bathroom—in a fucking trash can!? How imbecilic could you be? You were supposed to destroy it after using it—not lose it in the nearest trash receptacle!" he growled, throwing the phone across the room where it bounced off the wall, landing haphazardly at the other's feet.

"It was an accident ... it must have fallen out of my—never mind! I knew I'd misplaced it somewhere. It doesn't matter now, you've got it in your possession, just destroy it!"

Birdie gave a sour smile. "Yes, well, there's the rub. Missy expects me to be able to hack it for information, specifically to find out who sent her the texts. But even with this being a burner phone, it *can* be traced."

"I don't see the problem, even if they can trace it, that would only show the general location by GPS, what's the BFD?!" was the belligerent reply.

Birdie shook his head impatiently, "You don't understand—it leaves a trail leading straight to my door by just having it here. But I can't just dispose of it, she expects it back! I guess I can tell her I couldn't get into it or that I destroyed the information on it by hacking it, and then give it back to her. Either way *you* won't be implicated, unless ..."

"Unless *what*?" Apprehensively.

"Unless you foolishly gave someone else the number, and they in turn, give it to the cops, who can then get a warrant to get the number and cell phone records of whoever you've called or texted! Then you've put *my* ass on the line!" he accused.

"There is no one else that I've texted except Missy, you and ..." there was a hesitant pause.

Birdie raised an eyebrow and glowering said, "Yes??"

"Just an old friend down south, and only once, but she won't text or call!"

Birdie's interest perked up "And why is that?"

There was a long silence. *"She thinks I'm dead!"* was the whispered answer.

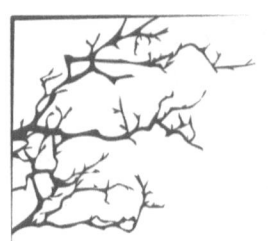

Chapter Nineteen

The butcher knife came down with a resounding *whack,* cleanly decapitating the unfortunate carrot from its top!

Jake just shook his head "You need to dice em', not chop, unless you want to end up like me!" he observed, waving his right hand in Missy's face.

She pushed his arm gently away, gave him an antagonistic look and replied, "Never criticize a woman with a big-ass knife in her hand, Bud!"

Jake took a cautious step backward, "Point taken," he said, glancing at the twelve-inch knife, as she continued to cut up the veggies for the salad she was preparing.

"Is there *anything* I can help you with?" Jake asked feeling very "kitchen-challenged" at present.

"Not a thing that I can think of ... well, you can turn on the oven and set it to 350 degrees for me. Oh, and fill that pan three-fourths full of water to heat," she told him, as she finished chopping red onion, sweet pepper, and mushrooms, placing them on top of romaine lettuce. She sprinkled some shredded feta cheese and bacon bits, topped it off with garlic croutons and placed the glass bowl in the fridge.

"By the way, I made another appointment with Birdie for this coming Thursday," Jake informed her.

"Missy, do you really think he'll be able to get any info off that phone? It's more than likely a burner phone," he said, filling the pan as she had instructed and putting it on the stove to heat.

"You noticed he skirted the issue of whether or not he believed what we were telling him about the creature. I told you he'd never believe us! And he never did tell us what happened to *his* shoulder, did he?" Jake stated suspiciously.

Missy declined to comment as she prepared the chicken breasts for the oven. Finally, she answered, "Well, I'm sure there's a perfectly plausible explanation for that—surely you don't think Birdie had anything to do with those attacks?" But the very thought had made her uneasy for some reason.

Birdie had no reason to harm Jake—they never even met until today! Ben, on the other hand, had a long-standing grudge with Jake over money allegedly still owed him concerning Jake's land. If anyone had a motive to harm Jake, it would be Ben. Then who had sent the texts warning her away from Jake? Did the mystery phone she'd given Birdie to hack hold the answer? Good questions!

These thoughts scrambled around in Missy's head like mice in a maze as she placed the chicken parmesan in the oven and set the egg timer for forty minutes. The mountain tops to the west were just obscuring the last bit of sun—casting lengthening shadows over the surrounding forest, pulling darkness over the land as the night fell quickly in the deep forest.

"I don't mean to be nosy, Jake, but this business with Ben, is he the only one you can think of who might be holding a grudge against you?" she asked, as he placed plates and silverware on the table. She could tell Jake clearly didn't want to discuss the matter.

"You mean other than my publisher?" His joke fell flat. "Ben's had a bee up his ass about the land deal ever since my old man died. I told Ben when he can prove my dad didn't pay his old man all the money owed, then I'll pay up, but not a damn dime until then!" he replied brusquely, wedging a can of diet soda between his right forearm and chest and popping the top.

"He can be an asshole, he got picked on a lot in school because of... well, his name, for one thing. Plus, he was a skinny kid. He bulked up, after that nobody jacked with him! But do I think he would have something to do with this madness these past few days? No... I don't." He sat down at the table to wait for the chicken to bake while Missy dumped pasta in the water boiling on the stove.

"I don't know, Jake. Ben's about the same size as that *thing* that attacked you. But it couldn't have been him, Ben was working night shift, plus I'd just got off the phone with him when you called about that *thing* trying to smoke you out! He couldn't be in two places at the same time," she said, sitting down facing him at the table.

He poured some soda over ice and handed it to her. She smiled, took a sip and put it down.

"You know, I haven't really seen Birdie around much, maybe a couple of times in town the past few years, did you know, he dated Elisa some back in school? Til mama found out, and she put a cork in *that* bottle! But I suppose he's changed over the years, just like everyone. The only constant in life is change, I guess." she said wistfully.

Missy's phone chimed with an incoming call. She looked at the phone, frowning, as she saw who was calling. She answered it, staring at Jake, "Hello, Ben, what's up?" Jake could hear a one-sided conversation coming from the phone, Missy didn't look happy!

"Uh-huh. Yeah, I understand ... no, no, I can do that. I'm okay. Alright, I'll be there ... Yes, sir, goodbye!" was all she said. She ended the call.

"Crap! Apparently, Bob can't cover my shift tomorrow, got the flu or some shit. I gotta go in tomorrow morning," she told him. "Could I borrow your truck? You can't really drive it right now, anyway," she asked logically.

Jake smiled, his ice blue eyes locked on to hers, "Only if you keep me company tonight."

She raised an eyebrow, "Depends on your definition of 'company,' Bud!" she parried, as they gazed at one another over the sparsely set table. The timer went off by the stove, startling them and breaking the moment.

She got up, muttering something that sounded like, "*freaking horn-dog!*" Then she grabbed an oven mitt and pulled the chicken out of the oven.

Jake grinned, "I'm a big fan of 'corn dogs!'"

"That's *not* what I said, ass-wipe, and you know it!" she replied, with a crooked smile. She carried the dish to the table, then went to the fridge and got the salad bowl, placing it next to the chicken dish, and put the garlic bread in the oven.

SHE STOOD OUTSIDE THE window, staring in at the man and woman sitting at the small dining room table. Through the thin gauzy curtain covering the window, she watched them as they talked and ate their meal together. A mixture of jealousy, anger, and hate flowed through her veins like a poisonous

venom. The pistol in her right hand shook as adrenaline poured into her bloodstream.

"I'm gonna finish you myself, 'Tweedledumb,' no more second chances, you bum!" she quietly cackled, raising the pistol, aiming at the center of the oblivious man's back.

He sat only three feet away from the window. She was squeezing the trigger when something large sprang onto her back, knocking her to the ground, and she lost her grip on the gun as it tumbled into the dark. She stifled a scream, as pain shot through her back from multiple sharp claws. Jinx hissed and growled, then sank his teeth into her left ear and bit down.

Desperately, she rolled onto her back, dislodging the big cat's teeth from her ear. Jinx promptly clawed her left breast, then leaped off as if to view his handiwork. She finally let out a yelp of pain, scrambled up, and ran off into the cover of the darkness to escape from the deranged beast!

HEARING THE STRANGE noises from out back, Jake and Missy both jumped up from the table. Missy grabbed her gun, Jake his flashlight, and they slowly opened the back door. Missy had her gun arm extended, while Jake held the flashlight, the beam penetrating out into the inky darkness of the night. He hadn't turned on the so-called "security light" earlier but did so now. *Nothing. He'd forgotten the light bulb was history. Shit!*

They pulled the door three-quarters open and a brown streak of fur raced past them, frightening Missy, who almost pulled the trigger before realizing it was Jinx. The cat went straight to his water bowl, which was empty.

"Damn it, Jinx! What the fuck is the matter with you? You scared the crap out of us!" Jake snapped at the big cat—who'd probably just saved his life. Jake got the water pitcher and as he bent over to pour it into the water bowl, noticed some red substance Jinx was licking off his whiskers.

"What have you been into?" He reached down and touched a splotch on the cat's nose. His finger came away smeared with red. "It's blood! He's either injured or killed something or got hurt trying!" He examined Jinx's body but didn't find any more blood or an injury.

Missy had suggested they look outside to see if he'd dragged any "kill" into the yard when they heard a car engine start somewhere down the drive leading to the highway. They rushed outside in time to see distant taillights glowing red and racing toward the highway. As it neared the "T" intersection of drive and highway, headlights flashed on, as the car turned onto the highway heading to town.

"Looks like you had an unwelcome visitor, Bud! One of several lately, I might add!" Missy declared.

They scoured the ground with the flashlight beam, 'til it caught a spot of reddish-black on the ground outside the window. They walked closer and saw a couple large drops of fresh blood on the ground. Jake shined the light in a wider arc, and it reflected off something metallic and shiny. A Colt Python revolver with a four-inch barrel was half-hidden in some weeds. Jake was reaching down to pick it up when Missy stopped him.

"Don't touch it, Jake! The cops should be able to get prints off it if they weren't wearing gloves. I think maybe Jinx might have saved your ass tonight. Go get a small piece of paper towel or tissue."

Jake gave her a questioning look but went to retrieve whatever he could find. He came back with a Kleenex. Missy tore off a piece and touched it to the quickly drying blood spot. The tissue soaked it up. They went back inside in search of sandwich bags.

He opened a drawer in the kitchen and took one out of a box, handing it to Missy. She placed the small blood-soaked tissue inside and sealed the bag, placing it in the refrigerator. Taking another plastic bag, she walked back out to where the gun lay. She asked Jake for his knife. He dug it out of his pocket, handing it to her. She opened the knife and the bag, then inserted the blade through the trigger-guard, carefully lifted the weapon and slid it into the bag, zipping it shut.

"Do we *really* have to call the cops? We don't know for sure whoever was here was actually trying to kill me—they might have just panicked when Jinx attacked and dropped the gun!" Jake desperately did not want the cops involved and was grasping at straws.

"Get real, Jake! Who the hell would be out here, at *night*, doesn't knock on the door, is carrying a freaking gun, and parks 150 yards away in the dark?! I'd say they were probably standing right outside the window, looking in.

They'd have had a clear shot at you!" Missy retorted angrily. She walked back inside. Jake looked miserable as she put the plastic bag with the gun in the fridge.

They heard a sound behind them and turned to see Jinx up on the table. He was finishing off Jake's mostly eaten chicken parmesan with vigor. He stopped eating and gave Jake a look that said, *I saved your sorry ass, I deserve this!* Grabbing the last piece, he jumped off the table with his stolen bounty and disappeared into Jake's bedroom to finish masticating in private.

"Guess I better call the cops, but we don't say *anything* about the *you-know-what*, right?' Jake groused, dialing 911. He told the operator about the prowler and the gun found outside. She said an officer would be dispatched shortly. He gave her directions to his place and said he'd be waiting.

"Whoever the hell it was has *got* to be connected to all this! First, I've got some *creature,* straight out of a fucking horror flick trying to kill me, and now some nut with a gun! I don't know whose cornflakes I pissed on, but I'm beginning to think it was God's! My freaking cat probably saved my ass from getting a bullet to the back. My ex-wife is presumed dead, and her sister saved my life twice already, or was it three times? I can't keep track!" Jake rambled, pacing the floor, near nervous exhaustion.

"Chill out, Bud, there's nothing you can do about it right now, let the cops handle it when they get here. When was the last time you had a pain pill?" Missy asked, trying to calm and distract him before the police arrived.

"I don't know, sometime before we went to Birdie's, I think. I'm overdue, I guess," he mumbled, as he went to his bedroom and grabbed a pill from the bottle and returned to the kitchen to chase it down with some water. A few minutes later, headlights cut through the dark as a sheriff's car pulled to a halt outside the house.

The deputy got out of the car, turning on a powerful flashlight, shining it around outside the perimeter of the house, then proceeded to the front door. He peered curiously at the four new nine-mm "peepholes" in Jake's front door, then knocked loudly.

Jake opened the door. "Hello, I'm Jake Anderson, th-thank you for getting here so soon. Come in, please," Jake told the cop nervously. The young officer removed his cap, walked inside and glanced around. He had an open, honest face with a square jaw, dark hair and brown eyes. He was about thirty years old.

"I'm Deputy Sykes, we had a report of a possible prowler at this address. Are you the complainant, sir?" he announced, offering Jake his left hand.

Jake looked at Missy, then nodded to the cop shaking his hand. "Yes, I am. My friend and I were having dinner and my, ah, pet bobcat ... I think he may have attacked a prowler outside my window there," he pointed, showing the cop the window facing the table in the kitchen.

"Your, uh, pet ... *bobcat*?" the cop asked incredulously, his eyes widening.

"Yeah, it's a long story, anyway, we heard a scream, we ran outside and found blood on the ground, also on my cat's mouth and face. Oh, and we found a revolver lying on the ground close to the window. Missy, that's my friend here, she collected a sample of the blood and put it in a bag, it's in the fridge with the gun."

The deputy shook his head. "You shouldn't have touched anything, you could have contaminated the crime scene!"

Missy cocked an eyebrow, crossed her arms and said, "There was no *crime* committed, except for maybe trespassing. But someone *was* sneaking around out there. We think they were injured, and they were also armed!"

Deputy Sykes was writing in a little notebook. "Let's have a look outside, show me where you found the blood and the gun."

Jake led him outside, Missy followed. They showed him the drying blood spot on the ground and approximately where she found the gun.

"I wish you hadn't removed the gun, it will be hard as hell to reconstruct what happened out here," he reprimanded, as he searched the ground for other evidence. "There's some shoe prints here in the dirt, but they could be anyone's," he reported, after scouring the area with his flashlight.

Missy then told him how she had collected the gun and stored it in the bag in the fridge. "Well, *that* was smart of you, maybe we can get some prints off it, anyway. Possibly see who it's registered to, that is, if it wasn't stolen!" he told them, as they made their way back inside. Jake opened the fridge and gave the deputy both bags of potential evidence.

"Well, we can run the blood for DNA. But it could take a month to process. It will tell us the gender of the 'unsub,' and by checking through VICAP and NCIC, see if they have any previous convictions. If they get any solid prints off the gun, they'll run it through AFIS," the deputy informed them.

"What's AFIS?" Jake asked.

"It's an automated fingerprint identification system," he patiently replied.

Jake shook his head. "Too many acronyms for me!"

"Do you have any description of the vehicle that the 'unsub' was driving?" the deputy asked them.

"Excuse my stupidity, but just what is an 'unsub?'" Jake asked.

"'Unknown Subject,'" the deputy replied, looking a bit surprised.

"Apparently I don't watch enough crime shows on TV," Jake allowed. "We didn't see the car. It was parked almost at the end of the drive. Probably to make a quick unseen getaway after they shot—never mind." Jake felt queasy thinking about it.

Deputy Sykes made some more entries on his note pad, then told them there wasn't much more he could do at present. He asked if Jake had a weapon, Jake told him he did.

"Keep your eyes and ears open, if you see anything suspicious, give us a call. We'll call you as soon as we have any results."

They shook hands and he turned to leave, stopped at the door. "What's up with all the holes in the door?" he asked curiously.

"The better to see you with!" Jake said wryly. Deputy Sykes looked at him oddly, then shook his head and bidding them goodnight, returned to his cruiser. He drove off down Jake's lane toward the highway.

Jake closed the door, locking it. He looked at Missy, then went into his bedroom. He came back out and plopped down on the couch. "That was nerve-wracking! I need to relax a little," he told Missy, producing a rolled joint.

She sat down beside him on the couch with a cold soda. "I've gotta get up early, I'll have to go back home and change clothes before I go on shift," she remarked, as he took a couple of tokes off the joint. He offered it to her, but she declined.

"Listen, I think Ben is pissed at me for helping you. I feel like I'm getting caught up in this feud over money or whatever it is between you two. Nothing personal, Bud, but I like my job and I *need* my job. I'll still help you—as long as my career's not threatened. You understand that, right?" she stated with a tight smile.

Jake took another toke, then put the joint out. "I appreciate everything you've done for me the last couple days, Missy. I never intended for you to be put between the proverbial 'rock and a hard place. You do what you gotta do. Don't worry about me, I can take care of myself. Just don't wreck my truck, okay?" he replied with a smile.

She got up from the couch and stretched. "Well, it's 10:30, I'm gonna hit it. I hope you enjoyed your dinner as much as *Jinx* did. Good night," she teased, walking to the spare bedroom, closing the door behind her.

"Yeah, good night, it was great," he said unenthusiastically, more to himself than her, as he stared at the four new holes in his front door. After a few minutes of stoned contemplation, he got up and locked the back door. Then he cleaned up the dishes and put them away. He turned off the kitchen lights and made his way to his room across from hers.

He paused outside her door for a moment, raised his hand to knock, then shook his head, went into his room and closed the door. Jinx was curled up at the end of the bed, watching as he took his bandage off, cleaned his wounded hand and rewrapped it. He lay down and stared at Jinx, "Thanks again for today, Buddy!" The big cat just closed his eyes, ignoring him.

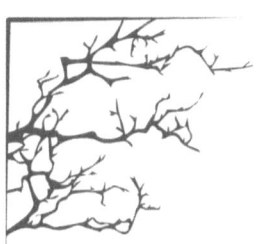

Chapter Twenty

S he was standing in the living room of her old house, when a knock came at the front door. She didn't want to answer it, but her feet moved of their own volition. She seemed to glide toward the door as if on a thin veneer of ice, fear and apprehension building as she floated closer. She stopped when she was standing in front of the door. She tried to turn the handle, but it was locked. Now she stood in front of an elevator. The doors slid to the side smoothly in slow motion—revealing the horrible visage of her long-dead father. It was dressed in his park uniform, standing on the other side of the doorway. Its greenish-black flesh was putrescence and peeling off in tatters, its long-dead eyes were shriveled and sunken into the sockets of its skull, floating in a viscous black fluid. The grinning horror opened its rotted mouth and thick, dark blood poured out in a small flood, cascading down the front of its moldy uniform.

Small black beetles poured out of its rotting nasal cavity and dropped into the gore at its feet, puddling like an unholy rain. The father-thing raised its skeletal arms to embrace her. "Missssyyy, dadddy missss youuu, givve dadddy kissss!" it burbled horribly, as part of its decaying black tongue fell off, splashing into the dark puddle at its feet, where it lay twisting about like some obscene worm. The remainder protruded from the daddy-thing's mouth, swarming with yellowish maggots. Its clawed hands reached for her, and she screamed. She tried to turn and run but her legs seemed mired in molasses. The boogey-dad had reached out with a bony claw, clutching her by her hair and was pulling her back toward its rotted mouth, the stench of the grave was overpowering. "Jusss one kissss, Missssyy!" it hissed. Missy screamed again as it leaned in close, hovering inches from her face as skeletal fingers forced her horrified mouth to open and the decomposed remainder of its tongue dripped squirming maggots into her open mouth like a leaky faucet, as it kissed her...

"MISSY! MISSY! WAKE up! You're having a nightmare!" Jake was shaking her as she woke up in a cold sweat, shivering badly, and realized she was still screaming from the horrid dream.

"Oh my God, what a hideous nightmare! M-my father was back from the dead! H-he was all rotted and trying to... oh God, it was terrible!" she sobbed, clutching the sheet around her naked breasts, as Jake sat on the side of the bed sympathetically rubbing her shoulder.

"It's okay, you're okay! It was just a bad dream. We all have those occasionally. Granted, more than usual lately. Are you alright? Can I get you anything? You scared the hell out of me when I heard you screaming like that!" he said with concern.

"What time is it?" she asked, calming down slightly.

"It's a little after 4:00 a.m., you want some water or a soda?"

"Some water would be nice, thanks." He went to the kitchen and took a glass of ice water back to her, then watched as she greedily drank it down.

She handed the glass back, and then looking at him, she said, "I don't know if I can or even *want* to go back to sleep. I'm scared of having another nightmare like that."

Jake sat back down on the side of the bed. He smiled, "Well, if you want some company, I'd be glad to loan you Jinx, but I warn you he's a bed hog!"

She laughed, then was silent as she stared deeply into his azure eyes.

He leaned forward hesitantly, then seeing she wasn't backing away, kissed her gently. She kissed him back, her tongue probing between his lips as her arms encircled his neck, pulling him down. His left hand tentatively caressed her breasts, her nipples stiffening as his thumb ran circles around them. She moaned, breathing heavily into his mouth, as she reached into the fly in his boxers and stroked him. He broke the kiss long enough to tell her he didn't have any condoms—they were in the truck.

"No time, I'll chance it! I need you *now*! Lay down, I'm gonna ride you!" she hissed breathlessly as she pulled his shorts off, watching his boner bounce at attention.

She climbed on top and reaching down, she slowly sank his shaft into her hot, wet core with a groan of pleasure. Jake sucked on her nipples, lightly nipping them as she rode him, twisting her hips like a corkscrew. He drew her down with his left hand and kissed her deeply as waves of pleasure rolled over them. They both climaxed just as Jinx jumped up on the bed. Observing them with a cat's disdain, he swatted Missy on the ass with a paw, making her yelp in surprise, then jumped back off the bed, leaving the room to them.

"He's just jealous, you know," Jake gasped, trying to catch his breath. He lay there until his heart rate slowed.

He glanced over at Missy—she was sound asleep. He leaned over and kissed her lightly on her sweat-flecked forehead. Then, pulling the bed covers over her, he grabbed his shorts and left the room quietly, closing the door behind him.

AFTER WRAPPING A PLASTIC sandwich bag over his right hand to protect it, he took a shower. He toweled off and climbed naked back into his bed. *What the hell, she's already seen my junk!* he thought, as he closed his eyes and thought about what had just happened.

He knew they had taken a huge step, crossing the invisible boundary between friends and lovers. He pondered if that was a good thing, or possibly one of the worst decisions he had *ever* made. He fell asleep, frowning.

MISSY JERKED AWAKE at the beeping of the alarm on her phone. It was 7:00 a.m. She felt the stickiness between her thighs, immediately felt her cheeks redden as she recalled the lovemaking of a few hours before.

Damn it! I should've had better control of my emotions than that! She chastised herself belatedly, donning her robe she'd brought from home. She opened the bedroom door a crack to see if Jake was up yet. His door was open, and she smelled coffee brewing. She hurried into the bathroom, closing the door and locking it. Then she got in the steaming shower, scrubbing herself clean and shampooing her hair.

She was rinsing her hair when the hot water suddenly turned to ice! She let out a yelp, leaped out of the freezing cold water and banged on the wall separating the bathroom and the kitchen.

He ran into his bedroom and shouted through the door, "Are you okay?"

"Hell no! There's no hot water. It's freezing cold. You used it all when you showered, didn't you?" she yelled accusingly.

Jake chuckled. "Sorry, it's an old water heater, doesn't hold much hot water and it hasn't had time to fully reheat," he said through the door.

"That's just *great*! I've still got soap in my hair. How long before it gets hot again?" she asked.

"Oh, probably another twenty minutes or so," he replied, grinning. "Long enough for another 'ride' if you feel like it," he suggested hopefully. For a moment, there was nothing but silence from the bathroom.

"I don't think that's a good idea, Bud! Last night was nice. I needed the release, so did you. But I've got to be on shift in about thirty minutes and that would be pushing it. I'm gonna finish washing my hair in this cold-ass water, get some coffee, then head out, if you don't mind."

"That's fine," he said, a little disappointed. "I'll have some coffee ready when you get out."

Missy dressed, pulled her still-damp curls back with a clip, then went to the kitchen table and sat down. Her coffee was waiting on a coaster. Jake was pulling a couple of toaster waffles from the toaster. He plated them, then set them in front of her and sat down across from her.

"Ah, about last night, I—" Jake began before she cut him off.

"No worries, no regrets, okay? I'm a big girl, I knew what I was doing," she said, as she took a huge bite of syrup-drowned waffle. She washed it down with some coffee and smiled. "You're kinda cute, in a 'scaredy-cat' sorta way, for such a big, strong dude! It's sort of endearing," she added, chewing on a bite of faux waffle.

Jake frowned, "Yeah, cowards *run* in my family, hah-hah! Listen, what time do you think you'll get back?"

She was silent for a moment. "I'm gonna go back to my place tonight, Jake. It's nothing you've done, it's just that I need time to process all this shit that's been going on the last few days. Plus, Ben may want me to do some water quality tests out on the lake before dark. I'll text you and let you know. If you need anything... I mean, if anything out of the ordinary pops up, just call me."

Jake didn't like it, but he *had* loaned her the truck. She gathered her stuff and waved goodbye, then left in his truck. He opened his phone, making sure it was charged. After all, he was *stranded* here and ... a shiver went down his spine as he saw today's date—October 31st, *Halloween*.

MISSY'S DAY WAS UNEVENTFUL, to a point. She cited a couple camping for staying an extra day without a permit. Caught a guy making a campfire outside of the designated *"fire-ring"* area, made him put it out and gave him a warning citation. She ate some fruit she'd brought from her house for lunch. Her fridge was still toxic to her psyche.

Ben called her around 3:00 p.m., asking her to take some water samples from the lake, just as she'd predicted. After patrolling the area, she drove to her cabin. She had started gathering her testing equipment out of the storage shed when she felt a stunning blow to the back of her head, and everything went black.

JAKE WAS TRYING TO watch stupid cat videos on his phone late that afternoon to pass the time. But his concentration just wasn't there. He kept replaying last night's events leading up to and following the sex in an endless loop in his head. First, he's nearly shot in the back, his freaking *cat* saves his ass, next he's making love with Missy. Somebody up there had a twisted sense of humor! He shook his head, got up, took a diet soda out of the fridge and was just sitting down when he got a text on his phone. It was from Missy's number. What he read stunned him:

"Trick or treat! Asshole! Just letting you know Missy's going to be tied up tonight, literally! *If you* ever *want to see her alive again, get your sorry fucking ass to the Joseph Cemetery Crypt at 12:00 am sharp! Don't even think about calling the cops! If you do, bye-bye Missy! I know you're ride-less. Now you're a big-shot writer, so let's see if you can write your way out of this shit! If you're one minute late, it's adios to the bitch! Happy Halloween, pencil-dick!"*

The color drained from his face as he read the text. What the *fuck* was happening? Had Missy been kidnapped!?

He quickly texted back, "Who are you?" He waited, but there was nothing. When five minutes had passed with no response, he re-texted, "What have you done to Missy?" He tried calling her number, it went straight to voice mail. He looked at the time: 6:00 p.m. Shit! He had six hours to find a ride and figure out what the fuck he was gonna do when he got there.

Who could he call? Maybe Ben, he would probably have been the last person she talked to. Or should I call Dr. Boucher and tell him about the text? Fuck! His mind was racing almost as fast as his heart. *Fuck it, I'll call them both!* he decided.

He quickly realized that he didn't have Ben's number. *And why would I, we haven't spoken in years! Crap! No good.* So, he called Birdie and got his voicemail. Jake had forgotten about the time. Birdie would have already gone for the day. He left an urgent message asking him to please call back ASAP! *Who else could he call without getting the cops involved?* The only name that came to mind was *Pete Chandler.* Jake *really* didn't want to re-involve the him in this shit, but he was running out of choices.

Besides, Pete knew from up-close experience what they might be up against. He opened the contacts on his phone, then realized the young man's personal number was on *Missy's* phone, not his! Shit! He called the Pizza Palace and Dan, the "Pizza Man," answered. Jake asked to speak to Pete.

"I'm sorry, dude, but he's on delivery tonight. It's Halloween, we get a shi—a lotta orders usually, and we're already short-handed. Ya want I should, like, give him a message?" he answered Jake.

"Yes, could you ask him to call Jake Anderson as soon as he can? Please, tell him it's *very* important!" Jake said giving him his cell number.

"No worries, dude. We, um, close at 10:00 p.m. tonight! He should get back to ya by then," Dan assured him.

Jake thanked him and hung up. His right hand was throbbing like a rotten tooth. He shook out a painkiller from the bottle, chased it down with some water, then paced back and forth between the living room and kitchen. He got his nine mm and checked to make sure he had a full magazine, then sat down anxiously on the couch to wait. *I'm coming, Missy!* At least, he *hoped* so. "Dammit, *someone* fucking *call* me!"

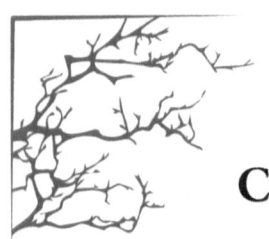

Chapter Twenty-One

The back of Missy's head felt like someone had dropped an anvil on it. Her hands were duct-taped behind her back and her feet bound, as well. She'd been blindfolded and duct-tape sealed her mouth. She was lying on her side on what felt like a cold cement floor, dizzy from the pain shrieking through her skull with every heartbeat.

"Well, it looks like *'Tweedle-Dee'* is awake!" a raspy voice snarled, making Missy jump. The air was frigid, and Missy shivered with fear, the glacial air made it worse.

"Pissy-Missy just wouldn't listen, even though you were warned, *twice,* to stay away from *him!"* the harsh voice hissed sarcastically.

Missy stiffened at the words, *"Pissy-Missy."* It was a phrase her sister Elisa had used when they were kids. Especially when Missy angered her, and it didn't take much!

She hadn't heard her sister's voice in over ten years—but could it really be Elisa? It didn't *sound* like her at all. Her captor was her *sister? But how the hell was that possible? Unless... unless Elisa had been playing the ultimate game of "hide and seek" these past six months and had somehow faked her own death!*

She let out a terrified groan as a wave of nausea threatened to send her lunch rocketing back up to visit her back teeth. She knew she could quickly choke to death on her own puke, courtesy of the duct-tape covering her mouth! Missy felt a hand grab one edge of the tape and rip it painfully off her lips.

"Can't have you puke and die—not yet, 'Tweedle-Dee!' I have a nice surprise lined up for 'Tweedledumb' as soon as he comes to rescue the 'maiden in distress.' You *are* in distress, are you *not?"* her captor cackled gleefully. "Pissy-Missy, trick or treat! Jakey's going to be *dead* meat!" The nasty rhyme was followed by maniacal laughter. Missy promptly threw up everything in her stomach onto the concrete floor.

JAKE WAS GETTING MORE worried and impatient by the moment. The clock on the wall told him it had been two hours since he'd left the message on Birdie's phone. Still no answer, so he left another urgent message, telling him that it was a matter of life or death for Missy!

This is all my fault! If she hadn't saved me from drowning, she wouldn't be *in this mess in the first place!* he thought miserably, mentally kicking his own ass. He jumped when his phone rang, startling him, and immediately answered it.

"Hello, Jake, I'm sorry, I just got your message. I've been counseling a patient. What on earth is going on?" Birdie asked, sounding out of breath.

Jake hesitated before answering, "Ah, Dr. Boucher, Missy's in big trouble, and I need your professional advice. I-I got a text from her number about two hours ago—at first, I thought it was from Missy, but then it I realized it was from some deranged nut who's apparently holding Missy hostage! I'm gonna send you the text... please read it and tell me what you think I should do at this point. This is driving me crazy!"

Jake then told him of the attempted attack on him by some unknown person the night before and about calling the cops.

"I can't call the cops this time, the text said they'd kill her if I did. I don't have my truck and I have to *be* at the crypt at exactly 12:00 a.m. I can't be a fucking minute late or she'll be hurt or worse!" his voice filled with anguish, as he sent the text to Birdie. Jake waited in agonized silence as Birdie read the message.

"Obviously, we're dealing with a mentally-unstable individual here. You're right, I don't think you can involve the police, this person sounds emotionally unbalanced and has serious anger issues directed toward you! Also, I think this person may know or has known you *intimately* at some point in your life!" he suggested, finishing his hypothesis.

Jake thought about Birdie's choice of words. "Dr. Boucher, why would you say it may be someone who has known me intimately?"

"Well, for one, they used the word "*now*" before proceeding with "*you're a big-time writer,*" which would indicate that they knew you at some point in time either before you were a writer or had become a successful one. That by itself is not indicative of a close relationship. However, the phrase, ah, 'pencil-dick' might suggest someone who has had, er, sexual relations with you and was knowledgeable about your, um, anatomy. Or they could just be trying to goad you into doing something foolish—a logical reaction to anger and feeling impotent at the need to locate Missy with extreme haste!" Birdie lectured on in a clinically detached voice, eerily reminding Jake of Mr. Spock from "Star Trek."

"Yeah, well, the angry part is working just fine! I still need to know how to proceed from here. If I go out there by myself, what's to stop them from killing us both?" he snapped back at Birdie.

"They are obviously using her to get to you, so my answer would be, your *life* in exchange for hers," he answered coldly.

Jake thought, *this is all fucking insane!* "Listen, Doc, can you give me a ride out to the—"

Birdie cut him off. "Jake, my best advice at this point would be to call the FBI! This is a kidnapping and that's what they are best at resolving. I would suggest you call them immediately. I'm empathetic to your situation, but I don't believe whoever is holding Missy would respond well to an on-the-spot 'anger management' session at this point. I'm sorry I can't be of more help."

Jake couldn't believe Birdie had just said that! "Listen, *asshole*! Missy's *life* is on the line! By the time the FB-fucking-I could get someone out here, she could be dead! I need someone to take me out there and—"

"This conversation is terminated as of *now*, Mr. Anderson!" Birdie snapped, hanging up abruptly.

"Fuck!" Jake screamed at the phone and almost threw it across the room in frustration. He looked at the time—it was pushing 10:00 p.m. He had just made up his mind to call the FBI in desperation when he got an incoming text. It was Pete.

"Hi, Mr. Anderson. Got your message. Dan said it was important, what's up?"

Jake hated to use the *auto dictate* feature on his phone. He used it, anyway, asking Pete to call him back instead of texting.

His phone rang and he answered, "Hey Pete, I—ah, got a serious situation here. Missy's in deep shit and I've gotta try to get her out. The thing is, I'm stranded here, and I need a ride to get to the cemetery. Someone has kidnapped her and threatens to kill her if I don't show up at 12:00 a.m. sharp!"

There was only silence on the other end. Jake then explained about the aborted attempt on his life and the text sent to him from Missy's phone. He left out the conversation with Birdie. *Fuck him!*

"Holy crap! Y-you think this has anything to do with that horror-show that attacked me the other night?" Pete asked nervously.

Jake thought about it before answering. "I can't be sure of anything anymore, but it's probable! Listen, I need a huge favor. This is a life or death situation for Missy." *And maybe me, too!* he thought. "Do you know how use a shotgun?" Jake asked, desperate but determined.

"Ah, yes sir, I do. My uncle used to take me bird hunting when I was twelve. What do you need me to do, like... shoot someone??" he laughed nervously, then was quiet when Jake didn't answer right away.

"I just need someone to be my back-up—I can't operate a shotgun because of my fucked-up right hand! I've got my nine mm, but I'm not much of a shot left-handed either, unless I'm practically at point-blank range. What do you say, can you help me try to get Missy back from these assholes?"

"Can't you just call the cops and let them handle it?" he asked.

"There's no time, Missy needs help now!" Jake exclaimed anxiously.

Pete was quiet for a second, then said firmly, "What the fuck, I'm your man!" Jake let out a suspended breath. *Thank you, God!*

Chapter Twenty-Two

"What the hell do you think you're doing? Kidnapping *her* was *not* part of the plan! I told you I'd take care of it—that's what you're paying me for, am I right?" Birdie barked into his phone. "No *harm* is to come to Missy! Is that understood?" he demanded.

There was a long silence. "There's been a change of plans, 'Tweetie-Bird!' You've had your three chances to do the job. Three strikes—you're out! Now I'm gonna do things. You just get your shrinky-ass out there and do what I ordered! Dudley Do-*write* is gonna show up to try and save the bitch, and you might *yet* earn your blood-money! Get the job done, then haul ass out here!" the voice rasped and hung up.

THROUGH HIS LIVING room window, Jake watched the headlights strobe through the pines lining his driveway, as Pete pulled up in front of his house and killed the engine on his Honda. He got out of the car wearing a red 'Pizza Palace' T-shirt and ball cap, he looked like a walking billboard for the place. Jake gave him an awkward-but-firm left handshake as he opened the door for him.

"Thanks for coming! I don't have to tell you this is gonna be dangerous, but I don't see any other way to roll right now. I have a spare key to my truck. I'm hoping whoever took Missy left my truck at her place and used their own vehicle to transport her," he told Pete, sticking his pistol in his jacket pocket.

"The shotgun will hopefully still be on the rifle-rack in the back seat, there's a box of twelve-gauge 00 buckshot and slugs in the console." He checked the time: 11:25 p.m. Jake locked the house and they climbed into the Honda.

Pete glanced nervously at Jake, "What do we do if the truck's not there?" he asked, as they buckled up.

Jake said soberly "In that case, we're in *really* deep shit!

"WHY ARE YOU DOING THIS, Elisa? It *is you*! Isn't it?" Missy moaned and tried to sit up, but her head throbbed and spun, nauseating her to the point of retching again. She laid back down. There was no answer from her captor.

"Elisa! What did I do to make you hate me so much? Is it Jake? Please... answer me!" she yelled, trying to get a reaction.

"Shut your trap, 'Tweedle-Dee!' This isn't about *you*! Keep your fucking voice down or I'll tape you up like a mummy!" the grating voice warned.

So, Missy lay quietly as tears leaked under the blindfold and streamed down her face. She pulled and tested the tape binding her wrists, but there was little give in it. *Dear God, please let Jake find me before it's too late!*

THE HONDA'S HEADLIGHTS found the turn-off to Missy's drive. Pete drove them up the lane until the bright halogens revealed Jake's truck sitting in front of her cabin. Jake blew out a huge sigh of relief. He'd had no back-up plan if it wasn't there. So far, his luck was holding.

Leaving the car running, Jake gave Pete the truck's spare key. Pete walked over, unlocked it and saw the shotgun on the rack, reached in and grabbed it. Then he opened the console and found the two boxes of shells inside. He walked back to his car and asked Jake what was next. Jake told him to load it first with buckshot, then the deer-slug and alternate until the magazine was full.

Pete loaded four in the mag and one in the chamber. Then he shook out the rest and put them in his coat pocket, on top of some Parmesan cheese and red pepper packets. He engaged the safety by the trigger and slid the Remington in the gap between the console and the driver's seat.

Then he climbed in and looked at Jake. "So, what's the plan when we get there? This sounds like a trap, you know! Don't you think that they're just waiting for you to show up—uh, am I really gonna have to *shoot* someone?" Pete's apprehension was mounting by the second.

Jake smiled grimly at him. "I honestly don't know, Pete. Your guess is as good as mine. Let's get this done."

SOMETHING WAS WRONG! At first, she thought it was just her imagination. She sniffed the air again—she knew that smell ... gasoline! The odor was getting stronger by the moment. She wavered briefly from curiosity to full-out panic! She could see nothing—the dark was absolute. Her crotch, legs and feet were suddenly cold and soaking wet. The smell of gas was overpowering as she frantically willed her body to move, but her brain didn't respond. Suddenly, there was the bright flare of a lighter. She watched helplessly in horror as a leering face was briefly illuminated in the lighter's glow, a hand slowly lowered the flame to her gas-covered extremities. There was a Woomph as the gas caught and began the unholy act of premeditated murder. She screamed her last thought out loud as the flames enveloped her lower body, "Hellpp, Misssy!!"

PETE AND JAKE WERE on the highway, Jake watching the digital clock on the dashboard display move to 11:40 p.m., sweat pouring off his face despite the frigid air coming in from his partially open window. He'd forgotten to bring a pain pill with him in the rush to get out of the house. His right hand throbbed, and he cursed himself for forgetting it!

"Can't you go a little faster, Pete, we've only got twenty fucking minutes to get there!" Jake growled. The posted limit on the winding highway was forty mph. "This is as fast as I can safely drive—I'm already doing fifty, as it is!" Pete added, resentfully.

As they came rapidly around a curve in the road, the headlights briefly reflected off a state trooper's car parked on the side of the road facing them. The cop had his radar gun hanging out the window. *Shit!* Pete thought as he glanced at the speedometer: *fifty-five mph*! He tapped the brakes, bringing his speed down to forty-five before checking the rearview mirror. Sure enough, he saw the headlights flash on, as the trooper shot up rooster-tails of gravel making a U-turn.

Five seconds later, the light-bar on the roof was strobing through the night as the police car came up fast behind them. The trooper's siren *whooped* a couple times as he raced past them and accelerated down the road. They looked at each other and both breathed a sigh of relief, and Pete brought the car back up to fifty mph as they continued toward town.

BEN HAD TRIED CALLING, then texting Missy several times since he'd asked her to take the water samples earlier in the day. The calls went straight to voicemail and the texts were ignored entirely. She'd never called him with the water results, either. She always sent the results back to him by the end of her shift. Something was clearly *wrong*!

He drove out to her cabin and saw Jake's truck in the driveway. He stopped, leaving the engine and the lights on as he got out and walked to the front door. He knocked three times loudly, getting no response, then tried calling her again.

It was answered on the second ring. "Fuck-off and die, asshole!" grated an angry, strident voice that was obviously *not* Missy's!

"Who the hell is this? And where is Missy?" he snapped angrily.

"Hey, Ben Dover—you can kiss Missy's ass good-bye, Ranger Rat-fuck!" the speaker cackled madly, then hung up.

Ben was left staring at his phone. *What the hell was* that *about? Whatever it was, Missy was in dire straits indeed, if that voice on the phone wasn't bullshitting!* He knew Missy had been driving Jake's truck, but there was no sign of either of them. He jumped back in his truck and drove like hell to Jake's house. No one answered when he anxiously pounded on the door. *Shit!* Nothing else he could do, so he dialed 911.

BIRDIE DROVE HIS MERCEDES-Benz with the headlights off he as approached the crypt in the middle of the Joseph cemetery. He parked behind it and got out, quietly closing the door, and walked down the steps leading into the encasement area of the mausoleum's lower level. Many prominent Indians of his tribe had been placed here. Including his own grandfather.

But he himself would never be laid to rest here, only the "holy-ones" were granted that honor. He was *Yeenaldlooshi*—an abomination of nature. Even he *himself* knew nothing of the origin of his existence, he just *was*. And he had little control of what occurred after he transformed, the beast seemed to have a mind of its own.

"About time you got here, Bird-turd! Did you get it done?" Elisa Morning Star snapped, as she lowered the nine mm pistol she'd taken from Missy. Birdie just nodded in the affirmative as he approached Elisa. She sniffed the air as he got near. "You smell like gas! Did she scream before you finished her?" she asked, with a high-pitched crazy laugh. "I bet she thought she was in hell in the end!" she laughed evilly.

"You are one loony-tune, cold-ass bitch—you always were!" he snarled at her, staring down at Missy's prostate body squirming on the cold cement.

Missy's insides turned to ice when she heard Birdie's voice. *What was he doing here? He must be involved in all of this! What the fuck have they done?* she thought, with mounting terror. She had managed to discreetly loosen the tape binding her wrists a little by flexing and relaxing her muscles after she'd regained consciousness. She had abraded the skin from both wrists in her effort to free herself and could no longer feel her hands. Thankfully, they had both gone numb from the lack of blood supply.

She'd almost freed her left hand when Elisa noticed her squirming and kicked her viciously in her side. Missy groaned in agony.

"I didn't give you permission to move! You didn't say *'mother may I!'* Red rover, red rover, fuck old Ben Dover!" Elisa cackled, her face twisted into a mask of psychotic rage. "Mommy can't help Pissy Missy anymore!"

The realization finally sank in that this madwoman must have had their mother killed. Missy screamed, "You crazy fucking bitch!! Why would you *do* such a horrible thing!? She did nothing but give you unconditional love, and this is how you repay her? Goddamn you! Why in hell did you *fake* your own death? I talked to Ava Farina. She told me you were dead! I guess the Elisa I knew *is*. What the fuck is wrong with you?"

Elisa was momentarily silent as Missy continued, "All those years, and never a phone call, a letter, *nothing*! You broke Mama's heart— after the stroke, she gave up hope that she'd ever see you again. I'll never forgive you for this! I hope you rot in hell for what you've done!" Missy snarled, as she flexed her left wrist and pulled it free from the tape binding it to the right.

She ripped the blindfold from her eyes and saw her sister for the first time in eleven years. She looked nothing like Missy remembered. Her hair was cut short and streaked with gray. Elisa was only two years older, but she had not aged well. Her raven-black hair was cut short and streaked through with premature gray. But it was her face that jolted Missy. Terrible scars disfigured her mouth and nose. When Elisa grinned, it was the terrible smile of the Joker from the 'Batman' movies. Her yellowed teeth were only stubs in gums encased by scar tissue.

"As you can see, dear sister, I'm already in hell!" She pointed to her face, "This is what happens when you gargle with battery acid! Hee-hee! I don't recommend it—it didn't hurt much going down—but coming back up was a dooozy! Didn't kill me, but I'll never 'drop acid' again!" Her insane, rasping laugh sent chills down Missy's already shaking body. "You should have heeded my warnings—I would have left *you* alone!"

Missy examined the immediate surrounding area, searching for anything that could be used as a weapon. The only objects she spied were the battery-powered lantern her sister must have stolen from the boat and was using to illuminate the crypt—and *her phone!* It was only a foot or so away from her, lying on the cold cement.

She stared up at Birdie with betrayal flashing in her eyes, "Why are you helping her, Birdie? What did she promise you? Money? Sex? Or both?" she accused, her voice shaking with anger.

Birdie's face was calm, but his dark eyes seethed with venom.

Finally, he spoke, "I have my reasons! *You* were never supposed to be part of this. If you hadn't had the unfortunate timing to be on the lake that night and fish Jake out of the water, this conversation would not be taking place! The wolverine should have eaten his balls, not his hand! Jake escaped me twice, it's not going to happen again."

"Three. Times!" Elisa hissed sarcastically.

He snapped his head toward her. "Shut up, you twisted, psychotic bitch! You owe me for the old woman!" he growled, taking a menacing step toward her. But he froze when they all heard a car moving slowly up the graveled road.

HENRY OVERTON WAS THE caretaker for the cemetery. He was a young sixty-four years of age, at least that's what he liked to think. Henry had worked there for damn near thirty years, he was retiring in two months. His sixty-fifth birthday had snuck up on him like a lion stalking its prey.

He *hated* Halloween more than any other time of year. The damn teenagers from town were always pulling some prank out here, tipping headstones, spraying graffiti, or some other juvenile bullshit. It just meant more work and aggravation for him.

So, he'd taken to staking out the cemetery on Halloween for the past couple of years trying to head off any mischief before it began. He'd seen the car pull up without its headlights on and park behind the mausoleum.

"Fucking little vandals!" he grumbled, as he started his car and drove slowly toward the trespassing vehicle with his own lights off. When he got closer, he noticed a soft glow of light filtering up from inside of the crypt.

Gotcha, you little assholes! he thought with a satisfied grunt, pulling his car to a stop ten feet behind the other vehicle. He quietly got out, carrying his five-cell heavy duty flashlight as both light and a weapon if needed.

JAKE SAW THE BRILLIANT flash an instant before the sharp crack of thunder followed, as lightning struck a tall pine maybe fifty feet away, causing Pete to swerve out of his lane and Jake to cringe. He had always hated thunderstorms. He understood the physics of them, but that didn't keep him from wanting to curl into a ball and hide when nature decided to remind humans how puny they really were!

"Jeez, that was close! Guess another front's pushing in, great fucking timing, right?" Pete nervously tried to make conversation, failing miserably, as they made their way through town—the cemetery was only a mile away. Rain started pouring. The lightning increased sending jagged bolts across the night sky.

"HOW DO YOU SPELL YOUR last name, sir?" the sheriff's deputy asked Ben.

"It's D-o-v-e-r! It's pronounced like the bird. Listen, I'm pretty damn sure Ms. Morning Star is in imminent danger, she's one of my rangers!" Ben frantically explained the brief conversation he'd had with the crazy woman a few minutes before.

"Is there any way you can locate where her phone *is* right now? I hope if you can find *it*, you'll find Missy—Ms. Morning Star. The person who answered it sounded like she'd escaped from the loony bin!"

The deputy said, "Well, we can '*ping*' her phone to acquire the GPS coordinates. Normally, we'd have to get a warrant to obtain the information. But if this is an emergency, we could skip the warrant and proceed immediately, except... the Chief's working a fire out at the nursing center. Arson, they think. Someone set one of the residents on fire, sorry scum—!"

Ben paled at this information and cut him off, "Officer, Ms. Morning Star's *mother* is a resident there! This could be somehow related to the crazy person I was just talking to! Please, if you *can* locate Missy's phone, for God's sake hurry up and do it *now*!" Ben beseeched the deputy.

He gave him Missy's number. "Please call me the minute you find her location! And thanks for your help."

"Yes sir, we'll get right on it!" the deputy replied.

Ben hung up, thinking, *Hang in there, Missy!*

PETE DROVE THEM THROUGH the walled gates of the cemetery, his windshield wipers fighting the deluge. Spotting the mausoleum up the incline, he cut the lights on the Honda and crept forward slowly in the pouring rain. Lightning flashed overhead several times, illuminating the road ahead.

Jake had briefly seen two cars parked behind the crypt before Pete had doused the lights. He glanced nervously at the clock: 11:58 p.m. *We made it in time. I hope!* He directed Pete to park in front of the car closest to the crypt's entrance. *Why were there two cars here, anyway?*

Pete parked the car and killed the engine. They were discussing how to proceed next, when suddenly five quick gunshots rang out over the din of the storm!

"I GOT HIM! I *got* Jakkkeeyy!" Elisa howled maniacally, after she sighted her pistol squarely on the beam of light moving slowly down the stairs and fired off five shots. She watched as the figure crumpled and tumbled down the last three steps of the stairs. The flashlight came to rest after spinning in a lazy circle, highlighting the face of the surprised and very dead Henry Overton.

Elisa's laughter abruptly shut off. She picked up the dead man's light and shined it from his head to his feet.

"Motherfucker!! I killed the wrong person! Where the fuck is *Jake*? That was supposed to be *him*! You made me kill the wrong person!" she shrieked, whirling on Birdie and shining the light in his eyes.

Birdie hissed in cold anger, "You always were a stupid, crazy bitch! You didn't even *wait* to see who it was before you started blasting away! If he *is* anywhere close by, you've just given away any element of surprise! Fuck *this*—and fuck *you*!!"

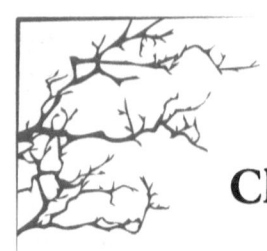

Chapter Twenty-Three

B irdie growled, as his eyes rolled back in his head—the metamorphosis starting. He threw his head back and an eerie wailing issued forth from his mouth as the agonizing transformation began. He ripped off his shirt and threw it on the ground at Elisa's feet.

Missy had watched in horror as Elisa shot the man now lying in a widening pool of dark blood on the cold cement. *Oh God! Jake! She's killed him!* was her first thought as he collapsed down the steps. Then she noticed his face and silver hair in the beam of the flashlight spotlighting him on the cold floor.

A huge sigh of relief escaped, seeing it was *not* Jake laying there. But then... *where was he?* She watched her deranged sister turning to scream at Birdie—as she did, Missy reached out and snatched her cell phone, keeping a watchful eye on Elisa and Birdie as they argued.

As Birdie began the unnerving high-pitched wailing, she quickly turned down the volume on her phone and dialed 911, then laid it back in about the same place. She believed if the police could not get a reply, they would try to track the cell signal to the nearest GPS coordinates. *I hope!* she thought as she bent down and began desperately removing the tape from around her ankles. She glanced up, then shook with awed terror at the rapid transformation of a man she'd thought she knew—into a monster, less than ten feet away!

Some fantastic amalgam of man and beast that nature had never intended now stood growling, eyes glowing malevolently in the weak light cast by the lantern's failing battery.

Elisa abruptly halted her tirade and backed quickly away from the Birdie-*thing,* tripping over Henry Overton's body and falling hard on the cement floor, Missy's pistol flying from her hand as she landed. The creature's harsh growl sounding like it had swallowed broken glass, it stepped toward the fallen woman. Elisa searched frantically around for the gun, but it had bounced out of her reach.

UPON HEARING THE GUNSHOTS, Jake anxiously told Pete, "Stay close beside me, sounds like the shit's hit the fan—and make sure the safety's off that gun. If that *thing* is in there, don't hesitate, blast it!"

Pete nodded nervously as they stepped out of the car. Instantly, they were drenched, as lightning danced across the sky, causing a strobing effect on the landscape. Pete slipped in the mud and almost lost the shotgun as they stole closer to the forbidding entrance of the old crypt.

"Be careful with that fucking thing!" Jake hissed at him. As they eased closer to the stairway, they could hear voices echoing from below.

A hand reached out and grabbed Jake's shoulder. *Shit!* Jake nearly jumped a foot straight up, nearly triggering his pistol and shooting himself in the foot.

Pete looked pathetic—half-drowned, his hair plastered to his head. "Sorry, Jake, uh ... can you see anything yet?" he asked softly, water pouring off his face in sheets.

"No, but I've got no *choice* but to go down there! Those shots we heard might have killed—never mind. Do you think you can *do* this? Because if you *can't*, it's okay. I'll think no less of you," Jake asked, starting to shake as the cold rain ran down his neck.

Pete looked like he was gonna "rabbit" at any moment. "I-I ... honestly, I'm s-scared shitless! *Okay*, l-let's go get her," Pete whispered, summoning the last of his courage.

MISSY SAW THAT HER pistol was lying just out of reach. If she moved to get it, the Birdie-*thing* would see and be on her before she could lift and fire it. It loomed over Elisa, its teeth glistening as ropy saliva dripped from its horrible mouth, pooling over Henry Overton's poor dead face. Its clawed fingers raised to strike at Elisa's once-beautiful face, now frozen in a rictus of terror and revulsion as she tried to scrabble backwards, crablike, to escape from the horror-show she'd hired to kill her ex-husband and her mother.

Sudden movement on the stairway caused the monstrosity to turn its attention away from Elisa. It growled in anger as Jake appeared in the fading light.

BEN WAS DRIVING LIKE a bat out of hell toward the Pleasant Valley Nursing Center, windshield wipers going full-tilt boogie. He didn't know what else he could do at present to locate Missy. He suspected the asshole on the phone might've had something to do with the fire, especially if Missy's mother was indeed the primary focus, but he couldn't be sure until he got better information.

He pulled into the parking lot, saw a group of people milling around in front of the building. The Fire Department was composed of mostly volunteers, and he saw only one fire truck and a patrol car from the Wallowa Sheriff's Department parked in front of nursing center as he threw his truck in park and got out into the downpour.

Ben didn't see much smoke, but the wind and rain probably had something to do with that. He ran over to the small crowd gathered under the eaves of the building, slipping once in his haste to get out of the deluge. He walked over to the deputy and quickly found his worst fears confirmed.

It appeared to be arson. Missy's mother's room was where the fire had apparently been set. The Sheriff's Office had called in a helicopter to transport her to Portland's Legacy Oregon Burn Center. They had contained the fire to her room and evacuated the other patients on the hall to spare rooms elsewhere in the facility.

Deputy Sykes was interrupted by his dispatch. He excused himself and walked a few feet away to talk. He nodded as he got the information, then came back over to where Ben was pacing anxiously back and forth.

"We've got a *ping* on Ms. Morning Star's phone—also just got a 911 'hang-up' call from that same number." Sykes motioned for Ben to follow him, and they ran toward the patrol car. Slogging through a small river of runoff from the thunderstorm overhead, they dove into the car, and Sykes turned on his overhead emergency lights.

"Where did they trace the phone to?" Ben asked, as they buckled up. Sykes grimaced and said, "Cemetery," as he accelerated out of the rain-slick parking lot.

MISSY SAW JAKE APPEAR on the steps at the same time the Birdie-*thing* did. She'd finally gotten the last of the tape off her ankles and, seeing the monster momentarily distracted, she lunged for her pistol lying halfway between her and Elisa.

Elisa anticipated Missy's intention, rolled and grabbed for it at the same time, clawing at Missy's face and screeching, "No, you don't, *bitch*!" as they grappled for control of the weapon.

Jake had barely been able to take in the scene of the two women fighting over the gun when the creature attacked in a blur of motion, leaping up the stairs, all teeth and claws.

Jake screamed as three-inch talons raked his left shoulder, knocking his pistol from his hand. It clattered down the steps and onto the floor just as the lantern's depleted battery gave out. Neither Pete nor he had thought to bring a flashlight. *Stupid!* Jake couldn't hold one in his right hand and Pete would've had to drop it to operate the shotgun. The dark instantly swallowed them all and with it, primal terror shot through their veins like ice water.

"Oh, shiit!!" both Jake and Pete exclaimed at the same time. Jake tried to take a step down the stairway but misjudged it. He fell the last couple of feet to the floor of the crypt, hitting his head and stunning him. Lightning flashed from outside, briefly highlighting the Birdie-*thing*—*it was standing directly over him!*

Pete panicked and froze as he got a good look at the creature staring back at Jake and him. Shaking with terror, he had raised the shotgun to shoot the hellish thing just as it had leaped up the stairs at Jake, but in that same moment, the fucking light had gone out. He couldn't pull the trigger without fear of blowing Jake away along with the creature!

Shit! No fucking flashlight, either! Pete desperately, despairingly tried to think of a way to illuminate the crypt well enough to shoot the *bastard* without killing Jake or Missy, too. Just as another brilliant flash of lightning briefly lit the horror standing over Jake, the incredibly loud report of a pistol firing momentarily deafened Pete.

Missy had just managed to wrestle control of the pistol from Elisa and saw the creature leap up the stairs to attack Jake, when the lantern gave out, plunging the crypt into jet-black dark.

Elisa shrieked hoarsely, "No-no-no-no-no!" over and over, getting to her feet blindly flailing at the darkness now enshrouding them. She had always been afraid of the dark, especially since the "wolf" attack when they were teens. Now she was beyond terrified.

She hadn't believed Birdie's claim to be *Yeenaldlooshi* when she hired him to kill Jake. She had even dated Birdie back in high school. She hadn't cared how Jake was killed, so long as it got done. She'd presumed Birdie would do in a normal fashion—with a gun, knife, or car bomb.

Now Elisa couldn't comprehend that he was, ironically, the "boogie-man" of all her youthful nightmares, come full-circle. *Had it been really Birdie himself at their window that terrifying night, so long ago?* She was paralyzed now with panic that she *herself* might be on the menu tonight, as well.

Missy tightened her grip on the gun. Her finger brace had been torn off wrestling for the pistol and, as feeling returned to her hand, her right index finger hurt like a *bitch!* She rolled away from Elisa as soon as the light went out, trying to keep Jake's last position on the stairway in her mind's eye, sweeping the nine mm from left to right in the cave-like dark. It would be impossible to get a shot off in the dark without possibly hitting Jake.

She needed some light! Abruptly, another brilliant flash briefly lit the room bright as day. Seeing the Birdie-*thing* reaching for Jake, she aimed quickly, but it was fully dark again as she squeezed the trigger.

THE PAIN EXPLODED JUST below the its collar bone as the slug tore through and out the right shoulder blade. The beast roared, enraged, having been shot—again! Its eyes had adjusted quickly to the dark and it now focused like a laser on the gray form of Elisa, who continued to shriek, her arms wildly sweeping the air in front of her blindly in the dark. With a growl, it leaped over Jake's still prostrate body and was on her in a heartbeat. It seized her by the throat and shook her like a rag doll, opening its jaws wide, as it prepared to tear her face off.

SUDDEN LIGHT FLOODED the crypt, causing the monster to quickly shut its eyes against the unexpected brightness. As it did so, it took a step back and slipped in the pool of blood draining from Henry Overton's bullet-riddled body. It howled as it fell hard on its wounded shoulder, its claws losing their grip on Elisa as she tumbled backwards to the ground.

Pete had activated his phone flashlight, plus the flash feature from his camera. Holding it in his left hand in front of him like a cross to ward away evil, he advanced down the stairs triggering the flash regularly for light and leveling the shotgun at the creature with his right.

Jake watched the Birdie-*beast* slip on the bloody floor, saw his own pistol lying a foot away and grabbed it. The monster leaped back up off the floor. Shielding its eyes from the flashlight's glare, it let out a roar, turning to charge at Pete.

Pete fired the shotgun, a long bright tongue of fire shooting out of its short barrel as the load of double-ought buckshot caught the creature full in the chest, blowing it off its feet. The recoil of the magnum round caused Pete to lose control of the shotgun. Being unable to brace it on his shoulder, he'd aimed and fired it like a pistol, and the recoil nearly broke his finger before it clattered to the floor. His phone slipped out of his rain-slicked left hand, bouncing down two steps to the floor, the face cracked, but amazingly, the flashlight still worked!

Pete seized the phone and held it up, incredulously watching the creature rise, slowly getting to its feet! *Un-fucking-believable!* Both Jake and Missy opened fire, emptying their weapons, blasting the monster with multiple rounds. The Birdie-*beast* danced like a deranged puppet on strings from the fusillade of lead directed at its mutated body. Sliding slowly down the crypt's blood-spattered wall, it let out one loud groan, then was still.

They were all deafened by the gunfire, so they didn't hear the approaching siren. Nor did they notice that Elisa had risen. She picked up the forgotten shotgun, aiming it at Jake's crotch, and pulled the trigger!

Click! Nothing happened. She pulled again, same result. Furious, she charged at Jake, intent on using it as a club. Jake saw the movement out of the corner of his eye just as she swung the shotgun at his head. He ducked the blow and caught her arms, pinning them to her sides, and forcing her to drop the gun as she fought him, screaming obscenities none of them could hear.

Missy rushed over to where they were struggling, leaned back and threw a hard, left uppercut to her sister's chin, knocking her out cold! She went limp in Jake's arms. Pete rushed over, picked up the shotgun off the floor and examined it.

A spent shell casing was jammed between the receiver and the breech—the firing pin had hit empty air. "No wonder she tried to club you with it, no way it would fire like this!" he hollered, showing them the gun. They both looked at him blankly, not understanding from the ringing in their ears.

Jake leaned close to Pete's ear, "Let's get the fuck out of here, *now!*" he yelled, as Missy gasped at the damage the Birdie-*thing's* claws had done to his left shoulder. Pete helped Jake carry the unconscious Elisa up and out of the crypt as Missy helped to steady Jake. When they reached the top, they saw the flashing blue and red lights of a Sheriff's patrol car parked behind Pete's CRV and walked slowly over to meet them.

The brunt of the storm had passed, ushering in a cold north wind that cleared the skies and quickly dropped the temperature in a matter of minutes. Deputy Sykes holstered his weapon and helped them put the still unconscious Elisa into the back of his patrol car, cuffing her hands behind her.

Ben got out of the patrol car, ignoring Jake, and took Missy's hand. "They traced your 911 call here, we just arrived. We heard gun fire. Deputy Sykes called for back-up. Thank God you're okay! We just came from the nursing center... there was a fire—I'm afraid your mother was badly burned, but she's alive. They flew her to Portland's burn center."

Missy just nodded sadly. Then she addressed the deputy loudly, "This is all horrible, but I think Elisa paid Bird—uh, Dr. Boucher to kill both Mother and Jake. Why, I don't know. She's insane! Dr. Boucher is-*was* a monster! He's tried to kill Jake at least three times—and almost killed Pete... Where *is* Pete?" she asked, looking around, finally spotting him over by his car, puking his guts out. Jake felt like he might join him any second.

Missy moved away from Ben, who stood glaring at Jake, and took Jake's hand, snapping, "We need to get Jake to the hospital, Boucher did a number on his shoulder. There's also another man down there, Elisa shot and killed him, thinking he was Jake."

Deputy Sykes just shook his head in disgust, shivering in the wind. "Where *is* Boucher?"

Missy looked at Jake, then said icily to Sykes, "In *hell,* I hope! He's down there, too," she pointed to the crypt. Two other patrol cars came roaring up to stop a few feet away.

Sykes asked, "Well, is he *alive?*"

Jake mumbled, "Well, if he is, you might need some *silver* bullets to remedy that!"

Sykes looked confused, "Need *what?*"

Missy broke in, "Officer Sykes, we need to go, *now!* We'll answer all your questions later, Jake's losing blood, he needs to get to the ER!" She led Jake to Pete's car, pulling Pete along by his shirt tail.

Deputy Sykes didn't look happy but nodded. "I'll catch up to you at the hospital, don't even think of leaving there 'til I get a handle on this mess." He told Ben to get in the cruiser. Then he backed it up, leaving room for Pete's car to back out. Missy insisted on driving and Pete didn't argue but climbed wearily in back, with Jake in the front. Missy reversed, then hauled ass to the hospital.

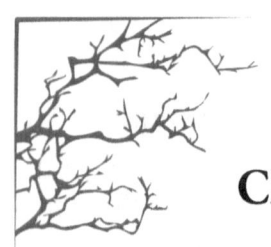

Chapter Twenty-Four

Missy got Jake to the ER in record time, nearly running over a couple of drunks leaving a bar. Pete asked loudly if she thought he should get his swollen trigger-finger looked at, holding it up for her to see.

"Hell, yes!" she replied loudly, as they got Jake inside the waiting room and on a chair.

A familiar-looking nurse came over, staring at him and Pete, "Third time's the charm? Or do you just like hospitals?" she asked Jake, smiling sweetly.

Jake ignored her and Pete didn't reply. She put Jake in a wheelchair and wheeled him back to triage, Missy and Pete following behind them.

They spent two hours waiting for the doctor to see both Pete and Jake. After 125 stitches for Jake's shoulder and a splint on Pete's finger, they all left the ER, just as Deputy Sykes pulled up beside Pete's Honda.

He got out, looking pissed. He marched over to them, "I need to know what the *hell* happened out there! *Where* is Dr. Boucher, and why was Henry Overton, the caretaker, shot? His was the only body we found inside. I need answers, people, or I'm gonna have to arrest the lot of you for murder and let the Sheriff sort this out!" he announced, his hand moving slowly closer to his weapon. Jake, Missy, and Pete all wore stunned expressions.

"What do you mean, *where* is Boucher? He's where we last *saw* him, lying dead on the floor of that fucking crypt!" Jake exclaimed hotly, his left shoulder beginning to ache despite the pain shot they'd given him.

"That's a problem—there was no one down there except poor Mr. Overton and a large pool of blood over by the back wall of the crypt!" Deputy Sykes spat back.

Pete interrupted timidly, "Ah, Deputy Sykes, these are pics I-I took of the, ah, *thing* down there!" Stepping forward, he brought out his phone, then pulled up the pictures he'd inadvertently taken in the crypt while trying to blind the creature and to provide enough light to shoot it. The pictures were a little fuzzy from the movement of both Pete and the Birdie-*thing,* but clearly showed it was truly *not* a man.

Deputy Sykes frowned, "What the fuck *is* this? Looks like a cross between Bigfoot and a Wookie! If this is some sort of sick Halloween prank—"

Now Missy interrupted, "Please, Officer Sykes, can we *just* get out of the cold, and we'll try to explain, as best as we can."

Sykes was still suspicious and worried about breaking protocol with the department, so he thought about it for a moment. "Alright—first, do you have any other weapons on you?" he asked tersely.

They all mumbled "no," then Jake said, "Well, there's a folding knife in my left pocket, but other than that, we left all the guns down in the crypt."

Sykes blew out a sigh. "I gotta have it, take it out slooow, and hand it over," he ordered, his hand hovering over his weapon again.

Jake did as he asked, groaning, and gently handed the knife to him. Sykes pulled out an evidence bag and placed it inside, being careful not to put his own prints on it. Then he locked it in the trunk, keeping an eye on all three while doing so.

"Technically, you should *all* be in cuffs right now. Let's take a booth at the Waffle-House, but if I don't like what I'm hearing, I'll book all three of you on suspicion of murder!" he informed them. The Waffle-House was conveniently located right next to the hospital, presumably for the visitors who were "hospital-food" intolerant.

Fortuitously, it stayed open late on Halloween and just about every other holiday it seemed, catering to the inebriated and those with the late-night munchies. Deputy Sykes herded them across the parking lot and out of the cold.

An exhausted waitress led them to a horseshoe shaped booth, where they sat down, just ordering sodas. The waitress gave them a nasty "no tips from these assholes!" look and walked off to flirt with the cook.

Missy asked, "First, where is Ben?"

Sykes looked annoyed. "I took him back to his car at the nursing center. Your sister is being questioned at central booking, then she'll have a psych evaluation or vice-versa. Now, do you want to tell me what the *hell* is going on? I've got a dead man's family to contact, and a missing doctor to locate!"

The deputy's dispatch called just then. He got up and moved away from the table to take the call. Garnering the attention of a couple of drunks waiting for their food, Jake said loudly to Missy and Pete, "How the *fuck* did that *thing* survive? We fired what? Over twenty rounds?"

"Maybe you weren't so far off in suggesting the use of silver bullets, Bud!" Missy whispered back. "Oh, by the way, thanks for coming to rescue me," she added.

Jake looked embarrassed. "I didn't do squat! Pete's the one you should be thanking, he managed to provide enough light for us to shoot that *bastard*. You basically saved yourself!"

They both looked at Pete, who alternated perusing the waffle-house menu and glancing enviously at a couple chowing down two tables away.

Deputy Sykes came back to the table. "We just got preliminary results back from forensics on the pistol recovered at Mr. Anderson's property, the prints came back an exact match for your sister's! The DNA test won't be back for at least a couple weeks. For now, she's being held for attempted murder, kidnapping, and trespassing. The sheriff ordered me to bring you all in for questioning," he said sternly.

He marched them out to his patrol car after throwing a ten-spot on the table for the snotty waitress. Pete, after a last envious look at the couple's food, led the way and got in first, followed by Missy, then Jake. After placing them in the back seat, Sykes drove off toward the Sheriff's office located in Enterprise, six miles northwest of Joseph.

Pete was panicking. He whispered, "I-I can't afford a lawyer, Mr. Anderson! Wh-what am I gonna tell them? I shot a fucking *monster*, not a man!"

Jake was starting to sweat again, despite the cold night. "We tell them the truth! You'll show 'em the pictures you took with your phone, it's the only proof we have that the *thing* truly exists."

Missy agreed, adding, "They also have the blood from the Birdie-*beast* that they can test to prove it's his DNA—Birdie's, that is. Plus, I'll testify Elisa used my gun to kill Mr. Overton, believing it was Jake on the stairs."

Jake was getting a headache trying to re-create the sequence of events that had unfolded in the crypt. "Missy, you picked up your gun to shoot the creature *after* Elisa had used it to shoot Mr. Overton. Your prints are gonna be the *last* ones on it!"

The implications began to dawn on Missy that *she* could be accused of murdering the old caretaker. It would be her word against Elisa's. *Fuck!* She was beginning to question her actions back in the crypt. *She hadn't really had a choice. Birdie would have killed them all.* Even though she despised her sister for her actions and knew Elisa was mentally ill and needed help, she would *not* take the rap for killing an innocent man.

THEY ARRIVED AT THE Wallowa County Sheriff's office at 2:30 a.m. It had been a busy night for the department. Between the fire at the nursing center and the kidnapping at the cemetery, it had been stretched thin.

Deputy Sykes brought the trio into the building and told them to have a seat in the booking area. He went in search of the sheriff, who came back with Sykes a minute later. The sheriff was in his mid-fifties, stood 6'4" and just shy of 220 pounds. His eyes were the color of polished onyx—no humor resided there.

He introduced himself with barely controlled fury, "I'm Sheriff Frank Blackstone—you people are in seriously hot water! You had better tell me what in blue blazes happened tonight out at the cemetery. I've got a dead caretaker and a seriously disturbed young woman screaming in my holding cell that some *monster's* trying to kill her, a fire at the nursing center that sent a poor woman to the burn center, and a large pool of blood on the floor of the Joseph Mausoleum, but no body to go with it!" he barked, leaning toward them menacingly.

"I'm *not* having a good day! *Yours* is not going to improve either, unless I can get some freaking answers! Let's go to the conference room and have a chat, shall we?" he said, leading the way. They all sat down around a large oval table.

Jake took a long drink of water from a bottle provided and related to the Sheriff everything that had happened, starting with the strange wailing in the forest four days previously, up to the present. It took him most of an hour and another bottle of water to explain it all, with Missy occasionally filling in some details.

Sheriff Blackstone sat listening, not interrupting, not saying a word, his face as still as a statue as Jake finished up, "I'm telling you, we *all* shot that *son-of-a-bitch* over twenty freaking times, Sheriff! Hell, my ears are still ringing. There's no way any *man* could survive that, then just get up and walk away!"

Sheriff Blackstone still hadn't said a word. He looked each of them in the eye, taking a swallow of rancid day-old cop coffee.

Missy then described her part of the action. Rescuing Jake from the lake, the attacks on Jake and her and later, on Pete, someone knocking her out this afternoon, then waking in the crypt to realize her sister had kidnapped her.

Diverting slightly, she related the terrifying visit by the wolf-*thing* when Elisa and she were teens. She related her mother's story of the *Yeenaldlooshi*, the "shape-shifter" of tribal lore, and ended with Elisa shooting the caretaker and overhearing Elisa say that she'd paid Birdie to kill both Jake and her mother.

"Deputy Sykes informed me that my mother was flown to the Portland Burn Center. Please, can you find out any information on her condition?" she implored the Sheriff.

Blackstone stared silently at her for a moment, his dark eyes seeming to suck the air from the room. Finally, he nodded at Sykes. The deputy left the room, closing the door behind him.

"You know, I don't believe any of this tribal-voodoo bullshit! You're basically telling me that you've been attacked by some Native American 'boogie-man' you believe your sister hired to kill both Mr. Anderson and your mother! Then Pete here just happened to be in the wrong place at the wrong time, and he was attacked by this same ... creature? *Why*, for delivering cold pizza?" Sheriff Blackstone sneered.

"Do you have *any* proof, anything at all to make me believe this barrel of hogwash you're trying to sell me?"

Pete nervously spoke up, "Uh, sir, earlier, I-I showed Deputy Sykes the pictures I took of that ... *thing* in the crypt—didn't he tell you?"

That got Blackstone's attention. "No, he didn't mention any pictures. If you had pictures, why the hell didn't you say so? Let's see 'em!" he ordered, glaring at Pete. Blackstone ordered one of the other deputies to go find Sykes.

Pete opened the photo app on his phone and brought up the pictures. There were only two that weren't blurred by motion from either Pete or the monster itself. Sheriff Blackstone used his fingers to enlarge the photos for closer inspection. He frowned after looking at them for a moment. Sykes and the other deputy entered. Closing the door, both looking uncomfortable, they sat down at the table.

"Sheriff, the burn center reports Ms. Morning Star's mother is stable but will have to undergo skin-grafts for her burns. She's has a sixty-forty chance of making a full recovery, barring any infection or unseen medical issue arising in the meantime," Sykes reported, glancing at Missy.

Sheriff Blackstone slid Pete's phone with the pictures of the *thing* across the table. "Just *when* were you going to inform me that you had seen these, Deputy?" he growled.

Sykes thumbed nervously through the pictures, "Uh, I-I thought they were something he just pulled off the internet, Chief, it kinda looks like Bigfoo—"

He was interrupted as another deputy knocked on the door and opened it. "Chief, we just got a call from Joe Donelly, he's got a place out behind the cemetery. He said something had attacked and, uh, eaten his dog. He said this happened in the last thirty minutes! He'd just let it out to pee and when it didn't come back, he found ... well, the remains on his driveway. Said nothing's left but the *head*!"

Sheriff Blackstone had heard enough! He angrily stood up from the table, "I want a car out at Donelly's ASAP! I'm going on this call. Sykes get over to Dr. Boucher's house. I want him found! If he's not there, check his office, call me pronto if he's not either place. Do we still have someone with tracking dogs on call? If so, call 'em and have 'em meet us at Donelly's—and bring the assault rifles!"

Jake, Missy, and Pete all got up from the table. "What are we supposed to do in the meantime?" Jake asked the Sheriff.

"You can catch a ride back to your vehicles with one of the deputies," Blackstone replied, heading for the door.

Jake looked at Missy and Pete, then turned back to the Sheriff. "You expect us to go back home and *pretend* that *thing* isn't still out there somewhere, waiting to get another chance to pick us off, one by one, at its convenience?" he asked incredulously. *Jake knew he was exaggerating—it probably only wanted to kill* him!

"It's already tried for me three times! I've got a feeling my luck's not gonna hold. I—we refuse to go back unarmed! The *least* you can do is give us back our weapons to protect ourselves, otherwise you might as well just invite that damned *thing* to have us for breakfast!" he said, challenging the Sheriff.

Blackstone stopped at the doorway, turned and stared at Jake with his coal black eyes. "No can do! We've got an unsolved murder that all three of you are involved in up to your necks, not excluding your sister, Ms. Morning Star! You're lucky I haven't booked you all for murder. We're running prints on your weapons as we speak.

"Sykes! These people are free to go—for now. Escort 'em back to their respective vehicles and see they get safely home. Oh, and please feel free to call us if you see the '*boogie-man.*' Don't any of you even *think* about leaving town!" he finished, as he stalked out.

"This is bullshit!" Jake complained to the deputy, as they were led from the room.

Missy grabbed Deputy Sykes' arm, "Can I see Elisa before we go? I need to speak to her, it's important!" she begged.

"I don't think that's a good idea, she's been given an anti-psychotic and a Xanax. The doc from the hospital said not to do anything that might excite her until the medication's had time to calm her down," he replied firmly, gently prying her grip from his arm.

Missy persisted, "Please, Deputy, just give me a couple of minutes with her, I have to ask her something ... crucial!"

Sykes looked away, then frowning said, "I'll give you three minutes. Then we leave."

He walked her back to the holding cells, leaving Jake and Pete by themselves in the booking area. They looked around the room, the only officer left was the one behind a desk who performed the bookings. Jake shrugged, motioned for Pete to take a seat and sat down beside him while they waited for Missy. Sykes came back in the room and conversed quietly with the officer behind the desk.

Jake whispered, "We're going to be sitting ducks if they take us back without any weapons. That fucking '*horror-show*' isn't dead, I know it! Apparently, bullets aren't the answer. If we let 'em take us out of here, we might not have a rat's-ass chance of surviving 'til sun-up with that *thing* still out there! Not acceptable!" he growled, standing.

Pete looked on anxiously as Jake strode over to Sykes, tapped him on the shoulder. As Sykes turned toward him, Jake said heatedly, "Deputy Sykes, you saw the pictures Pete took, I promise you it's no bullshit! Our *lives* are in jeopardy! If you take us back before that *monster* is caught or killed, you might as well be ringing the dinner bell. We'll have no way to protect ourselves. It *knows* where Missy and I live, possibly Pete, too! And it has nothing to lose, now that others know of its existence!"

Jake caught a brief glimpse of reticence and wavering in Sykes' eyes, quickly replaced with a fear of reprisal from the Sheriff if he failed to follow orders.

"I'm sorry, but we don't have the manpower to spare. We can't provide personal bodyguards for all of you! You *should* have called the FBI in the first place Mr. Anderson. They have the resources for this kinda thing. Ms. Morning Star's three minutes are up!" Sykes replied curtly, turning and opening the door to the holding cells to retrieve Missy.

Jake thought it ironic that Birdie had told him the same thing only hours ago. *Yeah, well, I got Pete instead, a damn good thing too!* he thought.

Missy came out of the holding area looking pale, followed by the Deputy. "I'll give you all a ride back to your vehicles, let's go."

Jake gave Missy a questioning look, she shook her head and mouthed silently "*not right now*," as they followed Sykes outside to the car, Pete bringing up the rear. They scrambled inside, and the deputy headed down the highway toward the Joseph Cemetery.

JAKE MURMURED TO MISSY, "Well, we're in deep shit if they don't find that fucker fast! It sure as hell will find *me*! We're gonna need to stick together until this is over. You okay with that, Pete? Or you can go it alone if you want. Your choice. Safety in numbers, is all I'm saying," Jake finished nervously.

Pete didn't look happy with either option. "I just wish we knew of some other way to kill it—like you said, bullets don't, like, seem to work too well! I'm sorry, Mr. Anderson, but I wish I'd never gone to your house to deliver that damn pizza! I'll have nightmares the rest of my life!" *However long that might be!* he thought dismally.

Missy whispered conspiratorially, "Elisa's terrified Birdie's going to kill her—she told me there might be a way to do it ... I hope! I'll tell you more when we're alone," she finished, afraid Deputy Sykes might be trying to listen in.

Sykes pulled into the cemetery and parked his car behind Pete's Honda. As they got out, Missy noticed that the caretaker's car was still there, but Birdie's was missing. She rapped on the Deputy's window, he rolled it down.

"Did you have Dr. Boucher's car towed?" she asked anxiously.

He looked over to where the Mercedes had been parked earlier. *Boucher's car? Shit!* With all that had transpired in the past hour, he'd completely forgotten to ask who the owner of the Mercedes was! He'd assumed it was either Elisa's or Missy's—a fucking rookie mistake!

"No, I *didn't*!" he snapped, grabbing his radio mic and asking dispatch to put out an immediate BOLO for the Doctor's car.

There was a pause before dispatch informed him that Sheriff Blackstone had already had it impounded until Boucher could be found. Sykes was only marginally relieved, as he knew the Sheriff would still chew his ass later for the oversight.

"Okay, thanks for the 'heads-up,'" he replied.

Missy had heard the exchange and was a little relieved to know that the car wasn't being driven around with Birdie behind the wheel.

"I'll follow you back and make sure you get home okay," Sykes told Missy. The three got into the Honda, Pete told Missy he'd drive.

Deputy Sykes followed them out of the cemetery, through town, then onto the highway and back to Missy's house, where she got out and hurried over to Jake's truck, starting it, then headed for Jake's house with the Deputy following.

Pete parked the car close to the house, then watched as Jake walked up to the deputy's window, rapping on the glass, as Missy parked the truck close to Pete's car.

"You *really* expect us to survive with no weapons if that thing decides to come back and finish the job? What do we use to stop it, harsh language??" Jake snarled angrily.

Sykes didn't meet his eyes, "Just stay inside and lock the doors and windows, you should be fine. Sorry, I'm just following orders."

Jake gave him the finger as the Deputy turned his vehicle around and left them all staring at his retreating taillights.

"Let's get inside, it's not safe out here!" Jake told the other two, as he walked up to open the front door. He felt in his left pocket. *His keys were gone! Shit!*

He felt around frantically with his left hand in both front pockets until Missy tapped his shoulder, holding them out to him, "You lookin' for these, Bud?" she smirked.

Embarrassed, he took them from her and opened the door—and was immediately attacked by Jinx! He'd forgotten to put him out before leaving earlier with Pete. He pried the anxious cat off his legs, surely leaving fresh bleeding claw marks in them, as they all pushed inside and locked the door.

"Excuse me, I gotta get a pain pill, my hand feels like it's been hammered," he said, walking to his bedroom. Pete sat on the couch, Missy went in the kitchen and dumped a little cat chow in Jinx's bowl. The bobcat ate like he hadn't eaten in a week.

Missy sat down beside Pete, who was looking miserable. "Do you need to call someone—your mother or girlfriend, let them know you're okay?"

Pete stared at his splinted finger, "My mother... we don't talk. She booted me out when I was eighteen. I beat up her boyfriend bad when I came home from work one night and found him punching her. They'd both been drinking, no excuse. Anyway, the cops arrested him, and she blamed me. We argued, and well, I've been pretty much on my own since then. My dad split when I was a little kid. He knocked up some woman and my mother booted his ass out. He ended up in Texas, I think."

Missy looked at him sympathetically. "What about a girlfriend?"

He just shook his head. "Can't seem to keep one for long, my latest, Sheena, is *mostly* just a friend. She works the day shift, I work nights, so we don't get to hang out much. I'm taking online classes hoping to get my B.S. degree in botany." The conversation lapsed into an awkward silence.

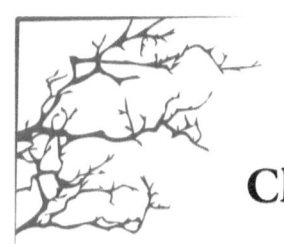

Chapter Twenty-Five

Jake came back in the room carrying an old, rusty double-barreled shotgun tucked under his arm—the old gun had been his dad's gift to him on his thirteenth birthday. He'd forgotten he had it. He assumed it would still fire, but he wouldn't want to bet his life on it!

He handed the gun to Missy, then turned to Pete, "Did you take both boxes of shells out of the console in my truck earlier or just one?" he inquired.

Pete thought for a second, "Only one! The other shotgun only held four rounds, including one in the chamber. So, I didn't bother taking the other box—I figured, if those five didn't do the job ..." he left it hanging.

Jake opened the front door, carefully looking around the yard with his flashlight, then walked hurriedly to the truck. He opened the door, reached in and retrieved the remaining shells, relocked the truck and quickly returned inside. The box contained only three shells, two deer slugs and one buckshot.

"There should be two more," he said to Pete.

Pete felt in his pockets. He'd stuffed the other two in there, just in case. "Got em' right here," he replied, digging them out and handing them to Missy. "I don't know why you think this is going to be any help, didn't stop him last time!" Pete observed, indicating the shotgun. Jake just had a sickening thought, *was dad's shotgun chambered for twenty-gauge or twelve?* Shit! He'd forgotten. He quickly checked the gun and was relieved to find it was twelve.

"It's better than nothing! Missy, you said Elisa told you it was possible we might be able kill that *thing*? Well, let's hear her idea," he said, opening a soda, then sitting on the couch beside her.

"Well, basically you have to call out its full name, addressing it in person. Then you call out the list of 'sins' or transgressions it's committed against others. Then it *should* die. Other than that, only a silver bullet to the neck or a silver knife to the heart can kill it—*supposedly*! Oh, and of course, fire and decapitation should work," she added hesitantly.

Jake and Pete exchanged glances. "Why, that's so simple! All we have to do is make sure it stands still—in *front* of us—then waits patiently, twiddling its claws, while we *accuse* it of all its 'bad behavior,' then it graciously allows us to shoot or stab it to death with something made of silver!" Jake proclaimed sarcastically.

"You got a *better* idea, Mr. 'Know-it-all'?" Missy shot back heatedly.

Pete spoke up, "How about fire? We lure it here and ... I don't know—burn it up!"

Jake thought about it for a moment. "I've got a pressurized bug sprayer. If we filled it with gas and could get close enough with a lighter, it would act like a flame-thrower. That just might work!" he said excitedly.

"What happens if your lighter fails to light on the first try? Presuming you could get close enough to use it in the first place. Or say you have a small leak in the sprayer-wand when you try to light up to barbeque that thing? You'll either toast *it* or end up cremating yourself, Bud! Fifty/fifty that you'd succeed in pulling it off. Do you *really* want to toss that coin?" Missy observed wryly. Jake's hard-on for that idea quickly waned.

Pete said, "Maybe we could set a trap for it, you know, like... punji sticks in a pit? Or maybe spray some battery acid in its eyes to blind it? If it can't see us, it can't kill us!"

Missy reappraised Pete through squinted eyes, "I've misjudged you, Pete, you're more devious than I thought, and just might be on the right track!" Pete looked pleased. Jake just shook his head as they continued bouncing ideas around to try and come up with a plan.

IT HURT TO BREATHE! The holes in its body were closing fast, mostly healed, thanks to the large dog it had devoured in the man's driveway. But it needed more blood—human blood. In order to gain its full strength, it would have to eat again—soon. It knew it would be hunted now. They'd come, with more guns and possibly tracking dogs. It didn't fear their bullets, for only fire

could destroy it. Its pain fueled the burning rage to find and kill Jake. The boy and Missy would be eaten slowly ... for dessert. Then finally, it would take exquisite pleasure in feasting on Elisa's demented, tasty brain while she was still alive, fully aware of every single bite!

SHERIFF BLACKSTONE gaped at the pitiful remains of Joe Donnelly's dog Jenny in the beam of his flashlight.

"What the hell could have done this, Sheriff?" Donnelly cried, wiping the snot from his nose on his shirtsleeve. "We've got wolves and some bear in the area, but I don't know of nothin' that could do *that* kind of damage, in such a short time. Damn it, she was only gone for maybe all of ten minutes!"

Blackstone was shocked by the condition of the corpse. The dog had been ripped open like a pita-pocket sandwich and gutted. All the entrails and organs were missing, blood and gore splattered in all directions. The head lay a couple feet away, having apparently been ripped from the poor thing's body. A shiver of fear rippled up his spine at the thought of what could do this kind of damage in such a short time.

DEPUTY SYKES KILLED his lights before pulling into the driveway of Dr. Boucher's house. It was a small two-story bungalow with weeds growing wild in a yard that hadn't seen a lawn mower in years. An old four-foot high cast-iron spiked fence ran around the perimeter of the yard, a rusted gate swung half-open in the front yard facing the street. A sidewalk led to three small steps and a tiny porch. Sykes grabbed his flashlight and his shotgun off the rack. He opened the door of his cruiser, the wind nearly slamming it on his leg as he stepped out. He locked the flashlight onto the barrel-clamp of the shotgun, securing it, and turned it on.

He could see no lights inside. He didn't expect any at this time of night. He radioed dispatch that he'd arrived at the doctor's house, then made his way up the sidewalk to the porch, sweeping the front entrance with his light. A sudden gust of wind slammed the gate behind him with a *clang,* startling him. Wooden steps creaked under him as he reached the front door and tried turning the door handle, which was locked. He was about to knock, when he heard a noise from inside the house! *Shit! Someone or something was inside, moving around.*

THE TRACKING DOGS ARRIVED at the Donelly place. When the handler took them over to the corpse of the dog, they sniffed and wandered around the general area, whining as they looked up at their handler quizzically and then sat, as if waiting for a command.

"*Shit*, they need a scent to track whoever it is you're looking for. You got a piece of clothing or something from the guy for them to use for a scent trail?" the handler asked Blackstone.

Frustrated, the Sheriff got on the radio, "Sykes, you copy?" Sykes replied "ten-four."

Blackstone continued, "We need a piece of the Doctor's clothing for the dogs to scent. I presume you didn't find him home, am I right?"

Sykes replied, "Uh, not yet, Chief. But I just arrived, heard a noise from inside, am going to investigate further."

"If you happen to find an unlocked door or window, I'm giving you the authority to enter and remove an article of clothing and bring it here ASAP! And if the doctor *does* happen to be there, arrest him!" Blackstone ordered.

"Uh... what do I charge him with?" Sykes asked nervously.

"Let's see, how about attempted murder, kidnapping, arson, impersonating a human being—damn it all, Deputy, just take your pick!" Blackstone snapped.

Sykes replied, "Ten-four, out."

THE DEPUTY SWITCHED off the flashlight on the shotgun and crept around the side of the house. Thankfully, there was enough moonlight to see by, now the cold front's passing had thinned the clouds. Two windows on the side were too far off the ground to reach. He continued to the back and saw another door. Despite the cold, he was sweating as he tried the door handle. To his surprise and *dismay*, it was unlocked.

He pushed the door open slowly, expecting the hinges to squeal as it swung, but there was no sound. He fumbled around in the dark for a light switch, found it and flipped it on. No light. *Shit!* He switched his gun light back on. Pointing it toward the ceiling, he saw the light bulb was missing. Then he spotted it, rocking gently back and forth on a table. *Someone had just removed it!*

Deputy Sykes considered himself a moderately brave man. But at that moment alarm bells were going off in his head. His gut told him to call for back-up. But being the "newbie" on the force, he didn't want to be thought of as a wuss either.

He flipped the safety off on his shotgun and hollered, "This is the Police! Dr. Boucher, if you're in here, come out with your hands up! You're under arrest!"

No reply came from the darkened house. Sykes' hands were sweating profusely, he was having a hard time breathing as his heart raced from adrenaline and the knowledge that he wasn't *alone*. He advanced slowly from the kitchen to a doorway leading to the living room. Something smelled disgusting—a rancid combination of wet dog, feces and the coppery odor of blood!

Suddenly Sykes wanted desperately to be anywhere but here. He heard a low growling sound issuing from a room off to his left that raised his" sphincter pucker factor" to a ten. *Fuck this shit!* he thought, turning to run back the way he came. *Gotta call for backup!* he thought wildly as he ran into the table, knocking the light bulb onto the floor with a loud *pop*. The growling in the other room grew to a snarling roar! Sykes' shotgun was slippery from his sweat-slick hands, as he tried to run through the back door holding it sideways. He bounced backward and the gun clattered to the floor along with the flashlight.

Fuck it, no time to get it now! Gotta get out! Gotta get to the car! was the mantra looping in his head, as he fled out the back door.

He made it as far as the corner of the house when something sharp savagely sliced across his neck. He choked on his blood as it sprayed up and out in a dark fountain of death from both of his severed carotid arteries. He fell to his knees, clutching frantically at his throat trying to stop the hot jets of blood pumping his life away—an exercise in futility. Surprisingly, he felt very little pain.

The last thing he saw was a horrible mouth full of razor-sharp teeth descending swiftly to rip out the rest of his throat.

ELISA SCREAMED, "I need help! Please help me, oh God, I'm hurt!" from her six- by eight-foot jail cell.

The only deputy remaining on duty inside the station was used to prisoners calling out to get attention or simply to harass their jailers to pass the time. But their incarcerated constituents were usually men. Consequently, he reacted differently to the screams of a woman. The reflex to protect women was inbred in most males' psychological makeup.

The deputy rolled his eyes. He pushed away from his computer, stood and opened the door to the holding cells. He walked in and saw Elisa curled in a ball on the floor of her cell, blood staining the front of her shirt.

The deputy thought, *what the hell now?* He asked, "What's your problem, ma'am? Do I need to call the doctor again?"

Elisa groaned and looked up at him. "Please help me, that fucking monster bit me!"

The deputy looked skeptical, "What 'monster' would that be, ma'am?" *Probably the one in her head,* he thought.

"The one at the cemetery tonight! Please, I'm bleeding again! I can't stop the bleeding!" she screeched hoarsely, writhing on the floor.

The deputy said, "Okay, okay, let me get a bandage and some gloves." He went to the Emergency supply cabinet on the wall and opened it.

Funny, I don't remember her bleeding when they had brought her in earlier! The deputy thought, tugging on a pair of gloves a size too small for his hands. He walked back to her cell door, selected a key from his key ring, opened the cell door and walked inside. She was still curled up and moaning on the floor. He leaned down and grasped her under her arms.

"You're gonna have to stand up," he said, pulling her to her feet. "Now, where's all the blood coming from?"

She straightened and croaked, "Right ... *here*!" kneeing him viciously in the balls. As he doubled over in agony, she backed up and kicked him in the face, knocking him to the ground semi-conscious.

She quickly reached down and snatched the keys off his belt and then his pistol. "Where's the key to your personal car?" she snarled. The deputy moaned and shook his head.

"Last chance, asshole!" she rasped, cocking the hammer on the pistol back with an audible *snick*. That got his full attention. "They're in... the... drawer, desk out front!" He groaned with relief when she un-cocked the pistol.

"If you lie, you die!" she hissed, then stepped outside the cell and slammed the door shut, which locked it automatically. She heard some drunks shout out something unintelligible as she cautiously opened the door to the holding area. She fully expected to be met with force when she stepped into the booking area, but it appeared to be empty. She hurriedly opened drawers until she found what she was looking for.

She grabbed what seemed to be the only car key in the drawer. *Better be the right one!* she thought, as she ran to the front door, cracking it a couple of inches and peering out. There were four civilian cars parked out front. She hurled the jail keys taken from the deputy up onto the roof of the building.

She pushed the key-fob and a blue Ford mustang's lights flashed on-off. She heard the *chirp-chirp*, and ran to it, sliding behind the wheel just as bright lights reflected in the rear-view. *Shit!*

A patrol car pulled into the parking lot, heading straight for the space next to her! She panicked for a second, then slid down as far as she could, until her chest was almost under the steering column. She reached up and locked the doors. She heard the cruiser pull up beside her and stop.

She had the pistol aimed up at the window as she heard the car doors open and shut. Thankfully, for both the officers and her, the windows in the car had been tinted dark. Her heart was beating like a racehorse's. The cops were laughing at some joke as they walked into the building.

She pushed herself back up in the seat, started the car and quickly left the parking lot, then turned onto to the highway. *Coming for you, Jake!*

JAKE, MISSY, AND PETE sat around his dining table in complete frustration. They hadn't been able to agree on *any* plan of action, and the conversation about any potential future confrontation with the creature had taken a toll on all of them. Jake's *everything* hurt, his body was one big throbbing pain.

"We need to take a break! This isn't getting us any closer to figuring out what do if Mr. 'Big Bad and Ugly' shows up to finish his meal. I gotta take another pill, my body feels like it's been through a blender!" he exclaimed, getting up from the table, trudging into his room and returning with his pain pills.

"Jake, I know you're hurting, but don't you think you'll need a clear mind, in case you have to—oh, I don't know, maybe run for your *life*? Seriously? That would be the second pill in two hours. I don't have to tell you addiction is a bitch, Bud! Percocet will *not* improve your survival skills either," Missy chided gently, as she rubbed her eyes, struggling to stay awake at 3:30 a.m.

Jake looked wistfully at the pill in his hand, then dumped it back in the bottle and capped it. "You're right, I guess I'll stick with ibuprofen ... for now anyway."

Pete was feeling and looking a little bit like a zombie. He was having a hard time concentrating on the conversation in the room and developing a thousand-yard stare.

He pushed away from the table, "I need some fresh air, and do you have any more coffee? I could use another shot of caffeine," he said, standing up and walking to the back door.

"I'll put another pot on, there's a soda in the little fridge out back—and Pete, I want to thank you again for your help tonight at the cemetery. You were very brave, kiddo!" Jake said.

Missy added, "If you hadn't thought to use your phone flash when you did, I-I don't think we'd be sitting here having this conversation."

Pete smiled and shrugged, "You're both welcome. Feels good to be useful for a change." Then he opened the back door and stepped out onto the porch, embracing the cold north wind whistling through the forest, causing goosebumps to rise on his exposed flesh.

SHERIFF BLACKSTONE wasn't a particularly patient man at the best of times. Right now, he was stressed and pissed because it had been half an hour since he'd heard from Deputy Sykes. Blackstone got on the radio, "Sykes, do you copy?" He heard nothing except some "cross-talk" from other deputies.

"Officer Sykes, do you need back-up? Please acknowledge!" He didn't like this at all. His mind was telling him not to panic, but his gut was saying *trouble!* Sykes was relatively new to the force, as he'd only been on the job for two years.

The Sheriff made up his mind. He called in a "ten-two" meaning, "Officer needs assistance!"

"I gotta check on Deputy Sykes! Stay here until you hear from me. In the meantime, keep an eye out for *anything* out of the ordinary. We've got a dangerous... *individual* loose. Until he's been located and in custody, I want you to be extra vigilant, am I understood?"

The dog handler snapped back, "Yes sir, Chief, I won't budge until I hear from you.

Sheriff Blackstone nodded affirmative, speeding off with emergency lights flashing to find Deputy Sykes.

IT HAD FEASTED RAVENOUSLY on Sykes' body, no part left untouched. After slurping up all the man's cooling jellied blood and devouring most of his organs, it savored the last bloody bite of the unfortunate man's eyeball, which burst in its mouth like an over-ripe grape. It now felt fully rejuvenated. The Yeenaldlooshi could assume any form it needed. It chose the form of a black panther. The unearthly wailing echoing off the trees as its body morphed quickly from one beast to the other. It now had agility, night vision, camouflage and, most of all, speed. Dr. Boucher's house sat on a cul-de-sac just south of the outskirts of town—only three miles from Jake's house. It could run fast, but it wouldn't need to. Jake would either be in jail or at his house. It desperately wanted revenge for the shooting in the crypt. Didn't matter, either way it would find and kill him ... slowly!

BEN WAS PISSED. NOT only had Missy basically ignored him at the cemetery, she hadn't bothered to call him and fill him in on just what the hell had happened down in that crypt. *Why had she been kidnapped in the first place? Why did fucking Jake just happen to be in the right place at the right time to rescue her, him and that kid? Why indeed. Just when he'd finally worked up the nerve to make a move on her, Jake popped up like an unwelcome house guest, getting her to swoon over him like he was God's gift to women. She was probably already sleeping with that asshole hack!* The thought made him sick to his stomach.

He'd fallen in love with Missy when he first set eyes on her. But he'd always been nervous around beautiful women, and he'd always considered her out of his league. Also, the Park System discouraged fraternization between the sexes and he was her supervisor. Guess his timing sucked, but it didn't make any difference now—it looked like Jake had cast some spell over her. Love was not only blind, it was a cruel bitch, ready to tear your heart out and eat it.

Well, Fuck You, *Jake! You screwed me out of my money and now the only woman I'll probably ever love!* he thought morosely.

Angrily, he unscrewed the cap on a half-empty pint bottle of "Old Granddad," taking a long pull, swallowing the fiery liquid along with his misery and pain, as he glared out the windshield of his truck parked in front of Missy's cabin. A shooting star blazed an eerie emerald green trail briefly across the night sky, winking out in a second as Ben drained the last of the bottle.

SHERIFF BLACKSTONE pulled up behind Sykes' cruiser, which sat empty. He got out after radioing dispatch that he'd arrived still with no report from Sykes. He turned on his flashlight and with gun out, walked through the rusty gate up to the front porch and stopped. He inspected the front door and windows. They seemed intact. He tried the door, which was locked. Then he made his way to the side of the house, instantly spotting the grisly remains of Deputy Sykes at the side of the house. *"Holy mother of God!"*

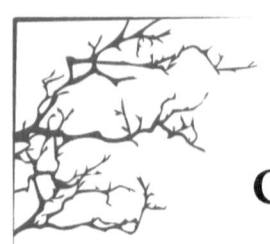

Chapter Twenty-Six

Pete opened a can of soda and was just taking a sip when he heard it. An eerie wailing sound that seemed to be coming from the deep black of the forest, somewhere just beyond the boundary of Jake's property. He felt the hackles rise on the back of his neck even as his feet were propelling him toward the back door. He'd just reached the door when it was flung open and Jake pulled him inside, slammed and locked it.

You *heard* it, right?" Jake barked anxiously, as they all moved into the living room.

Pete's face was sweaty and pale, "It's out there, isn't it?" he said shakily.

Jake looked at Missy, then Pete, "*Nobody* goes back outside, unless we absolutely have to!"

His phone rang, startling him, and he dropped the already beat-to-shit device on the floor. He picked it up, amazed it still worked.

"This is Jake, who's this?"

"Mr. Anderson this is the Sheriff's Office. Sir, I'm afraid I've got some bad news, your ex-wife has somehow, ah, escaped her cell. We think she took a deputy's personal vehicle—and she may be headed your way!"

They all three looked at one another, stunned, "Well, that's just fucking great! Any other 'good news' while I have you on the phone?"

The deputy cleared his throat, then stammered, "Ah... she's probably armed. She seems to have stolen an officer's side-arm during the escape."

Un-fucking-believable! "You need to get someone out here *right away*! You haven't found that *thing* yet, have you? I know that for a fact—because it's *here!* We heard it just before you called. It's somewhere close by, damn it!" Jake practically screamed into the phone.

"I'm sorry, sir, but we have an emergency of our own right now. We've got an officer, uh, down. We'll send someone as soon as we can, but for now I'm afraid you're on your own!"

"Will you *please* tell the Sheriff what I just told you, officer?" Jake pleaded.

There was a slight hesitation. "Ah, roger that, he'll be informed," the man replied, disconnecting the call.

"Fucking deja-vu all over again, folks!" Jake growled, as he loaded the shotgun.

ELISA DROVE THE STOLEN Mustang onto Jake's gravel lane, killed the headlights, pulling off the road to the house, and parked behind a thick copse of pines just beyond the entrance—the same place she'd left her car the last time she'd been here. She faced a dilemma. Though she was crazy as a shit-house mouse, she wasn't stupid. She knew that the Birdie-*beast* was probably not dead, she'd researched that *Yeenaldlooshi* couldn't be killed by bullets alone, at least not *regular* ones it seemed. She was torn between leaving the car, walking up to the house and blowing Jake away, or sitting in the car to await sun-up in case the Birdie-*thing* was lurking in the surrounding dark.

For some unknown reason, the rays of the sun would *supposedly* interfere with the transmogrification from man to beast and it *purportedly* would revert to its original form. It was a lot of supposition on her part. The Indian folklore she had researched could be nothing more than bullshit.

She had seen what Birdie had become, and it terrified her to think that *monster* was still alive and pissed-off at her. Also, the cops would be looking for the stolen car. She had kicked a hornets' nest and knew she would pay a steep price for it. But her obsession prevailed, and she only wavered for a couple of minutes before grabbing the cop's pistol and getting quietly out of the car.

"Here I come, Jake, ready or not!" she hissed in the dark.

BEN FINISHED OFF THE dregs of "Old Granddad" and tossed the empty bottle out the window of the car. He started his truck and slowly made his way back to the highway. He sat, momentarily staring into the dark outside the truck. He realized he was drunk, but he also didn't give a shit! He wasn't gonna play second fiddle to that Jake-flake, no sireee! He was gonna go and punch the fucker's lights out! Then maybe Missy would see how much he cared for her!

Yeah, that's the ticket! he thought drunkenly, as he pulled onto the highway, closing one eye to keep from seeing two of everything as he weaved slowly down the road toward Jake's place.

SHERIFF BLACKSTONE was horrified! So much damage had been done to his deputy's body that it was unrecognizable as a human being. Except for the tattered uniform and name tag hanging off the ragged remains of Sykes' uniform shirt, he wouldn't have known *who* or *what* he was looking at. Blackstone was horrified—and beyond pissed!

One of his deputies had just pulled up a few moments ago and ran over to assist him. He was now bent over, retching into Birdie's weedy flowerbed.

"Soon as you're done puking, call Fire Chief Hardilek, tell him I need a favor ASAP! Ask him to call me on my 'personal.' Then call crime scene and get 'em out here. Now I've gotta call his wife and wreck her world! *Shit*!" he barked through gritted teeth, turning away as two tears rolled down his cheek.

BEN WAS MORE THAN HALFWAY to Jake's when something large and black dashed across the road in front of him. He threw on the brakes, but it had already vanished into the dark forest ahead of him. He didn't know if he'd hallucinated it or not, but he was so plastered, he didn't give a fuck *what* it was. He passed Jake's turn-off, stopped in the middle of the road, backed up and pulled onto the lane running up to the house. He didn't dare turn off his headlights for fear of creaming himself on one of the many trees lining the road. So, the element of surprise was gone.

"Fuck it!" He growled, haphazardly braking the truck near the back of Jake's truck, nearly hitting it before he came to a stop.

He climbed drunkenly out of his truck, leaving it running. He stumbled once as he slowly weaved his way toward the front door. Suddenly, he saw what seemed to be two women walking towards him out of the darkness. They both had something in their hands. He squinted and closed one eye, so now there was only *one* of her. He recognized her as the woman who'd been carried out of the crypt and arrested earlier.

"Whaa the fuck *yah* doin' here?" he slurred to her, just as she raised the gun and shot him, and everything went black.

JAKE WAS REDUNDANTLY explaining to Missy and Pete why they needed to stay alert when Pete looked through the curtains on the front window and saw headlights moving slowly up the drive.

"Ah, someone's coming," he said, pointing toward the window. They watched the truck come to a halt just short of slamming into Jake's vehicle. Then saw a man stumble out, wobbling as he moved into the edge of light from the porch.

"It's Ben! What's he doing out here this late? He looks like he's been ... drinking? Ben doesn't *drink,* that I know of," Missy said concernedly.

They watched as he stopped abruptly, staring at something beyond the light that they couldn't see. It appeared he was talking to someone. Suddenly, everyone flinched at the sound of a gunshot—and watched Ben jerk backward and collapse.

IT RAN THROUGH THE underbrush, winding its way through the tall pines. It could see the house ahead through the scrub. Then it came to a sudden halt, hearing a gunshot.

The panther-thing transformed back to its wolf-like form. The dreadful wailing it produced was caused by the extreme pain of the metamorphosis. It was ravenous again, the metabolic changes burning huge amounts of energy in a short time. It loped closer to the house in time to see Elisa standing over a man lying on the ground, a pistol in her hand. Nooo!! The rotten bitch had somehow gotten to Jake first and killed him! It let out a horrifying roar of anger, charging toward the crazy woman.

SHERIFF BLACKSTONE sat stiffly inside the state police chopper, Fire Chief Scott Hardilek beside him, piloting as they lifted off the helipad. Hardilek was giving the sheriff last minute instructions on how to use the device resembling a diving rig that was strapped to his back, until the chopper blades made conversation impossible. Hardilek pointed to his headset as they flew rapidly over the forest, deep, dark Lake Wallowa sliding by below them. Blackstone put on his headset.

"Frank, you've got to be *really* careful with that thing! We don't want a disaster on our hands. You're absolutely positive that this action is warranted?" Hardilek asked loudly over the mic.

Blackstone answered grimly, "You want to tell Sykes' *widow* it isn't? Dispatch said that Anderson insisted it's out there, right now! Just get me there ASAP!"

Chief Hardilek shook his head. "Roger that." *He was wishing he was back home in his warm, comfortable bed.*

JAKE QUICKLY HANDED the shotgun to Pete, who cocked both barrels, yanked the curtain aside and they saw—Elisa standing over Ben, still pointing the pistol down at him.

Pete whispered nervously to Missy, "Should I shoot her or not?"

As much as Missy hated the violence her sister's illness had caused, she still didn't wish to see her harmed.

"Don't shoot unless you have to Pete, we can ..." she stopped mid-sentence as they heard the high-pitched wailing again outside—very *close* now!

Elisa heard it, as well! Terrified, she swung her gun around toward the sound just as the creature slammed into her, knocking her to the ground. She somehow managed to keep hold of the pistol as the wolf-*thing* leaped on top of her, its jaws opened wide for the killing bite.

Elisa pushed the gun's muzzle against its chest and fired rapidly three times as it sank its teeth into her lower neck and shoulder, narrowly missing her carotid. A great gaping wound was opened in her shoulder as its teeth were ripped from her flesh by the impact of the three shots to its torso. Blood sprayed the air as the creature was knocked on its back and away from her momentarily, leaving them both howling in pain.

Elisa scrambled up and ran, bleeding profusely, toward Ben's still-idling truck. Jumping inside and slamming the door, she locked it, threw the truck in reverse. Even as she was turning it around to escape, she saw the fucking Birdie-*bastard* get to its feet! Roaring madly, it ran and dived into the back of the escaping truck as Elisa swerved wildly back and forth, trying to shake it loose. Like some nasty parasite stuck to the bed of the truck, it wouldn't let go!

SHERIFF BLACKSTONE was getting airsick. He'd never liked to fly at the best of times and flying at night in a helicopter *really* sucked! But he damn well wasn't gonna puke in the state police chopper. Chief Hardilek didn't seem bothered at all by the turbulence. In fact, he seemed to relish flying in pitch dark at 100 knots and 200 feet in the air over the cold dark lake. Blackstone's palms were slick with sweat.

"Coming up on the property in one minute, Frank," Hardileks's voice crackled through the speakers on Blackstone's headset.

"Frank, remember what I told you earlier. Take three deep breaths before getting out onto the skid. Don't worry, the safety-harness won't let you fall. And for God's sake, make damn sure you've got the right ... *man* before you pull the trigger on that thing!" Hardilek instructed, latching the safety-harness from Blackstone's rig and securing it to a thick ringbolt on the chopper's inside frame.

Blackstone tried to smile at his friend, but it was more of a grimace. "Thanks, Scott, I'll do my best!" He opened the door on the chopper to the rush of cold wind and noise of rotor-chop.

"Okay, we're here," Chief Hardilek announced, "Good luck, Frank!"

He hit the switch for the outside spotlight, illuminating the tree-tops and ground 100 feet below. Blackstone stepped carefully out onto the landing skid. The wind was buffeting him as he hit the igniter on the device. The safety-harness went taut, holding him in place as he looked down and saw what appeared to be a woman running and climbing into a truck. A man's body lay on the ground and another figure, which surely was the *creature*, stood nearby. It glanced up briefly at the chopper hanging above it, then began racing after the truck. The *thing* jumped into the bed of the moving vehicle as the woman drove erratically down the lane leading to the highway.

"Follow that truck! That *thing's* in the back! She's trying to shake it off. Try to get me a little lower, Scott!" Blackstone yelled over the rotor noise.

"Roger," the chief replied. He lowered the chopper until it was about sixty feet above the weaving truck.

"Can't go any lower, 'cause of the damn trees! Take your shot, Frank, but be careful, a little of that shit goes a long way!"

Blackstone aimed the device at the creature below as the truck zig-zagged erratically back and forth across the narrow lane and slowly squeezed the trigger.

JAKE AND THE OTHERS watched mesmerized, as all this played out in seconds. They'd heard a *thump-thump-thumping* overhead. *A helicopter!* A moment later they saw a brilliant circle of light shining down through the branches of the surrounding pines.

Jake remarked that it looked like a scene out of that old *"Close Encounters"* movie, as the chopper's light found the swerving pickup in its beam.

"I've had enough 'close encounters' in the past three days to last a lifetime, Bud!" Missy muttered.

All three watched in awe as a long, blazing stream of fire shot down from the chopper, reaching out toward the fleeing truck like a fiery angel of death! It quickly engulfed the monster and the cab of the truck, evoking a blood-curdling scream of agony from it that reverberated throughout the forest.

INSIDE THE TRUCK, ELISA screamed, seeing the flames that suddenly appeared from nowhere immersing the monster in liquid flame! The truck itself was now a blazing inferno on wheels!

Missy, I love you, please forgive me. No way out of this shit now! See you in hell, asshole!" she screamed at the monster flailing around in the firestorm that was engulfing the truck.

The whole vehicle was a roaring bed of flame as she purposely slammed the burning truck directly into a large pine at nearly fifty mph. The air bag deployed, but having neglected to put on her seatbelt, the impact snapped her neck like a twig, killing her instantly. The *creature* flew over the top of the cab like a launched missile, smashing into the large tree head-on, its skull disintegrating in a spray of boiling blood and gore as its burning body slid slowly to the ground.

BLACKSTONE WAS FURIOUS at himself—he'd depressed the trigger on the flame-thrower just a hair too long, setting not only the monster on fire, but the whole damn pickup!

He watched helplessly as the truck swerved into a large pine at high speed. He didn't know who'd been at the wheel, but the driver was most certainly dead. *Shit!* Scott had warned him about the rig's trigger.

"Set us down, Scott, over there where the highway meets the road!" he yelled over the rotor noise, pointing to the ground, as he climbed back inside after turning off the rig's igniter. The Chief angled the chopper over the highway and set it down in the eastbound lane. The burning truck had almost made it to the highway before veering into the pine.

Hardilek threw out a couple of road flares on either side of the chopper to warn off any oncoming traffic. Then he grabbed a fire extinguisher and they rushed over to the burning vehicle and sprayed it, extinguishing most of the flames. But it was too late for the driver, who looked like a melted mannequin, with its clothes still smoldering.

The thing on the ground was nothing but a charred piece of meat and bone. It smelled like roast pork. Another vehicle arrived from the house, skidding to a stop a few feet away.

Missy, Jake and Pete all scrambled out of the truck and walked over to where the Sheriff and Fire Chief stood staring at the carnage in front of them. Missy was crying, as Jake wrapped his arms around her and held her tight, the sheriff informed her that the driver was dead, and finally, so was the creature.

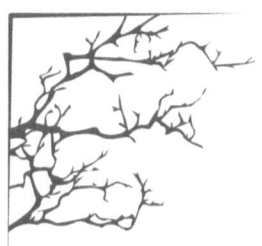

Epilogue

Eight Months Later

Jake heard his front door open, then slam shut. He got up from the keyboard at his desk after hitting the *'save'* box on the story he was close to finishing. Closing the new laptop, he walked into the living room and greeted the door-slammer with a deep kiss, and a firm squeeze of her right ass-cheek.

"Whoa there, Romeo, you're definitely getting your hand strength back! Maybe a little less tongue, though, I think I felt it in my ovaries! Here, make yourself useful," Missy teased, handing him one of two bags of groceries she was carrying. He took it, pretending it weighed a ton.

"If you had waited a minute, I would have come out and got 'em for you. Are you sure you should be carrying this much, I mean, in your...*condition*?"

She cocked an eyebrow, "And what *condition* would that be, Bud? I happen to think I'm in very *good* condition for a person carrying a seven-pound bowling ball inside her!" she said smiling, patting her belly lightly as she carried the other bag into the kitchen, setting it on the counter and dumping out the contents.

She saw him grinning at her. "What?" she asked, frowning.

"Think you got enough food there? You got some lumberjacks hidden in the attic to feed?" he responded, laughing.

"They had a sale on ice cream, okay? If I hadn't bought it, they'd probably just... throw it out! You know I hate to waste ice cream," she told him, taking out four cartons and sticking them quickly in the freezer.

Jake grinned, "If you keep eating it at that rate you have been, it'll go to *your 'waist'* alright!" He ducked the spatula she threw at him.

"You let *me* worry about my waist, Bud! If I were you, I'd be worrying about another part of your anatomy going to *'waste'* if you continue going down this road!" she warned, reaching over to give his junk a playful squeeze.

Jake leaned in and kissed her. "I'm just sayin', God help us if they have a sale on pickles anytime soon!" he said, putting his arms around her and hugging her close.

All the trauma of the past year had brought them closer together than either would have thought possible. That, and the coming baby, had clenched the deal.

Suddenly he was attacked from behind, knocking them both up against the sink counter. Jinx had flanked them while they were occupied with each other and decided to "assassinate" Jake's ass with his claws. Jake shook him loose.

"I swear that cat is fucking jealous! He never does that to you!" he exclaimed rubbing his butt, which he was pretty sure looked like swiss cheese by now. Missy was laughing so hard tears were rolling down her cheek.

Jinx gave him a look that said, *feed me now or I'll piss in your shoe!* Then the bobcat wandered over and sat by his food bowl, staring up at him.

Jake mumbled something about "cats behaving a lot like women" as he opened the cat chow and filled the bowl.

"You said your mother was getting out of the hospital soon, did they tell you when?" he asked, putting up the rest of the groceries.

"Tomorrow, or possibly the next day. It's such a relief, after all she's been through these past months," Missy replied, arching and stretching her aching back.

THEY HAD BURIED ELISA—THIS time, for certain, she lay next to their father. Her mother was never told of Elisa's death, her involvement in the death of the caretaker or the shooting of Ben Dover, who had survived that night, but at a cost. The bullet had creased his spine, causing partial paralysis in his right side. The doctors were optimistic that he would make a full recovery in time. Meanwhile, he had lost his job with the Park Service and was on full disability. With Missy's help, and donations from the Sheriff's office, Jake had bought Ben a used handicap-equipped van and had a wheelchair ramp installed leading from his driveway to his front door.

In return, Ben forgave any hard feelings and debt involving the previous land squabble created by their fathers. They became 'friendly' if not exactly friends.

Missy had been promoted to manager of the Park in his absence, which she felt guilty about since it was *her* sister who had nearly killed him. Of course, his jealousy of Jake played a part. If he hadn't been drinking, he'd never have had the courage to try to confront Jake in the first place. Just bad timing on his part. If Ben was bitter, he hadn't shown it the last time they had visited him at his home.

MISSY EASED HERSELF down onto the new sofa they had bought to replace the ratty old one. Jinx had done his best to break this one in right. There were already runners in several of the cushions.

"Oh, Pete texted that he can't make it to dinner tomorrow, he's starting his new job," Missy said.

Jake punched the time in on the microwave, then grabbed them both a cold soda and sat next to her. "Yeah? Where's that?"

"I, ah, got him into Ranger training with the Park Service. It pays a lot better than the Pizza Palace ..." she said, then hesitated.

Jake looked at her expectantly "And..."

"And ... I owe it to the kid after all he went through to help us—so maybe my karma will be in better harmony with the universe now!" she explained, smiling.

"I don't even know what that means, but if it makes you feel better any better, *my* karma seems much improved since you came into my life!" he told her, leaning in for a kiss.

Jinx picked that moment to jump up in the narrow space between them on the couch and swat him lightly on his cheek with a paw before their lips could meet.

"I told you he's jealous!" Jake laughed, shoving him back onto the floor. The big cat strutted back toward the kitchen to lick his wounded pride.

FOLLOWING THAT NIGHT, there had been little left of Birdie to identify. No dental records could be found to match up with any of the teeth left intact in his charred jawbone. Sheriff Blackstone had the small pile of remains fully cremated with little fanfare, since there was never any physical proof that the doctor and the creature were one and the same. Missy was the only living witness to the transformation from man to beast, and she wasn't going to talk about it... ever!

Elisa's prints were all over the officer's stolen gun that she used to shoot Ben, also on the weapon used in the crypt to kill the caretaker. Although technically Missy's prints were also on the trigger, they cleared her of the murder in the crypt. Missy still couldn't understand why Elisa had targeted their mother.

A FEW DAYS AFTER THE catnage, they had found Jake's stolen laptop in the trunk of Elisa's car, along with the old picture of Elisa and him. Taped to the screen alongside it was a plain manila envelope dated one month earlier with a single word, "Missy," written on it that gave her the answer.

Missy opened it, sitting on the couch next to Jake, and read out loud:

"*Dear Missy, if you're reading this, I'm probably dead. I am truly sorry for the lost time and the wasted years, it's never what I wanted or intended. Nothing matters now. I am ill, I've been diagnosed with schizophrenia.*

"*I need to tell you that I was raped back in high school by Birdie Boucher. The asshole didn't use a rubber and three months later, I discovered I was pregnant! I never told anyone, except Mama! She didn't believe me until I started to show—remember how fat I looked that spring? Too fucking embarrassed that I'd 'let' myself get raped, I guess. Shit! I was only sixteen!! I'll never forgive her! Doesn't matter anymore. Anyway, if you recall, I 'went away' for most of that year. Mama told you I was visiting relatives.*

"Bullshit*! She took me to the tribal elders, and they kept me out of sight until the kid was born. I barely got to see him before they took him from me. They raised him there, I never saw him again—yes, you have a nephew, somewhere! Mama was terrified that her social position in the tribe was in jeopardy if word got out that I was raped and pregnant, who cares that I went through a silent hell twice! First the rape, then losing my son to the tribe. Yeah, fucking Birdie's a father! But I'll never tell him. That's one of his punishments for raping me body and soul! The schizophrenia developed after all that shit happened—or maybe I've always been like this, I can't remember.*

"I've blamed everyone but myself for the way I am. I should never have married Jake Anderson, he turned into a fucking drunk! But he was basically a good man. I was probably as much to blame as him for our marriage tanking. All he was guilty of was falling in love with the wrong fucking woman! I now slip in and out of full-blown psychosis and two guesses who I sought for treatment? The Bird-Turd, Ha! Shows you how fucked-up I am! I couldn't afford anyone else. Now I can't afford the meds anymore, can't find work and no one will hire a schizophrenic off her meds! All I have is the goodwill of my BFF, Ava Farina. She was the only one I could really trust.

"It's possible I might have hired Birdie to kill Jake Anderson for something he didn't really do. Sometimes it seems real, but I can't be sure of anything. If so, Jake didn't deserve it. I can't tell what's real or not anymore. The darkness keeps pushing me further away from the light. Please forgive me, please love me! No one else ever will.

Xxooxx, Elisa

"P.S. I think now it really was Birdie that night long ago outside our house, he claimed back then to be Yeenaldlooshi. I thought he was full of shit! I thought those were just folk tales! Now, not so sure!"

MISSY FELT HOT TEARS roll down her cheeks as she finished reading the letter. Now she understood Elisa's bitterness toward her mother. Sheriff Blackstone was satisfied that everything was now tied up nicely and considered it "case closed," anxious to put the whole thing to rest. He would find himself waking in a cold sweat with nightmares about that night for years to come. Deputy Sykes' widow sold the house they had just purchased and moved away, taking the kids to stay with her brother.

EARLY THAT EVENING, they had each finished eating a huge plate of spaghetti. They each had a bowl of ice cream for dessert. She had dill pickles with hers, yuck! Then they lounged on the sofa, discussing names for the coming baby. Later, Jake smoked a little herb, Missy didn't indulge but reminded him to partake outside so that the freaking house wouldn't reek! They lay in bed an hour later, exhausted but sated from the light lovemaking. They spooned together under the covers, Jake with Jake's right hand resting lightly on her swollen belly, feeling the small kicks of their unborn child.

"I love you, Missy," Jake whispered to her as they were drifting off.

"I love you too, Bud!" she replied sleepily, as Jinx jumped back up on the foot of the bed, having previously endured being rudely shoved off during their lovemaking. He looked over at them with feline disdain radiating from his amber eyes as if to say, *it's about freaking time,* then he curled up in a large ball at their feet and dozed off.

Suddenly, they were startled out of their torpor, brought fully awake, by a sound from their bedroom windowpane—*Skritchhh ... skritchhh ... skritchhh ...*

Don't miss out!

Visit the website below and you can sign up to receive emails whenever James Dobie publishes a new book. There's no charge and no obligation.

https://books2read.com/r/B-A-TZLV-GTBCC

BOOKS 2 READ

Connecting independent readers to independent writers.

www.ingramcontent.com/pod-product-compliance
Lightning Source LLC
Chambersburg PA
CBHW050040180626
46810CB00002B/825